The Millionaire
by Mic

"You're in my room.

Tess gazed up at him, drowsy and confused.

"When I knocked and you didn't answer, I thought something had happened to you," Ben said. "I shouldn't have come in uninvited."

No, he shouldn't have, but Tess couldn't seem to be angry with him. Anyway, it wasn't as if he'd never seen her in bed before. In bed *and* naked.

He moved to the door. "Good night, Tess. Sleep well."

She lay awake a long time, counting the reasons staying here was a good idea, so she could forget the reasons it wasn't.

Because if Ben kept touching her so tenderly, and looking at her with those bedroom eyes, she was going to do something stupid, like sleep with him again. Then she'd wind up doing something even *more* stupid.

Like fall in love.

Reflected Pleasures
by Linda Conrad

ଵ ✳ ଭ

"Are you OK? What did you think you were doing?" Ty roared through the noise of the rain.

"I…thought you were hurt," she sputtered.

Ty dragged her up into his arms, kicked open the cottage's back door and set her on her feet inside.

As he removed her glasses and picked tiny sticks and grass out of her hair, he tried not to crack a smile. Merri tipped her face up to his and let him dry her off.

It was a temptation, gently stroking her cheek and focusing on the full, thick lips so close to his own. He couldn't concentrate on his promises to just be her friend. All he could think of was how beautiful she looked without the glasses…

Available in June 2007
from Mills & Boon Desire

The Soldier's Seduction
by Anne Marie Winston
&
Betrothed for the Baby
by Kathie DeNosky

ᴆᴕᴂᴄ

Secret Lives of Society Wives
The Rags-To-Riches Wife
by Metsy Hingle
&
The Soon-To-Be-Disinherited Wife
by Jennifer Greene

ᴆᴕᴂᴄ

The Millionaire's Pregnant Mistress
by Michelle Celmer
&
Reflected Pleasures
by Linda Conrad

The Millionaire's Pregnant Mistress

MICHELLE CELMER

Reflected Pleasures

LINDA CONRAD

MILLS & BOON®

Desire™

First published in Great Britain 2007
Harlequin Mills & Boon Limited,
Eton House, 18-24 Paradise Road, Richmond, Surrey TW9 1SR

The publisher acknowledges the copyright holders of the
individual works as follows:

The Millionaire's Pregnant Mistress © Michelle Celmer 2006
Reflected Pleasures © Linda Lucas Sankpill 2005

ISBN: 978 0 263 85021 5

51-0607

Printed and bound in Spain
by Litografia Rosés S.A., Barcelona

THE MILLIONAIRE'S PREGNANT MISTRESS

by
Michelle Celmer

Dear Reader,

As a young and naive newly wed mother (emphasis on the words *young and naive*), I used to place an awful lot of importance on making money and buying stuff. I just took for granted that every year our income would climb and some day in the not-so-distant future we would have our dream house, expensive cars, designer clothes and enough money to live comfortably for the rest of our lives.

Remember, young and naive.

Needless to say, it didn't happen that way. A bad economy, chronic illness and plain old dumb luck have taught me many important lessons over the past eighteen years.

If given the chance, would I go back and change things? If I could start my life over again, what would I do different?

Not a thing.

Because despite the fact that my life didn't turn out exactly as I'd planned all those years ago, I'm happy. I have a roof over my head, a husband who completes me, three great kids and a career I absolutely love. What more could I possibly ask for?

I thought it would be interesting to take a man who has everything money could buy and is so devastated by loss, he has to be reminded that it is the simple things that make life worth living.

Hope you enjoy it!

Michelle Celmer

MICHELLE CELMER

Bestselling author Michelle Celmer lives in southeastern Michigan with her husband, their three children, two dogs and two cats. When she's not writing or busy being a mum, you can find her in the garden or curled up with a romance novel. And if you twist her arm really hard, you can usually persuade her into a day of power shopping.

Michelle loves to hear from readers. Visit her website at: www.michellecelmer.com, or write to her at PO Box 300, Clawson, MI 48017, USA.

Though they aren't likely to ever read this, I dedicate this book to my dogs Spunky, Rocko and Combat, and my cats PeeWee and Bubba. They love me unconditionally, keep me company when I'm lonely and always make me smile.

One

In her twenty-four years, Tess McDonald had made
her share of bad judgment calls, but this one topped
them all. All of her life she'd been determined not to
turn out like her mother, but here she was, making
the same stupid mistakes. Maybe it was destiny.

Or just dumb luck.

She stared up at the sprawling structure of
marble and granite. Dark and foreboding under
overcast, gloomy skies, it loomed before her like a
castle out of a modern-day fairy tale. An enchanted
castle where nothing was as it seemed and
monsters lay in wait, ready to devour unsuspecting
maidens. And what fairy tale would be complete
without an embittered, cagey prince? A loner af-

flicted by some disfiguring curse, set free only by love in its purest form.

But Tess had abandoned the mystical for the practical a long time ago. Fairy tales weren't real. There were no princes—cursed or otherwise—no enchanted castles and the only monster she knew was still living with her mother back in Utah.

She climbed the wide marble steps to the front door, and lifted a reluctant hand—*come on Tess, just do it*—and forced herself to press the bell. The hollow ring penetrated the massive, intricately carved double doors, kicking her heart into a frantic beat. Seconds ticked by as she waited for someone to answer. Seconds that felt like hours. When she'd almost convinced herself no one was home, the door opened.

She'd expected a maid or a butler, one in full uniform of course—possibly looking like Lurch from the Addams Family. Instead it was Ben, looking much like he had when they'd met.

Mysteriously and intriguingly dark.

His raven hair lay at his collar in silky waves and heavy lidded bedroom eyes in the darkest, richest shade of brown, studied her. Everything about him reeked of prestige and wealth, from the expensive looking black cashmere sweater and custom tailored slacks, to the tantalizing scent of his cologne.

She felt the same shiver of excitement as she had when she'd caught him staring at her from across the bar that night. Their eyes had met, and the heat penetrating in the dark, bottomless depths made her heart go berserk with anticipation.

The way it was now.

He hadn't said a word. He'd just held out his hand in silent invitation and she'd taken it. He'd led her to the dance floor and when he pulled her into his arms, pressed her to the lean length of his body, she melted against him. Then he'd dipped his head and brushed his lips over hers.

Now, there were kisses, and there were *kisses*.

Kissing Ben had felt like two pieces of a puzzle locking together in a perfect fit. Her knees had gone weak, and the room had spun around her like a carousel. She knew in that instant that she would sleep with him. It wasn't even a conscious decision. It was just something she had to do. An opportunity she would regret for the rest of her life if she let it pass.

She also knew that he was just interested in one night. The, I'm-not-looking-for-a-relationship line he fed her between kisses in the elevator on the way up to his room had been a big tip-off. She'd never expected to see him again.

Considering the look on his face now, neither had he.

She knew she should say something, but she couldn't seem to make her mouth work. All she could do was stare, wondering if he knew who she was. If he remembered her. If he was wondering how she'd managed to track him down. She'd never been one to read the tabloids and she didn't have cable television so it had been weeks later that she'd learned from the girls at work who he really was.

What he'd been hiding.

He wedged his shoulder in the doorjamb and folded his arms over his chest, looking her up and down, those dark eyes putting a chink in the man-resistant armor she wore these days.

"And here I thought you'd been abducted by aliens," he finally said, in that velvety dark-chocolate voice.

Okay, so he did remember her.

He wasn't really going to pretend she'd wronged him somehow, was he? To stay the night in his room would have only been delaying the inevitable. The morning brush-off. The *gee-it-was-nice, have-a-good-life* speech men like him were notorious for.

At the time, she didn't think her heart could take that, because she had fallen stupidly and completely in love with Ben that night.

"You weren't looking for a relationship," she reminded him.

His eyes narrowed. The same bottomless pools she'd found so entrancing that night. How could she have known what he'd really been hiding behind that dark exterior?

The smoldering look in his eyes burned hotter. "I'm still not looking for a relationship."

"I just came to talk. Can I come inside?"

Though he looked hesitant, he held the door open wider and stepped back, all but disappearing into the dark interior.

The rubber soles of her work shoes squeaked on the marble floor as she stepped inside the cavernous foyer, and hazy darkness swallowed her like a hungry beast. As her eyes adjusted to the dim light, oddly shaped, ominous shadows crept soundlessly around her like restless spirits.

You don't believe in spooks, she reminded herself.

The door closed behind her with a thud that bounced off the walls and echoed up the cathedral ceiling. Ben simply stood there, towering over her, arms folded over his chest, biceps straining against the sleeves of his shirt, his face hidden in shadow. His intimidating size, ropes of lean, corded muscle, were part of what had intrigued her that night, what had drawn her to him. As if she hadn't learned her lesson so many times before. Dark angsty men were nothing but trouble.

But, boy they could be fun for a night or two.

He may have been dark and reserved in the bar, but under the covers she'd never had a more attentive, exciting or *imaginative* lover. It was all coming back now. How alive and beautiful he'd made her feel.

And why she'd run like hell in the middle of the night.

What he didn't know is that he'd given her a gift. The piece of her that had always been missing, even if she hadn't realized it. For the first time in her life she had a purpose. She wasn't alone. And for that she owed him everything.

That included an explanation.

True, the timing couldn't have been worse, but that didn't mean she wasn't happy. And scared of course. This would change everything.

She'd considered not telling him. Odds are he never would have found out. They didn't exactly run in the same social circles. In fact, she had worked so many hours since moving here, she wasn't even part of a social circle. And after everything he'd been through in the past year, well, he probably would have been better off left in the dark.

And considering the lack of light in here, that was exactly where he preferred to be.

She thought she could handle the burden alone, but as hard as she'd tried, her best efforts just weren't cutting it anymore. She needed his help. And since there was no easy way to say it, to soften the blow, she decided it was best to just get it out.

She took a deep breath and held her chin high. "I just thought you should know that I'm pregnant and you're the father."

Her words hit Ben like a sucker punch.

For months now he'd considered going back to the resort bar in the hopes that she would be there. That they could reconnect. Something inside him had changed that night with her. He'd begun living again.

But this he'd never expected.

She may have acted as if she hadn't known who he was that night in the resort, but clearly he'd been set up.

How could he have been so stupid?

He knew exactly how, and why now, months later, he still felt that tug of longing when she stood in his foyer. She'd been the first woman he'd connected with since the crash. The only one who had been able to make him forget the pain.

He used to believe that his heart had died along with his wife and unborn son, but something had clicked between himself and Tess that night.

Maybe it was because she was so different from Jeanette. Slim and angular and schoolgirl pretty to his wife's lush figure and exotic beauty. She'd looked so petite and nymphlike. Sweet and innocent.

What a joke.

He never should have left the house that night, but the idea of spending the holidays in solitude had forced him out of his self-imposed isolation. He should have known what was up when he woke the next morning alone. Yes, it was true he told her he wasn't looking for a relationship, but he hadn't asked her to leave, either. He thought there had been a connection.

Apparently, he'd thought wrong.

He wondered how many other men she'd picked up in that bar. How many she'd used. And why she'd picked him to seal the deal. Because he was vulnerable? Or was it his bank balance?

And to think that he'd been *this close* to falling in love with her.

"You neglected to mention that you worked at the resort," he said. She hadn't told him much of anything about herself. Not that he'd asked. He hadn't been looking for conversation, just a sweet, warm body to lose himself in. Kind of like a Christmas present to himself. By the time he realized he wanted more, she'd already disappeared.

She lifted her chin and looked him in the eye. "We didn't spend a whole lot of time getting to know each other."

"Actually, I thought we got to know each other rather…*intimately.*"

Tess bit her lip and her cheeks flushed bright pink. It would have been charming if he believed it were anything but an act.

"Maybe you don't remember, but we used protection," he said, sure that she would come up with some creative excuse why the condom had failed. All three of them, or had it been four?

She didn't. "Believe me, I was just as surprised as you are. I didn't plan this, either."

"Let's say it is mine. What do you want from me?" Like he didn't already know. She probably had a long list of demands. Would she expect him to marry her? Did she think they would settle down together and play house? Or maybe she was looking for a break into acting.

She wouldn't be the first who'd tried to use him for his connections.

She lowered her eyes to the floor, looking genuinely humbled. Give the girl an Oscar, she was one hell of an actress. "I need your help. I thought I could do this alone, but with the doctor bills and all the things I need for the baby…"

Just as he suspected.

"I want a paternity test," he told her. "Before I give you a penny, I need to know if this really is my baby."

Tess nodded, thankful he wasn't going to make her beg. Her mother had struggled for years to make Tess's wealthy father own up to his responsibility and pay child support. Tess had been sure Ben would fight her tooth and nail.

"I figured you would. I've already talked to my doctor about it. She said they can do the test next week, when I go in for my ultrasound."

"Fine. I'll contact my attorney."

"If you want, you could come with me," she said, figuring it was the least she could do. It was his baby as much as hers. Maybe they could reach some sort of accord, find some middle ground and maybe even learn not to resent each other.

Maybe they could even be friends.

"Come where?" he asked.

"To the appointment. To see the baby."

Something dark and unsettling flashed across his face. He closed in on her, his eyes sparking with anger. "Let's get something straight. If this is really my child, I'll see that it's taken care of, but I can't be a part of its life."

She took a step back and bumped into the door. He moved forward, boxing her in. If he was trying to intimidate her, it was working.

And he knew it.

"Why so nervous?" he said, easing even nearer, bracing his hands on either side of her head. Black hair framed his face, settling it deeper into the shadows, but she could still see his eyes—dark and penetrating pinned on her face. And so cold it made her shiver. "You didn't mind being this close that night in my room. In fact, I was under the impression you rather enjoyed it."

She glared up at him, refusing to be the one who backed down. She'd almost forgotten how beautiful he was. Beautiful in a completely masculine, testosterone driven way of course. But that was to be expected being the product of two gorgeous Academy Award winning actors.

He smelled good, too. The scent of his cologne and sheer male heat swirled through the narrow space between them. He smelled expensive and refined and…

My God, was she actually getting turned on by this he-man macho crap? It had to be the pregnancy hormones making her feel so loopy.

After that night with Ben she had forever sworn off men like him. They were nothing but trouble. If she ever did date again—and that was a big *if*—she was going to find herself a quiet, average, boring guy. She'd take safe and unexciting over sizzling and sexy any day.

She poked the solid mass of his chest with her index finger, feeling his body-heat soak through the silky softness of his sweater, enjoying the look of surprise on his face.

"You must think pretty highly of yourself if you believe I would want a relationship with you. Just like you, I went up to your room expecting one night. Go ahead and pin the blame on me if it eases your guilty conscience, but this is as much your fault as it is mine. I wasn't in that room alone. If I recall correctly, you *rather enjoyed it,* too. And need I remind you that you were the one with the condoms? How do I know you didn't do this on purpose? Maybe you get some sort of depraved thrill knocking up unsuspecting women. For all I know, you have illegitimate children all over the place."

His expression shifted and he looked almost… wounded.

Was it possible she'd hurt his feelings? That he actually *had* feelings?

Ben dropped his hands from beside her head and backed away, his face somber. He looked so…sad. The brief charge of satisfaction hissed away like a deflating balloon.

"May as well take off your jacket and get comfortable," he said. "We have a lot to discuss."

Ben sat at his desk and ripped open the envelope his lawyer had messaged over. With a heavy heart, he read the results of the paternity test she'd taken last week. The wounds that had begun to heal in the year since his son's death ripped open and grief twisted his insides.

Tess had been telling the truth. The baby was his.

If he had been able to talk Jeanette out of taking the trip to Tahoe while he wrapped up postproduction on his last film, she and his son would be alive. Even the doctor had said it was late in her pregnancy to be flying. Ben should have insisted, but when Jeanette wanted something she usually got it.

He would never forgive himself for letting them down, and he wouldn't let it happen again. This baby was his, whether he wanted it or not. He would see that it was taken care of and raised properly.

In his son's honor, he wouldn't let anything bad happen to this child.

"I take it the news wasn't what you'd hoped."

He looked up to find Mildred Smith, his housekeeper, watching him from the doorway. Any other of his employees would have been fired for insinuating themselves into his business, but Mrs. Smith had been with his family since before Ben was born. It had only been natural to hire her when his parents moved permanently to Europe three years ago. She'd been with him those horrible months after the crash and had nursed him through the worst of it. She was more like family than hired help. More of a mother to him than his own mother had ever been.

"It's mine," he told her.

"What do you plan to do now?" she asked.

The only thing he could do. "I'm going to make sure she and the baby are safe. I'll bring her here to live with us until it's born."

"You know nothing about this girl." Her tone was

stern, bordering on cold, but that was just her way. He knew she cared deeply for him. The past year hadn't been easy for her, either. Though Mrs. Smith had never cared for Ben's wife, the loss had hit her hard.

"I don't know her, which is exactly the reason I need to keep her close. That's my child she's carrying."

The one thing he didn't get, that didn't make sense about this whole situation, was why she'd waited so long to tell him. According to her due date, she had to be close to sixteen weeks pregnant. Meaning she'd known she was pregnant for at least a couple of months already.

He was sure she had her reasons.

He found the number Tess had jotted down on a slip of paper. It had been sitting there on his desk, taunting him for days. He hadn't yet written it in his book, on the slim hope it was all a mistake. Since her visit last week, all communication had been through his attorney. Now it was time to make his position clear. Face-to-face.

"Suppose she doesn't want to live here?" Mrs. Smith asked. "What then?"

He gave her a look, one that said he didn't antici-pate that being an issue. "You think a girl like that, with a menial job at the resort and next to nothing to her name, would pass up the opportunity to live in luxury? I know her kind. She'll take whatever I have to offer."

Two

"Absolutely not! There is no way I'm moving in with you." All that Hollywood fame must have gone to Ben's head if he thought he could boss her around. He hadn't even asked. Instead he'd issued an order.

He sat casually behind his enormous desk like a king on his throne addressing his royal subjects. The only thing missing was a scepter and crown.

And tights—which she had to admit would be well worth seeing.

Instead he wore black again. Black shirt, black slacks. Did he own a single article of clothing in color?

Tess turned to see if the stern woman who had let her in was still standing in the doorway listening.

Thankfully she wasn't.

Ben, Tess could handle. At least, she was going to give it a valiant effort. His housekeeper on the other hand—Lurch's twin sister—gave her a serious case of the creeps.

"I have an apartment," she said. "I don't need or want to live here."

"I didn't need or want a child, yet one is being forced on me."

"I did not make this baby all by myself," she reminded him. "Besides, what has that got to do with where I live?"

"You live in a disreputable part of town. It's not safe."

"I do the best I can." Not everyone was born with a silver spoon in their mouth—or in his case, an entire service for twelve. She was quite sure he had no concept of what it was like to struggle, to live on canned spaghetti and Wonder Bread until the next payday.

"If geography is such a problem for you, we can compromise. If you help me out financially, I can get a place in a part of town you deem as safe. Then we'll both be happy."

"Not acceptable. I need you here."

"As I said, I don't want to live here."

"Shall I send someone over to help you pack?" he asked, as if she hadn't just *emphatically* stated that she *would not* be moving.

She normally had interminable patience, but this guy was pushing all her buttons. "Are you hearing impaired? I said that I'm not moving into your house. That's final."

He went on as though she hadn't spoken. "I also think it would be best if you quit your job. As a maid, you probably work with harmful cleaning solvents, and heavy lifting must be involved. It could be damaging for the baby."

Whoa. Someone had serious control issues. Did he really think she would allow herself to become totally dependent on him? She'd been on her own since she was sixteen. She knew how to take care of herself, and she would take care of her baby. She just needed a little help—emphasis on *little*. A couple hundred bucks a month to help cover her extra expenses.

She glanced at the crystal tumbler filled with some sort of amber colored alcohol sitting on his desk. Warning bells clanged like crazy through her brain. She'd heard rumors from the other employees at the resort that he'd become a reclusive alcoholic since he'd lost his wife. The reclusive part she believed, the alcoholic part she'd only hoped wasn't true. Looks like she might have been wrong.

Not that everyone who drank was an alcoholic, but she wasn't taking any chances.

"I'm not quitting my job. I'll give you weekly updates on my condition if it will make you feel better, but that's it."

"That reminds me," he said. "I've picked an obstetrician I'd like you to see. He's the best in the area."

And it just kept getting weirder. Now he wanted

to pick her doctor? Next he would be telling her how to dress, and what to eat.

"I already have a doctor I'm comfortable with that takes my insurance," she told him.

"Expense isn't an issue."

"It is for me, since I'm the one paying for it."

He folded his arms across his chest and leaned back in his chair. His face was partially hidden in shadow, but if she could see it, she was sure he would look annoyed.

It was so darned dark in here.

"What are you, a vampire? Could we maybe open some drapes? Turn on a light or two?"

He unfolded his arms, leaned forward and switched on the desk lamp. Yep, he looked annoyed all right.

"You mean to make this as difficult as possible, don't you?" he asked.

Was he kidding? "*I'm* being difficult? You're not the one whose life is going to drastically change. You don't have to suffer the morning sickness and the weight gain and the stretch marks. And let's not forget hemorrhoids and heartburn and hours of hard labor. The day you can do all that for me, I'll let you start calling the shots. Until then, this is my body and my baby and I will go to whichever doctor I choose, and live wherever the heck I want. Is that clear?"

"If you don't cooperate I could fight you for custody. I have unlimited financial resources."

She knew he was desperate when he started tossing around legal threats.

"I've done my homework. I've got the numbers of half a dozen high profile bleeding heart attorneys who would just love to handle a case like mine pro bono."

She could swear she saw a hint of amusement in his eyes. "Would you really want to put yourself through that? Agree to my terms and I'll grant you full custody and adequate financial assistance to have you living in luxury for the rest of your life."

She took a deep, calming breath. "Apparently you're not hearing what I'm saying. I don't want to live in luxury. I want a *little* help. Got it?"

He stared up at her, a vague smile curling his lips.

She propped her hands on her hips and glared at him. "I fail to see what it is about this situation you find amusing."

He leaned back in his chair, gazing up at her. "I was just thinking about that night in the resort."

Oh great, now did he think sex would be a part of the deal? "What about it?"

"I knew there was a reason I liked you."

Now he *liked* her? That didn't make any sense.

"You are the most stubborn, self-centered, *confusing* person I have ever met," she said, and his grin widened. She never imagined a man so dark and sexy could look so…cute.

Cute? What was she thinking? He wasn't cute. He was a big pain in the neck.

She flung her hands up. "Fine, don't help me.

Because frankly, it isn't worth the trouble. The baby and I will manage without you."

She turned to leave and was halfway to the door when she heard him call, "Tess, wait."

No way. She was through arguing about this. She and the baby would make it without him. She wasn't sure how, but she would manage.

She made it to the door and had her hand on the knob when she heard him say, "Please, stay."

She reluctantly turned back to him.

"I know there has to be a way we can make this work."

"Unless you're willing to compromise, I don't see how."

"I am." He gestured to the chair across from his desk. "Please, sit."

Because he said please, she crossed the room and took a seat.

"Tell me what works for you, then we'll figure something out."

"You're serious?"

"Absolutely."

"First I have to ask, why the change of heart? Why are you willing to compromise now, when fifteen minutes ago you were being an ogre?"

He wasn't insulted by the observation, in fact, he smiled. "Fifteen minutes ago I thought I knew who you were."

"And now?"

"Now I realize I was wrong."

* * *

Tess prayed silently the way she did every morning as her old junker chugged its way up the mountain to the staff parking lot behind the resort. It had stalled twice on the way here. Once she'd flooded the engine and had to wait several minutes, holding up traffic, before it would turn over again.

Her carburetor was terminally ill, but it would be at least three or four months before she had the money saved to replace it. And that was if she did the work herself—which she was pretty sure she could manage given the time to figure it out. She'd blown her entire savings plus a week's groceries on a gas pump last month. The co-pay for her monthly doctor visits and prenatal vitamins was eating up the rest of her extra cash.

The downside to residing in a resort town was the astronomical cost of living. If she skipped grocery shopping again on Sunday, that would shave a week off her expenses, but the doctor had already expressed concern that she wasn't gaining enough weight, and a healthy diet was critical for a healthy pregnancy.

She'd spent the last few days thinking about Ben's offer. As far as she could tell, when she'd threatened to leave, he finally realized she was telling the truth. That the pregnancy was an accident and she wasn't after his money. Though for the life of her, she still didn't understand why it was so important that he have her living in his house. But when she stopped to think about it, there was no reason why she absolutely shouldn't live there. She would have her own suite and could come and go as she pleased.

Everything he'd had to offer sounded pretty good, except for one thing. Despite every other concession he'd made, he still insisted she quit her job.

Tess couldn't remember a time when she hadn't had some sort of job. Babysitting, delivering papers, stocking shelves at the party store—anything to earn a little extra spending cash. And later, hard work had been a way out of the hellhole that was her stepdad's house.

If she quit working now, what would she do for money? She already felt uncomfortable taking things from Ben. But to be totally dependent on him?

Frankly, she was scared. What if she gave up her job, then found out he was some kind of creep or weirdo? She'd be stuck, because she seriously doubted anyone would be jumping at the chance to hire a pregnant woman.

She'd told him to give her a few days to think about it, but she still wasn't sure what to do.

She pulled her car into a spot at the back of the employee lot, glanced at her watch, and cursed under her breath. She was ten minutes late.

Hopping from the car, she bolted for the back entrance. Olivia Montgomery, the owner of the resort, ruled like a foreign dictator, expecting one hundred and ten percent from her employees. Tardiness was not acceptable. And because of her temperamental carburetor, this was Tess's third time in two weeks.

Tess shoved her way through the door and headed to the employee locker room behind the kitchen. As she turned the corner, her heart sank when she saw the morning shift manager standing next to her locker waiting for her.

"I'm sorry I'm late," she said. "Car trouble."

His sour expression was tarter than usual. She was convinced the guy sucked lemons for breakfast. "Mrs. Montgomery would like a word with you."

Oh, swell. Getting chewed out by her boss was not her favorite way to start the day.

She shoved her jacket and purse into her locker and headed for Mrs. Montgomery's office, where the secretary greeted her with a sympathetic smile. "Go on in, she's waiting for you."

Tess opened the door and stepped inside the lush office. Her boss was on the phone, but gestured to the chair across from her desk, her expression unreadable.

She spoke for several minutes, then said goodbye to the person on the line, hung up the phone and turned to Tess.

Tess had learned that the best thing to do in a situation like this was to shelve her pride and take responsibility for her actions. "I'm very sorry for being late. I know it's unacceptable. I swear it won't happen again."

Her boss very calmly folded her hands atop her desk. "This is the third time in two weeks, Tess."

"I know, and I'm sorry."

"Well then, you can make it up by working a few

extra shifts this week," she said in that condescending, *I'm God and you're a peon* tone. "We have several people out with the flu."

Tess was already working over fifty hours a week. She'd been suffering a chronic backache and swollen knees from being on her feet too long, and her bad ankle had been stiff and sore. It also seemed that no matter how many hours she slept, she woke feeling exhausted. But she knew that if she didn't work the extra hours Mrs. Montgomery would find a reason to fire her. She knew Tess was pregnant, and that in several months she would be eligible for paid maternity leave.

She'd been looking for a reason to let Tess go.

And because of that, Tess had been working her tail off at a job that she quite frankly despised, for far less money than she deserved. Didn't she *deserve* a break? Hadn't she *earned* it?

She thought about Ben's enormous house and what it would be like to live there. What it would be like to not have to get up at 5 a.m. and drag herself to work. To stay up late watching movies and eating popcorn. To sleep until noon. How it would feel to relax and enjoy her pregnancy.

So maybe she wouldn't have a lot of extra spending money. So what? She was used to getting by on a tight budget.

But if she did this, that would be it, she would be stuck with Ben for five long months. Although, if she had to be *stuck* with someone, she could have done a lot worse.

"Well?" Mrs. Montgomery said tightly, expecting an answer.

"No," Tess said. "I'm afraid I can't do that."

Her boss's eyes narrowed. "I'm afraid you don't have a choice."

That wasn't true. For the first time in her life, Tess actually *did* have a choice.

What it all came down to was, what was best for her child? She grew up with nothing. Ben had everything. She wanted something in between for her baby.

If she accepted Ben's offer, the baby would never want for life's basic necessities, never feel threatened or abused. Her child would go to good schools and get a college education, would have all the opportunities she never had.

Ben could give them that, if she just had a little faith.

She still wasn't one hundred percent sure she could trust him, but she was so sick of feeling achy and tired and overworked. Maybe it was time she took a chance on him, the way he'd taken a chance on her.

She flashed her boss a smile, feeling that, for the first time in months, maybe she was doing the right thing. "I do have a choice, Mrs. Montgomery. And I choose to quit."

Three

"Benjamin, I'm sorry to interrupt, but there's someone here to see you."

Ben looked up from the computer screen to find Mrs. Smith standing in his office doorway. She opened the door wider and behind her stood Tess.

Her cheeks were pink from the cold and her eyes bright. She was dressed in a denim skirt and a fuzzy olive sweater that was just tight enough to reveal her stomach was no longer flat. She looked good. In spite of himself, he smiled.

He couldn't deny he was happy to see her. For reasons he probably shouldn't be.

He rose from his seat. "You're back."

She nodded and flashed him a tentative smile. "I'm back."

Mrs. Smith shot Ben a stern look. One that said she wasn't crazy about this arrangement—which she'd made clear on more than one occasion in the past few days—and she still thought he was making a mistake. Then she stepped out and shut the door behind her.

"I take it you've made a decision?"

"I have," she said. "I quit my job this morning. My bags are packed and I'm here to stay."

The news was an enormous weight off his mind. Things were now under control. She and the baby were finally safe.

"I should probably warn you that my car committed suicide about a hundred feet down the driveway."

"My condolences."

She shrugged. "The carburetor was terminally ill. I don't suppose you could spring for a new one. I'll reimburse you."

"I'll take care of it."

He might have worried it was just another scam, but he'd learned an awful lot about Tess these past few days. Since one could never be too careful in a situation like this, he'd hired a private detective to check her out. He'd found nothing in her past to indicate foul play. She had no criminal record, no past deviant or questionable activity. Nothing to suggest she might be conning him. Tess was exactly who she appeared to be. A hardworking woman just doing her best to get by. She had never wanted more from him than a little financial help.

With that knowledge, something deep in his soul felt oddly settled.

Not that he expected this to be easy. Making love with Tess had made him feel alive for the first time in months—had given him hope that he had a chance for happiness again. But even if he'd asked her to stay that night, if he'd let himself fall for her, a child would have never been part of the deal. Seeing Tess's growing belly would be a constant reminder of everything he'd lost.

He'd loved Jeanette, but she was gone. He'd accepted that. It was losing his son that still stung like a fresh wound. A slash through his heart that would never stop bleeding.

In some ways he felt ready to move on, in others he was still trapped in the past.

"So," Tess asked, dropping into the chair across from his desk, "how exactly is this going to work?"

"It will be exactly as we discussed the other day. You'll stay here with me until it's born. Afterward I'll set you and the baby up in a condo with a generous trust."

She gazed intently at him, as if she were trying to see into his head, to be sure what he said was true.

The color of her sweater seemed to draw out the yellow in her irises. He remembered thinking that night in the bar how unusual they were. How bright and full of curiosity, and maybe a little sad.

He'd watched her for a while before approaching her, fascinated by her petite, striking features. By her warm, genuine smile as she chatted with the bartender. And when she looked his way, and their eyes met and locked, there had been enough sparks to melt the snow on the entire mountain. It hit him with such force that it had nearly knocked him out of his chair.

Even now there was something about the woman that messed with his head.

"Sounds almost too good to be true," she said.

"Meaning…?"

"Look, it's not that I don't trust you, but…"

"But you *don't* trust me," he said, and she gave him a sheepish shrug. "I'm not offended. Put in your position, I wouldn't trust me, either."

"Honestly, you seem like an okay guy. A little overbearing maybe… It's just that I'm giving up an awful lot here. I'm watching my back, you know? I don't really know anything about you."

He understood completely. He would never enter into a business agreement on a handshake deal. "I've already spoken to my attorney about drawing up a contract."

She narrowed her eyes at him. "And I'm supposed to trust this attorney?"

"You're free to have the attorney of your choice look over the documents before you sign anything— at my expense of course."

"I guess that sounds fair."

"I should warn you that my lawyer has insisted on a confidentiality clause."

"*Confidentiality?* Who am I going to tell?"

"This is as much for yours and the baby's protection as mine. It was abhorrent the way the media exploited my wife's death. For months after, they made my life a living hell. There was an unauthorized biography written about her life and a made-for-television movie. Neither was what you could consider flattering, or had barely an ounce of truth. Trust me when I say that you don't ever want to know what that's like."

"When I found out from the girls at work who you were, I went to the library and did a little research."

"What kind of research?"

"Old newspaper articles and magazines, Internet stuff."

He wanted to feel indignant, but really he had done the same thing. "And what did you find?"

"There was a lot. So I get why you're worried."

"Things have finally died down. I don't want to stir the pot. The fewer people who know about this the better."

"I understand. I don't want that, either."

He didn't want to alarm her, but it was only fair that he caution her about what she might be getting herself into. "I'm not suggesting you should break all ties and avoid your friends—"

"I don't have any friends." She smiled and added. "I didn't mean that the way it sounded. Like, oh poor me I have no friends. It's just that I haven't lived here long and I work so many hours I never really found the time to make too many friends. Not close ones, anyway."

And now he was basically telling her not to make friends at all.

"Don't worry," she said. "I'll be careful."

"Then I guess that just about covers it," he said.

"Um, actually, there are a couple more things."

"Okay."

"I'm not sure how to say this, so I'm just going to say it. I won't live with an alcoholic. You have to stop drinking."

Her words took him aback. What had given her the impression he had a problem with alcohol? Because he had an occasional drink? Who didn't? Or had she read about him in the tabloids? Removing himself from the public eye, hiding away, had only served to fuel the media's interest. God only knows what rumors they had been spreading lately. He'd stopped paying attention a long time ago.

He opened his mouth to deny the accusation, then realized that was exactly what an alcoholic would do. Damned if he did, damned if he didn't.

Instead he asked, "If I refuse?"

"The deal is off."

Seeing as how he wasn't an alcoholic, it was a small sacrifice to make.

"I'll quit drinking," he told her.

She gave him a wary look, her pixie features sharpening with suspicion. "You'll quit drinking. Just like that?"

"Just like that." He walked over to the minibar, picked up the decanter of scotch he kept there and poured its contents into the sink. He enjoyed an occasional drink, but it wasn't something he couldn't live without.

She narrowed her eyes, as though she wasn't sure she could trust him. "You'll put it in the contract?"

"Done. Anything else?"

"After the baby is born, I'd like you to loan me the money to go back to school. I got my GED last year and I really want to go to college."

"I'll set up a trust that will ensure you'll never have to work another day in your life."

"Sitting around eating bonbons and getting facials may appeal to the women in your inner circle, but I want to do something with my life. I want to be able to look back and feel that I've accomplished something."

"I have nothing against working mothers. But I do believe a child should be raised by its parents, not a nanny or a babysitter."

Tess wondered if his movie star wife had been planning to give up her career once their child had been born.

Somehow she doubted it.

If Ben wanted to take care of his child financially, that was one thing. She was more than capable of taking care of herself.

"If it makes you feel any better," she said, "I agree completely with your values. I wouldn't even con-

sider going back to work until the baby is in school.
So it might take time for me to pay you back."

"I don't want you to pay me back."

"But I will anyway."

He looked as though he might argue, then gave his
head a shake, like he realized it was probably useless.
"Is there anything else?"

"The other day you said I could keep my doctor."

"If that's what you want."

"Good. Then, I guess that covers it."

One of those cute smiles curled his mouth and like
a silly school girl she felt her knees go weak. The
man was too good looking for his own good. He was
wearing black again, as he had every single time
she'd seen him—a good indication that he really
didn't own anything that wasn't black. Maybe it was
his trademark. She wondered if he wore black
boxers, too. Or maybe bikinis.

Whatever his underwear preference, it was clear
she'd made him happy, and for some reason that
made her feel really good. The man had been through
an awful lot. She'd tried to convince herself he was
just some guy who happened to be the father of her
baby. But when they were near each other she felt
so…*aware* of him. Connected in a way that she
didn't think had anything to do with the child she
was carrying.

Even worse, she was pretty sure he felt it, too.

"I'll call my attorney and have him draw up the
papers. Mrs. Smith will see you to your suite."

"Before you do, there's something about this that just doesn't make sense to me."

"What's that?"

"If you don't want the baby, why are you doing this?"

He was quiet for a moment and when he looked at her, his eyes were so sad. "I take responsibility for my actions."

She shook her head. "I don't think that's it. If you didn't care about this baby, it would have been a hell of a lot easier to pay me off and send me on my way."

"I never said I didn't care."

If he did care, why couldn't he be a part of the baby's life?

And just like that, something clicked. Suddenly this whole thing made sense. Why he insisted she stay here. Honestly, she didn't know why she hadn't figured it out before.

He blamed himself for his son's death. By keeping her here, he thought he was keeping her and the baby safe.

"Nothing is going to happen to me or the baby," she said. "I'm used to taking care of myself."

He gave her a look so full of pain and anguish she felt it straight through to her heart. "I didn't protect my son and now he's gone. That's one mistake I won't be making again."

The malevolent Mrs. Smith led Tess up the wide marble staircase to her room. Tess followed her through the ornately carved double doors—didn't they have any *normal* doors in this place—to what would be home for the next five months.

Her first impression was the sheer size of the room, but it mostly just looked dark and depressing. The scent of paint and new carpet lingered underneath the refreshing lilt of potpourri. She looked around for a light switch. "Don't you people ever turn on lights?"

Casting her a dour look, Mrs. Smith marched across the room and yanked open the heavy drapes shading the windows, flooding the room with warm afternoon sunshine. The transformation of dark to light made Tess gasp.

Decorated in warm beiges and soft greens, the room blossomed around her like a budding spring garden. The overstuffed furniture looked comfortable and inviting. The kind you could sink deeply into, curl up with a good book and lose yourself for an entire afternoon. She kicked off her shoes and dug her toes into carpeting so thick and luxuriant it felt like walking on pillows.

It was fresh and warm and alive. The perfect place to nurture the new life growing inside her.

If she had all the rooms in the world to choose, this would be the one she would pick.

"It's beautiful," she said. "And everything looks so new."

"And let's try to keep it that way," Mrs. Smith

said in that holier-than-thou tone. "Benjamin asked me to furnish you with whatever you need."

Orders she would follow, but not happily. But Tess was determined to remain marginally polite. She had the sneaking suspicion she would be running into this woman an awful lot over the next five months. Meaning that if she were so inclined, she could make Tess's life a living hell. "Thank you."

"I've taken the liberty of removing anything of value." She flashed Tess that condescending, distasteful look. As if Tess were not a houseguest, but something she'd scraped from the bottom of her shoe. Ben obviously hadn't instructed her to be nice.

Tess wouldn't give the old bird the satisfaction of knowing she'd bruised her pride. "Aw darn, my fence will be so disappointed."

With the ferocity of a mother bear protecting her cubs, she all but growled at Tess, "After all that Benjamin has been through, he doesn't deserve this. I won't let you hurt him."

Tess didn't point out that it took two to tango, and if Ben didn't want to be in this situation, maybe he should have become a monk. At the very least he shouldn't have taken Tess up to his room.

But what good would it do to try to defend herself when she was sure the frigid woman believed Tess had gotten pregnant on purpose? And Tess couldn't deny her own background. There was no escaping her social status. She'd been the last born in a long line of uneducated blue-collar workers. She hadn't even gone to college.

At least with her child Tess would be breaking the cycle.

"Dinner is at seven in the dining room," Mrs. Smith said in that cold, annoyed tone, then she turned and left, shutting the door behind her.

Tess let out a long, tired sigh and looked around, deciding the sooner she got herself settled in, the better. But she didn't see her bags. Across the room, through a second set of doors—ornate and gaudy of course—Tess found herself in an enormous bedroom. Not surprised that it was dark, she crossed the room and flung open the curtains, letting in a wash of golden sunshine. To her delight, the bedroom had been decorated in the same warm, earthy tones. She opened a set of French doors and stepped out onto the balcony, filling her lungs with fresh air. The view of the gardens below was breathtaking. Spring flowers exploded with color and rolling green grass seemed to stretch for miles. The white tips of the Scott Bar Mountains towered in the distance underneath a clear blue sky.

Wow.

This she could definitely live with.

She stepped back inside and found her bags waiting for her by the king-sized bed. She carried them to the cavernous walk-in closet, set them down then continued on into an enormous bathroom decorated in soft yellows with a Jacuzzi tub big enough for a family of four and an enclosed glass shower stall with two heads.

So this was how the other half lived. It was even more impressive than the presidential suite at the resort.

She rubbed her aching back and gazed longingly at the tub, then at her bags. Unpack first, bath later. But by the time she'd emptied her duffels and hung up all her things, she wanted nothing more than to lie down and rest.

Just a quick nap, she decided, then she would go exploring.

She stripped down to her birthday suit and pulled back the fluffy leaf patterned comforter and slipped beneath the cool, silky-soft vanilla-white sheets. She felt herself sinking as the mattress conformed to her body.

It was like curling up in a bowl of whipped cream. Within minutes she was sound asleep.

Ben pushed aside the drapes covering his office window and stood in a column of bright light, gazing out across acres of pristine rolling green grass and gardens blooming with vibrant shades of deep orange, sunny yellow and royal purple.

Jeanette would have loved this. It was exactly what she had envisioned when they bought this house. If he closed his eyes, he could imagine her out there, playing with their son. He would have been nearly a year old now. Maybe even walking. Saying his first words. In his imagination his little boy always had

Ben's dark hair and his mother's pale blue eyes and bright smile. He was always happy and laughing.

The door opened and he turned to see Mrs. Smith standing there, saving him from a landslide of painful memories. He let the curtain drop.

"Your guest is all settled in," she said.

"Thank you."

"Is there anything else?"

"No, nothing—oh wait, yes there is. I need you to go through the house and get rid of anything alcoholic."

She frowned. "Whatever for?"

"A condition of her staying here was that I stop drinking. She thinks I'm an alcoholic."

"And you let her believe—"

"It doesn't matter what she believes, I want her to feel comfortable here. Just do it please."

Mrs. Smith didn't look happy, but she didn't argue. "I'm going to say, again, that I don't like this arrangement."

"I know you don't." She hadn't liked Jeanette, either, but they had learned to coexist. She was so protective of him, the truth was, she would never think anyone was good enough.

"I know you still feel guilty, Ben, but it wasn't your fault."

He didn't have to ask what she meant. She had never said it to his face, but he knew she blamed his wife for his son's death. She'd always considered Jeanette spoiled and self-centered.

Her career had just been taking off when she found out she was pregnant. She'd been more annoyed than excited at the prospect of becoming a parent, by the physical limitations of her pregnancy. Afraid it would affect her career negatively—God forbid she get a stretch mark or two—she'd even talked briefly about terminating, but thankfully he'd managed to talk her out of it. He had been sure that given time to adjust, she would have enjoyed motherhood. At least, that had been his hope.

In the end, none of it had mattered.

"Have you called your parents?" Mrs. Smith asked.

His parents.

Having to explain this to his family was another problem altogether. They had never been overbearing or judgmental—quite the opposite in fact. He hadn't seen or heard from either of them since last Thanksgiving. That didn't mean it wouldn't be difficult for them to understand. In so many ways, they barely knew him. "Not yet."

"Don't you think you should?"

"Why? There's no point in getting them excited about a grandchild they're never going to see."

Four

Ben knocked on the door to Tess's suite, curious as to why she hadn't shown up for dinner. Why, in the three and a half hours since she'd arrived, she hadn't even ventured out of her suite.

No. He wasn't curious. He was downright worried.

According to Mrs. Smith she'd only had two bags and a couple of small boxes, so it couldn't have possibly taken her all this time to unpack. What if something was wrong? What if she was sick?

He knocked again, harder this time. "Tess, are you there?"

Knowing he probably shouldn't, he eased the door open. The sitting room was flooded with pinkish light from the setting sun. He'd always been fond of the color scheme, and Tess staying there seemed oddly appropriate somehow. Much like her, it was refreshing and cheerful and almost whimsical in its simplicity. And homey. That was what being with Tess had felt like.

Like coming home.

He stepped past the doorway and listened for the sound of movement. The suite was dead silent.

"Tess," he called, expecting an exasperated reply. In fact, if it meant she was all right, he welcomed a little sarcasm, but she didn't answer.

Fear looped like a noose around his neck, making it difficult to breathe.

What if she'd slipped and fallen?

What if she was hurt?

Without considering the consequences, he charged across the room to the partially open bedroom door and shoved his way through, his heart thumping against his rib cage. More muted sunshine and soft color—but no Tess. He stormed through her closet to the bathroom.

Empty.

Where had she gone? Had she snuck out? Had agreeing to stay here only been some sick joke to humor him?

He returned to the bedroom, teetering on the narrow ledge between anger and panic, when he heard a muffled snore from the vicinity of the bed. Only then did he notice the slight lump resting beneath a mountain of fluffy blankets.

Relief hit him so deep and swift his knees nearly buckled.

He'd been picturing her sprawled on the floor bleeding to death, and in reality she was only taking a nap.

He raked his hair back and shook his head. He had to get a grip, or this was going to be the longest five months of his life. He had to stop expecting the worst. She was safe here. The baby was safe. If he wasn't careful, he was going to drive her away. She wasn't his prisoner. She was a guest.

He considered waking her to see if she wanted something to eat, but decided against it. Though he hated the idea of her missing a meal, she obviously needed her sleep just as badly.

He walked over to the French doors and slid the drapes closed so the light wouldn't disturb her. Though his good sense told him to leave before she woke up and saw him there, he felt drawn to the bed. Drawn to her.

He couldn't screw this up. It was almost as if someone was giving him a second shot at this. The chance to keep this child and Tess safe. It wasn't a responsibility he planned to take lightly.

One quick look, he promised, just to be sure that she was all right, even though the steady cadence of soft breathing should have been assurance enough.

One quick look and he would leave.

The thick carpeting cushioned his steps as he crossed the room to the bed. Underneath an overstuffed comforter patterned with pale green leaves and yellow rose blooms, she lay curled on her side. She looked so small in the oversized bed, so vulnerable, like a nymph in a forest. Sweat beaded her forehead and dampened her upper lip and wisps of pale hair stuck to her cheek.

Would she overheat and make herself sick? It did feel awfully warm in here.

He very gently eased back the heavy comforter. Tess whimpered in her sleep and rolled onto her back. Only then, with the Egyptian cotton sheet clinging to her damp skin, exposing every dip and curve of her body in stark detail, did Ben realize she was naked.

Desire, swift and intense, rocked through him like a shock wave.

Get out now. And for God's sake don't touch her.

But she looked so pale against the cream-colored sheets. What if she wasn't just overheated? What if she was ill and burning up with a fever?

"Tess," he said softly, not wanting to startle her. She mumbled something incoherent and thrashed her head to one side. "Tess, wake up."

Don't do it, he warned himself, don't you dare touch her.

But the part of his brain that controlled his right arm apparently wasn't listening just then. He reached out and pressed the back of his wrist to her forehead, just as Mrs. Smith had when he was sick as a child, unsure of what it was exactly that he was supposed to feel.

Her skin was clammy and cool, which he took to be a good thing.

When he should have pulled away, he couldn't stop his hand from wandering over her skin, his fingers grazing the softness of her cheek. He liked her this way—all delicate and sweet and vulnerable. Her mouth looked soft and kissable. That night in the hotel he'd been addicted to her kisses. He'd been like an addict needing a fix, and when he woke the next morning to find her gone he'd craved her presence.

Even now, after all that had happened, there was something about Tess that he found irresistible.

Considering the position he held in Hollywood, not to mention coming from a wealthy family, he'd met his share of women with less than pure intentions. With Tess it had been different. As much as he hated the term, so *real*.

He wanted to feel that again. Which seemed unlikely now, given the circumstances. Or at the very least, not very smart. Even if these feelings he was having were mutual, she was having a child he could never accept. Definitely not the ingredients for a lasting relationship. Which is what she and the baby deserved. Someone to love them *both*.

Which would cause a person to wonder why he was still touching her.

He watched his thumb slip over the lush fullness of her lower lip, saw her lips part slightly and felt a puff of warm breath escape. The heat crawled up his thumb and into his hand, gaining momentum as it traveled through his arm and into his chest, kicking his pulse up a notch. He'd be damned if the woman didn't have a way of getting under his skin, making him feel.

From there the heat worked its way down in a swirl of sensation to his abdomen and settled firmly in the region just below his belt. The idea of bending down to brush his lips against hers, to feel that physical and emotional connection, was almost irresistible.

Almost.

Tess's eyes fluttered open and he jerked his hand away. She gazed up at him and her mouth curled into a drowsy, confused smile. "Hi."

Damn—she was pretty.

"Hi."

She looked around, puzzled by her surroundings, as if she'd forgot where she was. "You're in my room?"

She didn't sound angry, though she had every right to be. And he couldn't resist brushing the damp hair back from her forehead. What was it about her that made it so difficult to keep his hands to himself? "You didn't show up for dinner and I was worried. When I knocked and you didn't answer, I thought maybe something had happened to you."

Her eyes were still foggy from sleep and far too trusting. "Like what?"

Good question. It was obvious now that he'd over-reacted. "I don't know. I guess I just needed to know that you were okay. I should never have come in un-invited. I'm sorry."

No, he shouldn't have, but Tess couldn't work up

the will to be angry with him. She kept seeing the anguished look on his face when he talked about losing his son. Why didn't he just tell her how he really felt? Tell her he was scared?

Because he was a man, she reminded herself. And in her experience men didn't talk about their feelings. They never admitted fear. Especially men like him. They thought it made them weak.

Nothing about Ben Adams could be mistaken for weak. He was a walking powerhouse of pure testosterone and male perfection.

"I'm okay," she told him. "Just tired. It's been a long couple of days."

He stroked the hair back behind her ear. Despite how inappropriate his being here probably was, Tess didn't stop him. It was such a sweet gesture, and felt so good. Instead of telling him to leave, as she really should have, Tess closed her eyes and sighed.

After all, it's not as if he had never seen her in bed before. In bed *and* naked.

"That's nice," she said. "You did the same thing that night in the hotel."

"Did I?" He continued the gentle stroking, brushing past the shell of her ear, grazing her neck softly. Until it began to feel more than just *nice*. Exactly as it had that night. And for the same reason as then, she didn't reach up and wrap her arms around his neck, pull him down for a kiss. No matter how much she wanted to.

"You thought I was asleep. But I was only pretending."

"Why?"

She shrugged. "Maybe I was afraid that if I opened my eyes, you would tell me to leave. And maybe I wasn't ready to go."

"Why did you?" He stopped stroking and she looked up at him. His eyes were almost…sad. "Why did you leave?"

"What reason did I have to stay?"

"You tell me," he said. It was almost as if he wanted her to say she'd fallen for him. But at this point, what difference did it make?

"You can't deny we're both better off. Suppose I had stayed. Supposed we had fallen in love. And a month or so later I sprang the news on you that I was pregnant. Would you have been happy? Would it have made you want the baby any more than you do now?"

She could see by the look in his eyes and in the words that he didn't say, the answer to that question was no. It wouldn't have made any difference.

"It's not that I don't want it. I just…I can't do it." There was so much grief in his eyes, so much unresolved conflict. If he was ever going to get on with his life, he needed to learn to forgive himself.

She rolled on her side and propped herself up on her elbow, tucking the sheet under her arms. "Bad things happen to good people, Ben. Things we have no control over. It's no one's fault."

"And what about the things we do have control over? Who do we blame for that?"

She hated to see him sad and hurting when she

knew there wasn't a thing she could do or say to make him feel better. Only time would heal his wounds. The question was, how much time?

A year? Or ten? Or would he carry his guilt to the grave?

"Are you hungry?" he asked. "I could have something warmed for you."

Looked like their heart-to-heart was over. Would it always be this way? Every time she started to get close, would he push her away?

She rested her head back into the pillow. "I think I'd rather just sleep."

He nodded and rose to his feet. "I'll have a plate set aside in the fridge for you, just in case you change your mind."

"Thanks."

"Come find me tomorrow morning and I'll give you a tour of the house. I'm usually in my office."

"Okay."

"Good night, Tess. Sleep well."

"Good night."

He paused, looking as if he might say something else, then he turned and left. A second later she heard the door to her suite close.

She lay awake for a long time, watching the last traces of light disappear, counting the reasons why staying here was a good idea, so she could forget the reasons it wasn't.

The only thing she knew for certain is that she had to be careful. If Ben kept touching her so tenderly and looking at her with those lazy bedroom eyes she *was* going to do something stupid, like sleep with him. Then she would wind up doing something even *more* stupid.

Like fall in love.

Tess lay awake the following morning, not quite ready to roll out of bed. She'd slept over fifteen hours. Fifteen of the most restful hours she'd had in ages.

Despite everything, she felt comfortable here. And though yesterday she might not have been one hundred percent sure, she knew now that she was doing the right thing staying here. The right thing for her and the baby.

Knowing she no longer had to kill herself working too many hours, struggling to pay bills she couldn't afford, an enormous weight had been lifted from her shoulders. She felt a sense of peace she hadn't experienced in a long time.

The future was still blurry, but now at least she felt as if she were moving in the right direction.

She folded a hand over the little bump where her baby was growing. She couldn't wait to feel it move for the first time, and she was actually looking forward to getting big, even if that meant getting stretch marks. Since this first pregnancy could very well be her last, she wouldn't take a second of it for granted.

She only wished she had someone to share it with.

Some day soon she would have to think about getting maternity clothes. Though, without an income, she wasn't sure how she planned to pay for them. Her last check hadn't added up to much, and her savings were nearly depleted.

Maybe if she shopped at The Salvation Army. In the past she'd found some really awesome deals there. Designer labels—gently used—for dirt cheap. A girl did what she could to get by. No one could accuse her of not being resourceful.

And of course she could ask Ben to lend her money for clothes. She didn't doubt for a second that he would fall all over himself to accommodate her. In her experience, guilt could do that to a man. And if she were a different kind of woman she might take advantage of that. Lucky for him she had a conscience.

But Ben had done so much already. God only knows how she would ever pay him back.

She heard the door in the sitting room open.

Who could that be? Was it Ben coming to fetch her for the house tour. Or maybe he was coming to check on her, to see if she was still breathing.

She sat up, tucking the sheet close to her bare torso. Less than a minute passed before she heard the door close again. Whoever it was hadn't stayed long. Then the scent of bacon wafted her way. Her stomach rumbled and her mouth watered and she had to swallow to keep from drooling on herself.

She crawled out of bed, slipped her robe on and followed the scent to the table in the sitting room.

Someone had either anticipated her being ravenously hungry this morning, or they weren't sure what she liked.

There was a plate covered with three different types of eggs—omelet, scrambled and poached—and another piled high with pancakes, a delectable looking croissant and two slices of French toast. Beside that was yet another plate with sausage and bacon *and* a thick slab of ham. To drink she had a choice of orange juice, grapefruit juice, cranberry cocktail or hot tea.

Wow. Someone went all out. And because she hated seeing good food go to waste, she was sure she would eat way more than she should. She would have to ask Ben or the cook or whoever to take it easy on her portions or she was going to wind up gaining one hundred pounds.

With a body like hers, eight pounds of baby would be pushing the capacity.

On the table beside the tray lay a large white envelope with her name scrawled across the front. She picked it up and grazed her fingers over the letters, wondering if Ben had written it. She had no idea what his writing looked like. It was odd to be having a child with a man she knew virtually nothing about. To be living in his house.

She bit off a piece of bacon, grabbed the envelope and ripped it open. Inside she found a set of keys that did not belong to her car and a shiny new Visa card with her name on it.

The attached note read:

For whatever you and the baby need.

It was signed simply, B.

Wow.

She should have figured he would do something like this, yet every gesture of generosity still shocked her a little. He had an uncanny way of anticipating her every need. Not that she could accept this. But the polite thing to do would be to thank him. If her mother had taught her nothing else, she'd instilled Tess with good manners.

She quickly finished her breakfast, showered and dressed and headed down the stairs to Ben's office. She rapped on the door several times, but he didn't answer. Would it be okay to open the door and enter uninvited?

He'd come into her bedroom uninvited. Of course, that had been because he thought she might be maimed. Or dead. Besides, this was his office, not his bedroom. And he had told her to come get him this morning for a tour of the house.

So going in was probably just fine.

She reached for the knob…

"What are you doing?"

Tess jumped so high she nearly fell out of her shoes. She spun around and found Mrs. Smith standing there.

"You scared me," Tess said, her pulse pounding.

Mrs. Smith leered down her hook nose. "Why are you snooping around Benjamin's office?"

The old bat had an uncanny way of making Tess

feel like a deviant and she hadn't even done anything wrong. "I wasn't snooping. I was looking for him."

"He's not in his office."

Tess smothered an impatient sigh. "Where could I find him, then?"

"He's asked not to be disturbed."

It occurred to her just then that Mrs. Smith could be covering for him, hiding the fact that he was still drinking. Maybe he'd only said he would quit to get Tess to agree to stay.

Almost as quickly as the thought formed, she knew it wasn't true. Wouldn't she have smelled it on him last night when he came to her room? Wouldn't she have been able to tell by his behavior? She could spot a drunk a mile away.

Ben wouldn't have told her to come down to see him if he didn't mean it. No, there was only one person who didn't want Tess to see Ben.

Mrs. Smith.

"Tough," she told the old bag. "He left me something and I need to talk to him."

"If this is about the car, it's in the garage. The dark blue Mercedes."

A Mercedes? She'd never driven an import. In fact, she'd never driven anything under twenty years old and on its last leg. "I don't know if I feel right using his car."

"It's not his car. He ordered it for you. It was delivered this morning."

"Delivered?" Tess asked.

"From the dealership."

"Dealership?"

She gave Tess an exasperated look, as if she were addressing an obtuse child—or the village idiot. "Is English a second language for you? Yes, a *dealership*. Where they sell *cars*. You do know what a car is?"

Yeah, and there was no way the man actually bought her one. "So what, it's like a rental until mine is fixed?"

"No, it's a lease."

"He *leased* me a Mercedes?" What about her car? He said he would replace the carburetor.

"Benjamin is a very generous man," she said, looking at Tess with barely masked disdain. "Too much, I think."

Tess couldn't disagree with her. Generosity like Ben's was completely foreign to her. And unsettling.

"You know, I didn't ask for any of this," Tess told her.

"What you did or didn't ask for is of no consequence to me."

From the other side of the door Tess heard the phone ring. Only once, as if someone had answered it right away. Mrs. Smith's eyes widened a fraction and Tess knew instantly that she'd been lying about Ben not being in there. But when she made a move for the knob Mrs. Smith insinuated herself between Tess and the door.

She shot Tess a tight-lipped defiant look. "You're not going in there."

Five

"But Benji, I haven't seen you in so long!"

Ben sighed and shook his head. God how he hated that nickname. It was annoying when he was ten, downright embarrassing when he was a teenager, now he swore she did it just to piss him off. "I'm sorry, Mom, it's just not a good time for a visit."

Not for at least another five months. Why was it that he hadn't heard from his parents for months, and out of the blue his mom calls, determined to make the trip overseas to see him.

She always did have lousy timing. She had been on location filming for nearly every major event of his life. If she'd had the option of paying someone to give birth to him for her, she probably would have.

"I promise I won't get in the way. You won't even know I'm there."

"I have so much work I wouldn't be able to spend any time with you. In fact, I'll probably be going back to L.A. for a while." Big fat lie. He had no plans to leave the city. Or the house for that matter. "You know how much you hate it there."

He heard his mother sigh disappointedly and tried not to let it bother him. She hadn't been concerned with his feelings when she had to trot off and shoot a movie for eight weeks, or attend openings halfway around the globe. He didn't complain when his parents took their private vacations. Because they just *needed* to get away.

She had absolutely no right to expect anything from him. And still he felt guilty for telling her no.

From outside his office door he heard raised voices.

Aw hell, were Mrs. Smith and the cook going at it again?

"Mom, I have to let you go."

"But Benji—"

"Something's come up. I'll call you later. I promise." Much later. Like five months from now.

He hung up before she reduced herself to begging. He would have to stop answering the phone when she called.

He pushed himself up from his chair and crossed the room. He pulled the door open to find Mrs. Smith standing there with her back to him, arms spread as if she were guarding the doorway.

What the—?

Tess stood across the hall, cheeks bright with anger, fists clenched, looking ready for a fight.

A knock-down, drag-out brawl.

Mrs. Smith could be a mean old bird, but he'd put his money on Tess, hands down. She may have been little, but Tess has street smarts, and man was she tough.

"I told you that he doesn't want to be disturbed," Mrs. Smith snapped at Tess, in the scolding tone Ben recalled from his childhood. The tone that said she wasn't taking any crap.

"I don't care," Tess snapped back just as forcefully. "I need to talk to him."

Neither seemed to notice him standing there.

"Can't you just leave Benjamin alone?" she hissed. "Why is it that you insist on making this harder for him. He's giving that bastard child a decent life. Isn't that enough?"

Ouch.

Tess opened her mouth to reply, then noticed Ben standing there. Whatever she had been about to say evaporated, and by the look on her face he knew exactly what she was thinking. She was wondering if he'd heard that *bastard child* comment.

"What's going on here?" he asked.

Mrs. Smith let out an undignified gasp of surprise and swiveled to face him. The color leached from her already pasty face. "I—I told her before you don't like to be disturbed while you work, and I caught her sneaking in here."

"I wasn't *sneaking*," Tess said, giving Mrs. Smith the evil eye. And here he'd been under the impression Tess was afraid of his housekeeper. Most people were. Every now and then she even gave him the willies.

But if Tess had been, she'd apparently gotten over it.

"I asked Tess to come and see me today," Ben told Mrs. Smith. "I promised her a tour of the house."

Mrs. Smith forced a smile. "All you had to do was ask. I'd be happy to give her a tour."

He would bet his bank balance she'd be *happier* removing her own eye with a fork than spending time with Tess.

He leaned in the doorjamb and sighed. This was so not going to be fun. "Tess, could you excuse us please? Mrs. Smith and I need a quick word."

As his housekeeper moved silently past him into the room, Tess shot her a smug look. Ben had to fight a grin. It wouldn't have surprised him a bit to see her stick out her tongue.

Those two didn't realize just how alike they were. But to tell either would probably earn him a black eye.

"Give me five minutes," he told Tess. When he shut the door, she was smiling.

He turned to his housekeeper and could see by the starch in her spine she was going to make this difficult.

"Have a seat."

She looked down her nose at him—a real feat considering he was several inches taller than she was. "I'd rather stand."

"Please, Mildred."

She relented and sat primly on the edge of the seat opposite his desk.

"I know you won't like this, but I want you to stop interfering."

"I'm looking out for your best interests," she said, as if that justified her behavior.

"Be that as it may, I want it to stop. You don't even know her."

"Neither do you."

And it would seem Mrs. Smith wanted to keep it that way. "But I'd like to get to know her. Maybe I can't be a father to that *bastard child* she's carrying, but it's still mine."

She lowered her eyes to her lap.

"Have you forgotten that my parents weren't married when they had me?"

"It was said out of anger. I apologize for my thoughtlessness."

"Would you please drop the faithful employee martyr act?" He sat on the edge of his desk. "You're family, and I love you. I understand that you're only trying to protect me, but I want it to stop. Understand?"

She nodded.

"I know you still blame Jeanette for what happened."

She looked up at him. "Is that any worse than you blaming yourself?"

"And assigning blame hasn't gotten either of us anywhere. Has it?"

She shook her head.

"I know you didn't like Jeanette, and yes, she had her share of undesirable qualities. Who doesn't? Despite her faults, she was my wife and I loved her."

"And Tess?"

"What has she done to you to make you dislike her so? I think she's made it pretty clear that she wants nothing from me."

"She says that now."

"I know you don't like it, but as Tess reminded me, she didn't make this baby alone. I share equally in the responsibility."

"I still don't trust her."

"She may act tough, but I don't doubt for a minute that this is just as difficult for her as it is for me. If you take the time to get to know her, I think you might like her."

"And you?" she asked. "Do you like her?"

"I do like her." Probably too much for his own good. "So, do we understand each other?"

"Yes."

"You promise to stop meddling?"

She nodded.

"I want to hear you say it," he told her and she shot him an exasperated look. "Come on. Say, 'Ben, I promise not to meddle.'"

She rolled her eyes heavenward. "I promise not to meddle."

"See how easy that was?"

"May I go now?"

"Sure. Send Tess in on your way out."

He watched as she rose from the chair and walked to the door, and when she pulled it open, Tess all but fell into the room. Like perhaps she'd been leaning against it. Trying to hear their conversation maybe?

"Whoops!" she said, looking from Ben to Mrs. Smith. "I must have tripped."

Mrs. Smith shot him a look—one that asked, I'm supposed to be *nice* to her?—before she stepped past Tess and out the door. Ben folded his arms over his chest and grinned at Tess.

She shot him a look of pure innocence. "I wasn't listening, I swear. I was just…leaning."

"The door is sound proof," he said.

She made a *pfft* sound. "Which explains why I couldn't hear a darned thing."

He just shook his head.

"Oh, come on," she said. "Can you blame me? She hasn't exactly been nice to me."

"That shouldn't be an issue any longer."

"Yeah, sure," she said with a snort. "I'll believe that when I see it."

Man, did he like her. And he could see that having her around would, if nothing else, keep things interesting.

"How was your first night here? I take it you slept well."

"Like a baby."

"Did you enjoy your breakfast?"

"It was good. Although there was an awful lot of it."

"Sorry. I wasn't sure what you would like."

"That's what I figured. But I'm not picky. I'll eat pretty much everything. And in slightly smaller quantities next time, please."

"I'll let the cook know." He pushed off from his desk. "Are you ready for your tour?"

"I wanted to discuss something with you first." She stepped over to him. "I can't accept this."

She handed him the credit card he'd left in her room this morning.

"I got it for you," he said.

"And I appreciate the gesture. Really I do. I thought about it a lot and decided it's too much."

"No, it isn't, Tess."

"Yes. It really is. You're doing too much already."

"You can't tell me you don't need things. Just take it." He held out the card and she pushed his hand away.

"I have money, you know."

"Not that I enjoy playing *I can top that,* but I'm almost certain I have more. You and the baby are my responsibility now."

"The only person responsible for me, is *me.*"

What was he, a magnet for stubborn women?

She was so damned proud. It annoyed him almost as much as he admired her for it.

"And here," she said, handing him the car key. "I'd feel much more comfortable driving my own car."

Uh-oh. "That could be a problem."

She narrowed her eyes at him. *"Why?"*

"It's sort of…gone."

"Gone to be fixed?"

"Ah, no. Just gone."

"Gone where exactly?"

"Car heaven."

Now her eyes went wide. *"Car heaven?"*

He could see that she was losing her patience. Not that he could blame her. He wouldn't be real happy if someone had sent his car to the junkyard. Of course, his car wasn't a death trap on wheels. "I had a mechanic look at it. He said the car was worth half the cost of everything that needed to be fixed. Not to mention it was lacking most modern safety features. It wasn't safe."

"Ben, you said you would buy me a new carburetor."

"And I did. It's in the garage, in the Mercedes."

She closed her eyes and shook her head. "Cute."

"It was a sound investment, and it's a safe vehicle. Antilock brakes, air bags, GPS, the works."

"You sure you can even handle me operating a motor vehicle? What if I'm late? Suppose I'm out somewhere and I lose track of time. You may have an anxiety attack. Or call in the Marines."

"Nope. I have that covered." He leaned back and opened the top drawer of his desk, pulling out the phone he'd ordered for her. He held it up so she could see. "I'll just call you on this."

"Jeez! You bought me a phone, too? Is there anything else? A pony maybe?"

"Would you like a pony?"

She gave him that stern, squinty-eyed look. "You

would, wouldn't you? You would actually buy a pony just to spite me. You would probably build a stable, too. And hire a trainer, all because I dared you to."

Yeah, he probably would.

He just smiled. "Come on, Tess. You need a car, and I have an extra one. If you don't use it, no one will."

"What about Mrs. Smith? Can't she use it?"

"She has a Rolls."

"You bought your housekeeper a *Rolls-Royce?*"

He grinned. "Perk of the job. Now, will you drive it, or do I have buy that pony?"

She held out her hand. "Fine, I'll drive the car."

He dropped the key in her palm and handed her the phone. She stuck them both in the pocket of her jeans—jeans that were looking more than a little snug in the tummy. In fact, he was pretty sure she'd left the button undone.

"Now are you ready for the tour?" he asked.

"Let's do it."

She obviously needed new clothes and would eventually need things for the baby, but he wasn't going to push his luck with the credit card.

Not yet anyway.

After touring the house, Tess came to a conclusion.

Ben had *way* too much money.

Until she'd seen all the rooms, she'd never realized exactly how many of them there were. How freaking enormous the house really was. Four huge floors including the walkout basement.

Eight bedrooms, six full bathrooms and two half baths. Two full suites and servants' quarters. Two kitchens. A walk-in pantry stocked to the gills with enough canned and dry food to last an ice age.

He owned a library packed floor to ceiling with shelf after shelf of books. Biographies to classic literary fiction and everything in between. Hardback and paperback. And she was pleased to see that he even had a decent collection of romance and women's fiction—which he swore were sent to him by agents hoping to sell movie rights.

The lower level of the house was where he seemed to keep all his toys. There was a screening room scented of leather and new carpet with an attached projection room full of all kinds of funky electronic equipment that she assumed had something to with Ben's work as a producer. Next to the screening room he led her into a fully equipped exercise room that put most gyms to shame, which he told her she was free to use at any time day or night. The tour ended in a game room equipped with a dart board, a foosball and pool table and four full-size classic arcade games. There was also an attached kitchen and a full bar that was conspicuously devoid of alcohol.

Each room he led her into had been as dark and gray and depressing as the next. Until she hit a light switch or opened the drapes, revealing life and color and all of the subtleties and warmth that made a house a home.

And as interesting as the tour proved to be, Tess had been even more enthralled watching Ben as he led her from room to room. She found herself mesmerized by the casual yet confident way he carried himself. Sleeves rolled, hands dipped loosely in the pockets of his slacks. She'd never known a man who seemed so comfortable in his own skin. She was pretty sure he was oblivious to how gorgeous he was, or if he knew, he didn't care. Maybe that was part of what made him so attractive. She found herself hypnotized by the sound of his deep voice, drawn to his energy as he seemed to put his whole heart into everything he said and did.

Though they had yet to really connect on an intellectual level, she knew instinctively that she would be as attracted to his mind as to his killer body and handsome face. Despite his pampered upbringing and assumingly top-notch education, it was obvious Ben had never developed the over-inflated ego she would expect from a man in his position. As far as she could tell, he was generous and kind and an all-around nice guy—when he wasn't doing things to annoy her, that is.

She'd always had a tough time figuring men out. But despite his few slightly annoying habits—like stealing her car—being with Ben felt easier. More mature maybe. But in a way that had nothing to do with age or experience. She had dated *mature* men who psychologically never made it past their eighteenth birthday. The ones who say they're ready to take the relationship to the next level, then have kittens when they see the extra toothbrush on the bathroom sink.

Sharing space obviously wasn't a problem for Ben. In fact, she couldn't recall a single issue that he'd deemed a *problem*. He never seemed to complain about anything.

She didn't doubt that falling in love with him would be as natural and effortless as breathing.

Meaning she would have to work all the harder not to.

"So what do you think of my house?" he asked.

"It's nice," she told him. "Although, for some reason I wouldn't have pictured you in a house this big. I don't want to say it's pretentious. It's beautiful. It just doesn't seem to fit you."

"The big house was Jeanette's idea. She was a small-town girl with big dreams. I think that buying this house was her way of showing everyone back home that she'd made it. Despite the fact that I thought it was too big, I couldn't deny her that."

"I knew girls like that back in my hometown. Not that I can recall a single one accomplishing much though."

"Ironically, she never even spent the night here. The renovations weren't finished until after she died."

"Everything looks new."

"Most of it is. She worked with the decorator for months. She was so proud of it all."

She could see a lot of love in his eyes for his late

wife, but there was something else there. Regret maybe? Or was it just sadness?

"You must really miss her."

"Some things I miss, some I don't."

When she shot him a curious look, he simply said, "No marriage is perfect."

Was it possible that he and Jeanette didn't have a good marriage? Or that they'd been having problems?

She couldn't deny she was curious, but if he wanted her to know the intimate details of his relationship with Jeanette, he would tell her. She was in no position to go fishing.

"This isn't new." She ran a hand across the edge of the pool table, over the well-worn felt.

"I've had this since I was a kid." Ben followed her with those dark, inquisitive eyes, making her ultra-aware of every move she made. Aware of the way the soft felt tickled her fingers, how, depending on the mood, the move was almost enticing. Not that she'd meant it to be. At least, not consciously.

"You must play a lot."

"When I can't sleep, usually. It clears my head. Helps me sort things through. It's gotten a lot of use the past year. Do you play?"

"I'm more of a Ping-Pong girl. Not that I don't have fond memories of one pool table in particular."

"Really?" He gave her a look, one filled with playful curiosity, and she knew exactly what he was thinking. What every guy would think.

She couldn't resist smiling. "Get your mind out of

the gutter. It's nothing like that. It's where I had my first real kiss."

"Sounds romantic," he teased.

"It really was." She felt wistful just remembering. A girl never forgot the thrill of her first kiss. "It was a friend's older brother. I was fifteen and he was eighteen."

"An older man." Ben sat on the edge of the table, folding his arms across his chest, looking genuinely interested. "How did it happen?"

She sat beside him. It had been so long since she'd even thought about it, but she remembered every detail. "Well, my friend was upstairs helping her mom with dinner and I was in the basement with her brother Noah, watching him play pool. We were talking and somehow we got around to the subject of whether or not I had a boyfriend. When I told him no, he said he couldn't believe a pretty girl like me didn't have ten boyfriends. Then he asked if I'd ever kissed a boy. Of course I turned fifty shades of red."

"What did you tell him?"

"The truth. That I hadn't. Not really. Not a *real* kiss."

"So then what? He tossed you down on the table and planted one on you?"

She gave him a playful shove. "No. It was very sweet. He was sitting on the edge of the table, kind of like you are. I was standing in front of him." She pushed off the table and stood a couple feet in front of him. "Like this."

Ben unfolded his arms and rested his hands on the

table beside him, and for a minute he actually looked the way Noah had that day. They were both dark, and had that long-haired, simmering, rebellious look. And they were similar in personality. Very sweet when they wanted to be—with the potential to be thickheaded. Maybe that's why she was so attracted to Ben. He reminded her of her first crush.

"Then what happened?" he asked.

"He reached up and took one of my hands and kinda pulled me closer, so I was in between his legs."

"You mean like this?" Ben took her right hand in his and tugged her to him. Her heart fluttered wildly when her legs brushed against his inner thighs and all of the sudden they were this close.

"Uh-huh." Exactly like that. The memory of the awe and excitement and the rush of emotions came rolling back to her. She recalled the exact instant when she realized she was about to experience her first real kiss. She remembered exactly what his lips had felt like as they brushed across hers. How it was so slow and sweet, how he'd taken his time. The thrill of his lips parting and his tongue touching her. Some girls she knew still thought tongue kissing was gross, but Tess had just about melted. He tasted warm and exciting and forbidden. A blend of cigarettes, soda and lust.

At the time she didn't recognize what lust was exactly. She just knew it was a feeling she liked.

She still liked it.

Too much.

Ben's eyes searched her face. He was so close she could feel the warmth of his body through his clothes. She could feel the whisper of his breath on her lips when he asked, "Then what did he do?"

She knew that if she told Ben, he would kiss her. And then who knows what might happen? She wasn't a fifteen-year-old girl any longer with naiveté and fear still on her side to help stop things before they got out of control. She had needs and desires just like Ben and she didn't trust herself to put on the brakes.

As much as she wanted him to kiss her, she knew she couldn't let him do it.

"After a few heavy-duty make out sessions over the next couple of weeks, he got Tracy Fay Bejarski pregnant, got married in a shotgun wedding and moved into a single wide across town."

He took the hint and, with a trace of regret in his eyes, let go of her hand. Regret she could definitely identify with.

She took a step back.

"Not exactly a happy ending," he said.

"I was devastated. A couple of kisses and I thought it was true love. Things were pretty bad at home, and I used to fantasize we would fall in love and run away together. I should be grateful. He didn't make much of his life. He and Tracy Fay divorced after baby number four and last I heard he's working nights at the gas station and spends the better part of his days in the bar."

"Benjamin?"

They both turned to find Mrs. Smith in the doorway. Tess wondered how long she'd been standing there watching them. How much she'd heard.

"Lunch is ready," she said.

"We'll be right up," Ben told her.

Mrs. Smith shot them a slightly suspicious look, then turned and left.

"Actually, I think I'll skip it," Tess said. "I'm still pretty full from breakfast. I think I'll take a walk in the gardens instead."

"Are you sure?"

"Yeah. I think the fresh air will do me good." For some reason she felt as if she needed a little time alone. Time to clear the unpleasant memories.

And the pleasant ones.

"I'll have the cook put something aside for you, in case you change your mind."

"Thanks."

He turned to leave and made it as far as the door before he turned back. "You know, you're right. It was a good thing it didn't work out between you and your friend's brother. You deserve better."

Maybe he was right, but she'd learned the hard way that the less you expected from life, the less you were disappointed when you didn't get what you wanted.

Six

Ben sat at his computer hitting Delete to erase the dozen e-mails his mother had sent in the week since their last phone conversation, the day Tess had arrived. Why on earth was she suddenly so determined to insinuate herself into his life? Could her timing be any worse?

His office door swung open and he looked up to see Tess standing there.

"Back from your morning walk?" he asked.

She stormed over to his desk, wearing that squinty-eyed, furious look she'd had the other day when he informed her that he'd gotten rid of her car.

"What did you do with them?" she demanded,

hovering over his desk, looking as if she might lunge over and throttle him.

Well, someone's panties were in a twist. And damn, she was cute when she was angry. A compact package of attitude and sass.

"Do with what?"

"My clothes," she said through gritted teeth. "I came back from my walk to take a shower and they were all gone."

He had the almost overwhelming urge to pull her in his arms and kiss that scowl right of those pretty pink lips.

He was quite sure if he did, she would deck him.

"Are they?" He calmly folded his arms over his chest and leaned back in his chair. "Have you checked the laundry?"

She slammed her hands down on her hips. "Why would the clean clothes that were hanging in my closet this morning be in the dirty laundry? Even my underwear are missing!"

He shrugged. "It was just a thought. I could ask Mrs. Smith if she's seen them."

Her cheeks flushed red with anger. "Give them back."

"I can't give you back something I don't have." He pushed up from his chair and walked across the room to the fireplace. He grabbed the iron poker and jostled the embers smoldering there.

Her eyes went wide and her mouth fell open in horror. "You *didn't.*"

He set the poker back in the rack and turned to her, a confused look on his face. "Didn't what?"

She marched over to where he stood, gazing into the fireplace then looked up at him, aghast. "You *burned* my clothes?"

She was beside herself with anger—and completely adorable. He tried to look sympathetic, but a smile was breaking through.

"Oh my God! You think this is *funny?*" She darted a glance around the room, as if she were searching for something to throw at him. Or bludgeon him with.

"You need clothes, Tess. Otherwise you wouldn't be wearing shirts that are too tight and jeans you can't even button."

"What are you, the fashion police?" She tugged her shirt down in an attempt to cover the waist of her jeans, but it was—as he'd suspected—too small. "Besides, that is *not* the point."

"You said you have money, right? So what's the problem? Just buy new clothes."

"Yes, I have money, but not for an entire wardrobe!"

"Well then, I have the perfect solution." He slipped the credit card from his back pocket. The one she'd refused to take five days ago. "You can use this."

"You are unbelievable. Is there *nothing* you won't do to get your way?"

"Use this and you can save your money for a time when you really need it."

She looked as if she might burst with frustration.

"Don't you get it? I don't feel comfortable taking anything else from you. I hate owing people money."

If they were going to get into a debate on who owed whom, he owed her and the baby a hell of a lot more that she would ever know. More than he would ever be capable of giving. "You're not taking anything. I'm offering."

She looked at him like he was nuts. "What's the difference?"

"Tess, do you have any clue how much money I have?"

"Yeah," she snapped. "Way *too* much."

"Please," he said. "Let me do this for you."

Something in his face must have revealed his feelings, because her expression softened from anger to mild annoyance.

"Fine," she said after a moment. "But I'm going to pay you back. I don't know when, and I don't know how, but I'll return every penny that I spend."

"If that's what you want." He didn't bother to tell her he would never accept money from her.

He would burn that bridge when they came to it.

He held out the card and she reluctantly took it. "Don't believe for a second that you're completely off the hook here. I'm still mad as hell at you. If you do anything even remotely close to as stupid as this ever again, it's going to be your clothes in the fireplace next time. And you'll be shopping for new clothes completely naked, because I'll get it all."

A grin tugged at the corner of his mouth. He

didn't doubt for a second that she would do it. "I'll keep that in mind."

She shook her head, grumbling under her breath as she turned to leave.

"Will I see you at dinner tonight?" he asked. Every night since she'd arrived they had shared dinner together. And lunch.

She looked back at him over her shoulder. "Maybe I'll see you, maybe I won't. It just depends on how mad I still am at you." Then she left, slamming the door shut behind her.

No, she would be there. Because as angry as she might have been, he had seen something else dwelling just below the surface.

Relief.

She knew damned well she needed things, but she didn't want to spend the last of her money. She was the kind of woman who liked to keep a little extra for a rainy day. It made her feel safe.

What she didn't seem to get, or just hadn't accepted, was that she never had to worry about money again. She would be taken care of for the rest of her life, no exceptions. He would see to that.

Once he made a promise he didn't break it.

"That was wonderful," Tess said, wiping away any last traces of chocolate mousse from the corners of her mouth. She settled a hand on her overstuffed stomach. "I ate way too much again."

Ben sat across from her, sipping a steaming cup of coffee. "I'll tell the cook you enjoyed it."

She leaned back in her chair and sighed with contentment. Though she'd considered being a no-show, she'd decided to have dinner with him despite his stunt this afternoon.

She'd confronted him earlier feeling as if she would never forgive him, never trust him again, then he'd smiled—an adorable grin filled with amusement and affection—and it had been nearly impossible to hold on to the anger. He'd just looked so happy that he'd gotten what he wanted, and while normally that would have annoyed her even more, she realized in his own clueless male way, he meant well. Despite what she might have believed when she moved here, Ben really wasn't trying to manipulate or control her. He just wanted to take care of her.

It was tough to fault a guy for being generous and kind, even if his methods were slightly off the wall. And she couldn't deny driving a fifty thousand dollar car and shopping her heart out had been a blast.

After a couple of hours in town shopping, she'd begun to feel a little like Julia Roberts in *Pretty Woman*. Except, of course, that she wasn't a hooker, and Edward hadn't gotten Vivian pregnant.

And this wasn't a movie. It was real life. Ben wouldn't be sweeping her off her feet, or in Vivian's case, off a fire escape. They wouldn't ride off into the sunset together in his limo and live happily ever after.

"So," Ben said, dropping his napkin on the table. "What would you like to do now?"

She shrugged. "I don't know. What do you want to do?"

Although she already had a pretty good idea. He'd been teaching her to play pool. Rather unsuccessfully.

"Game room?"

"Why, so you can slaughter me at pool?"

"We don't have to play pool." He had this grin, like he knew something she didn't. What was he up to now?

Honestly, she was afraid to ask.

"I told you, video games were never really my thing and I suck at foosball."

"So we'll do something else," he said.

"Darts?"

"Nope."

Now she was getting curious, which with him could be a dangerous thing. In more ways than one. Since their almost kiss on the pool table the other day, they had both been pretty good about keeping their hands to themselves. Ben's eyes were another matter altogether. It seemed he was always watching her, studying her. But not in a way that made her feel uncomfortable. Instead she felt so...*aware* of herself. Aware of him.

Even though she shouldn't be.

"You'll see," he said, rising from his chair, motioning her to join him.

"All right." She got up and followed him downstairs to the game room, all the while feeling he had something up his sleeve. She found out what it was when he switched on the game room light, and she saw the brand new Ping-Pong table sitting there.

She groaned and shook her head. "You can't go a week without spending money on me, can you?"

He shrugged apologetically. "Sorry. It was this or the pony, and we both know how you feel about that."

The man was hopeless. "You really do have too much money, don't you?"

He grinned and handed her a paddle. "Want to play?"

Of course she did. She took the paddle from him. "I have to warn you, I'm pretty good. I might bruise your ego."

"It's been bruised before," he said, taking one side of the table.

"That's what you think." She flashed him a devilish smile. "Ten bucks says I whup your behind."

Tess did whup him. Repeatedly and shamelessly. But Ben redeemed himself by decimating her at a game of pool.

If it had been Jeanette playing, she would have pouted and complained over losing. If she couldn't do something perfectly, she didn't like to do it at all. She'd been incredibly competitive.

Tess on the other hand didn't seem to care who won or lost, as long as they were having fun. And they did have fun. She had a playful, almost silly side that was unexpectedly refreshing. She brought light into a world that had been too dark far too long. She gave him hope.

Though, hope for what, he hadn't figured out yet.

After an hour of fierce competition, they took a break and Ben got them each a bottle of water from the refrigerator behind the bar.

"That was fun," she said. "I haven't played Ping-Pong in a long time."

"It was fun," he agreed.

"If I wasn't here, what would you be doing? What was a typical Friday night for you?"

He leaned on the bar and took a swig of his water. "Either work or watch television."

"I thought you Hollywood types did exciting things, like going to parties or night clubs."

"Not anymore. All Jeanette ever used to want to do was go out barhopping and it seemed as though there was always someone throwing a party we just *had* to be at."

"You didn't like that?"

"Occasionally I don't mind getting out. But the truth is, I'm more of a homebody."

Tess leaned forward and rested her elbows on the bar, propping her chin on the backs of her hands. "I'm exactly the same way. Give me a good movie, a bowl of popcorn and a comfy couch to curl into and I'm in heaven."

"You like movies, huh?"

"I *love* movies."

"What kind?"

"I'll watch pretty much anything. I'm a movie junkie. The employees at Blockbuster know me by name."

"Then there's something I should show you."

Her brow furrowed. "Uh-oh, you have that look. The one you get just before you give me stuff. What did you buy this time?"

He flashed her a grin. "I didn't buy you a thing. I promise."

He led her upstairs to the den where he kept all of his entertainment equipment. Besides his office, he spent most of his time here. It was the one room in the house he'd insisted on having input in as far as interior design went.

He motioned to the door that was nearly hidden in the seams of the rich wood paneling. "See that door?"

She squinted in the direction of the wall. "Oh, yeah. A hidden door. Cool."

"Open it."

"How? There's no knob."

"Give the right side a push and the door will pop open."

She gave him a look, like she wasn't sure she should trust him. "You promise there isn't a pony in there?"

"I promise."

She gave the door a push. The latch clicked and the door swung open and Tess gasped.

"Oh my God." She stared openmouthed at row after row of DVDs, floor to ceiling, spanning either side of the narrow four foot deep closet. "You must have every DVD in existence."

"Probably close to it," he said. "You like it?"

"*Like* it? It's amazing."

He watched with a smile as she stepped inside and ran her hand along a row of cases, as if she were soaking up their essence through the pores in her hand, a look of pure delight on her face.

"You could say I'm a movie junkie, too."

"I guess. Have you watched them all?"

"Most of them I've seen at one point or another. A lot of the older movies I haven't watched on DVD yet."

"I love old movies. John Wayne and Jimmy Stewart. And I love Hitchcock. *Psycho* is my all time favorite horror flick."

"Would you like to watch something?"

Her eyes lit up. "Could we?"

"Sure. Unless you're too tired." She typically retired to her suite before ten, and it was almost nine-thirty.

"I won't kill me to stay up late one night."

"Pick something. They're in alphabetical order, sorted by genre."

She spun in a slow circle. "I don't even know where to begin. On this shelf alone I see four or five possibilities."

"I have a lot of television series sets, too."

He watched as she scanned shelf after shelf of titles, still shaking her head in amazement. She looked so…happy. He liked that he could do this for her. That her stay here would be a pleasant one. She deserved it.

"How about this one," she asked, choosing an old Spencer Tracy-Katharine Hepburn film still sealed in plastic. "I haven't seen this in years."

"Sounds good to me." He took it from her and started setting up the system. "Go ahead and take a seat."

"Hey, Ben?"

He switched on the DVD player. "Yeah?"

"I just wanted to thank you."

He turned to her. She had a smile on her face. But her eyes looked sad.

"For putting on a movie?"

"For everything."

He was about to tell her there was no need to thank him. He owed her and the baby, and he would do anything to see that they both came out of this healthy and happy. But he didn't think that was what she needed to hear. She already knew that.

So he said the only thing he could say. "You're welcome."

It was after eleven when the movie ended. Not that Ben had spent a whole lot of time with his eyes on the screen. As always, he found that watching the woman stretched out on the couch across the room was a much more pleasing way to pass the time.

How was it that he never tired of looking at her? She wasn't the kind of woman who strutted into a room and stunned every man with her breathtaking beauty. She was much more subtle than that. So soft and petite, but sturdy somehow. Cute and sassy, and almost wholesome, until she opened her mouth and fired off a dose of attitude.

In the same way he had been attracted to Jeanette's fire and lust for life, Tess's quiet, determined nature fascinated him. He'd met more than his share of women over the years, through business or socially, but he couldn't recall ever knowing anyone quite like her.

When the credits began to roll on the screen, Tess turned to him and smiled. "That was *so* good."

Since he hadn't really been paying attention, he would take her word for it.

She yawned and stretched. "I wish we had time for another one, but I'm exhausted. I'm usually sound asleep by now."

He switched on the lamp beside his chair and used the remote to shut off the television. "We can do it again tomorrow night."

He walked over to the couch and held out a hand to give her boost up. She accepted and let him pull her to her feet. "I'll walk you to your room."

She yawned again and walked with him to the stairs. Mrs. Smith had already gone to bed and most of the lights were turned off.

"I'll probably sleep in tomorrow. Lately, if I don't get at least eight hours, I'm like the walking dead."

"Jeanette had that, too," he found himself saying. He didn't mind talking about Jeanette, but talking about her pregnancy was tough. Too many memories.

She smoothed a hand over her belly, a look of pure and complete contentment on her face. "It's worth it."

Another way she and Jeanette were so very different. Jeanette had flat out told him he had better be happy with one child, because she wasn't planning on doing the *pregnancy thing* ever again. Not that he thought it made her a bad person. She just had different priorities. Her career meant everything to her. She'd worked damned hard and sacrificed a hell of a lot to make a name for herself.

As much as he admired and appreciated his wife, he admired and appreciated Tess for all her differences.

"Does it kick yet?" he heard himself ask.

Where had that come from? He didn't want to know any more about the baby than necessary. All that mattered was that it was healthy.

"Not yet. Although I have felt flutters that may or may not be Braxton Hicks or indigestion. I'll ask next week at my five month checkup."

Five months already, meaning it had been nearly a month since she'd first come to give him the news. It seemed like only yesterday, so why did he feel as if he'd known her a lifetime? What was it about her that made him feel so…connected?

"I can leave a note for Mrs. Smith to have your breakfast brought up a bit later tomorrow morning if you'd like."

"That would be nice," she said. "As long as it's no trouble."

He didn't ask any more questions about the baby

and thankfully she didn't offer any details. When they reached her suite, they both stopped outside the door. Tess gazed up at him through the dim light, a sleepy, contented smile on her face. "I had a *really* good time tonight."

"I did, too."

She looked at the door, then back at him, her bottom lip clamped between her teeth.

"Anything wrong?" he asked.

"No. I just…" She lowered her eyes.

"You just what?" he asked, and the next thing he knew, Tess's arms were around him in a bone crushingly enthusiastic hug.

Seven

Aw, hell.

Ben steeled himself for the slam of emotion as her belly bumped his stomach. He waited for the grief to grab hold and drag him down. But instead of feeling pain or guilt or even aversion—and ah, man, he almost wished he had—desire snuck up and pounced on him like a wild animal, digging its claws and teeth into his flesh, sinking through skin and muscle straight to the bone.

Her scent suddenly seemed to be all around him. The same as before—sweet and sexy and enticing as hell—but different somehow. Maternal, maybe, if that made any sense. Or was even possible. Could a woman smell pregnant? And if she did, would it be so damned...*erotic?*

Her cheek settled against his chest, the softness of her hair snagging in the stubble on his chin as her hands settled on the flat of his back just below his shoulder blades. And damn did it feel nice. He'd forgotten how it felt to be close to her. The excitement and contentment. As if he were right where he was supposed to be. If it weren't for the baby...

He had intended on patting her back a couple of times, then backing away, but his arms were already around her. One hand curling over the base of her skull, his fingers tangling through her short silky blond locks. The other had made itself right at home dangerously low on her back. An inch lower and he'd be copping a feel of her sweet behind.

Holding her now, months later and after all they had been through, still felt the same, like...coming home. A place where everything was warm and sweet and familiar. He wanted to crawl inside the feeling and hold himself there.

He wanted to be inside of her.

And she would know just how much in another ten seconds, when the last of his blood left his brain and drained into his crotch.

Tess sighed, melting a little deeper into Ben's arms. Though she knew it was probably just an illusion, she felt so close to him.

When he'd asked about the baby kicking, it had been close to impossible to contain her excitement.

To stop herself from gushing out every little mundane detail about her pregnancy. She knew if anything spooked him, that would be it.

She closed her eyes and breathed in the scent of spicy cologne and male heat, felt bands of lean muscle flex under her hands. She rubbed her cheek against the silky fabric of his shirt, heard the steady thump of his heart. His long hair hung down and tickled her forehead, and suddenly every cell in her body ached to be touched. Her lips begged to be kissed. And *oh,* what the man could do with his mouth.

Bone-melting, toe-curling, out-of-this-world kisses. It was all coming back to her now. Not that she'd ever completely forgotten. She'd just blocked out a few crucial details. Like the way he'd been demanding yet achingly tender when he'd touched her. The way he'd given back twofold whatever he took. She'd never been with a man more interested in satisfying her needs than his own. In fact, she'd lost count of how many times he'd *satisfied* her.

The truth is, it had been so perfect, so amazingly wonderful, it had scared her half to death. After he'd fallen asleep, she had lain there wondering what she'd done. She knew nothing about him. She'd met him in a bar for goodness' sake. Her days of acting irresponsibly, of taking stupid chances and getting mixed up with the wrong kind of man, were supposed to be over. Moving to Prospect had meant turning over a new leaf.

Even if he hadn't been completely bad news—

which at the time seemed unlikely given her tendency to attract men who were nothing but trouble—he'd already said that he didn't want a relationship.

And like a fool, she'd ignored all her instincts and had gone and fallen in love with him.

"Tess," Ben said softly. He cupped her cheek and tipped her face up to meet his. It was dark in the hallway, but she could see the desire in his eyes as he gazed down at her. So fiery and hot she felt herself melting.

He was actually going to do it. He was going to kiss her. She knew it was wrong, but she'd been aching for it for so long now, it was almost a relief to finally get it over with. To get past that unresolved thing that always seemed to hover between them.

Ben's head began to tip and drift lower, his lips closer and closer, his hair tickling her cheek. He smelled so good, felt so solid and strong. She let her eyes flutter closed, let her head sink down into the cradle of his palm.

Oh, yes…

She felt hot all over and dizzy with anticipation, as if the hall were spinning around her. Ben dipped lower and lower, hovered there for a second, his breath warm and sweet on her lips.

"Tess," he whispered, and she held her breath, waited for that first brush of his lips, the hot taste of his mouth. He came closer, closer and her knees began to tremble…

And his lips softly brushed her cheek, just below her right eye.

"Good night, Tess."

Then he was gone, swallowed up by the darkness, and she was left standing alone in the hallway, too stunned to utter a sound.

Several minutes passed before she realized what had happened, before her hormone drenched brain cleared enough for the message to get through.

She didn't know if she should feel dejected or relieved or just plain thankful that at least he had had the good sense to put the brakes on.

Right now all she could feel was hopelessly confused. Did he want her or didn't he? Okay, dumb question. There was no denying he had been more than a touch turned on. She'd felt it. So why did he walk away?

Tess leaned against the suite door, still warm, weak and shaky.

She couldn't deny feeling as if she and Ben had reached some sort of turning point.

The question was, which way should they go?

Ben sat in his office working on his second cup of morning coffee and reading e-mail when something compelled him to get up from his seat and look out the window. His Tess-radar as he'd come to call it. Sure enough, when he eased back the curtain, there she was wandering through the garden. As she had every morning since she'd come to stay with him.

They shared meals, played Ping-Pong and pool and watched movies and television together. Other times they lost themselves in conversation, talking for hours. Sometimes late into the night. Despite coming from completely different backgrounds, they had a common bond. They understood each other.

In only a month's time she had become such an integral part of his life, he could hardly recall what it had been like without her there. The thought of her leaving, of things changing, was difficult to grasp, though he knew it was inevitable.

He let his forehead rest against the cool pane of glass. As she strolled slowly down the path, he allowed himself the privilege of watching her, of noticing all the changes in her body. She was beginning to look soft and round where she was once lean and angular. With the arrival of summer just weeks away, she'd been spending more time outside and her once pale, milky complexion was golden tan from hours in the sun.

Since that night outside her suite, they'd managed to keep their hands to themselves. No more almost-kisses, cheek or otherwise, and limited physical contact. It was as if they had established a silent understanding. An unwritten law that dictated just how far they would allow themselves to go.

At times he would go an entire day without an impure thought. Then she would smile at him a certain way or lightly touch his arm as she brushed past him and he would have to fight to keep from ravaging her on the spot.

And despite their best efforts to behave, there was

a feeling in the air, a tension growing between them and eventually something was going to have to give.

Though he almost never went outside, his feet carried him out of his office, through the house and out the back kitchen door to the path that led into the garden. When he reached Tess, she was kneeling down, her nose buried in a fuchsia bloom.

For a minute he just looked at her. She wore a pair of white capri pants and a gauzy blouse that looked almost transparent in the sunshine. She was humming to herself, slightly off-key. Some tune he didn't recognize.

"Good morning," he said.

Tess looked up at him, shielding her eyes from the sun, a bright smile lighting her face. "Good morning. You came outside."

She sounded so surprised, and pleased. Probably because she'd never seen him do it. He didn't know when the idea of leaving the house had become so unappealing. It wasn't even something that had happened gradually. He'd just stopped going out. The one and only exception had been that night at the resort, and look what had happened then. "Yep. I came outside."

She sat back on her heels. "Huh, and you didn't turn to ash."

"Ash?"

"As dark as you keep it in the house, when I first moved in, I honestly considered wearing garlic around my neck. Just in case."

He could feel a grin tugging at the corners of his mouth. He nodded to the blooms resting beside her where she knelt on the path. "Picking flowers?"

"I hope you don't mind. The gardener was giving me the evil eye earlier."

"Someone should enjoy them." He offered his hand and helped her to her feet. Her hand was small, warm and soft in his and he resisted the urge to keep holding it.

To keep his hands safely to himself, he slipped them into the pockets of his slacks.

"Will you walk with me?" she asked, and when he looked back toward the house she said, "Just for a few minutes."

When she gave him that sweet, hopeful look, how could he say no? "Just for a few."

They walked side by side down the winding cobblestone path bordered on either side by lush perennial gardens, chatting about the film he was considering working on. He closed his eyes and filled his lungs with clean mountain air scented with sweet fragrant blooms. The sun felt soothing and warm on his face and soaked into the black fabric of his shirt like hot molasses. "It's really beautiful, isn't it?"

She nodded, looking just as content as he was feeling. Linking arms, or resting an arm across her shoulder would the be the most natural thing in the world right now, but he didn't let himself go there. And the longer they spent this way, the harder it would be to resist.

"This is nice, isn't it?" she asked him. "Taking a walk, I mean."

"It is," he admitted. "But I am going to have to get back to my office. I'm expecting a call at eleven."

She held up the bunch of flowers she clutched in her hand and inhaled the sweet-smelling blooms. "You wouldn't happen to have a spare vase lying around that I could keep these in."

"You could probably get one from the kitchen. Ask the cook."

"The one who doesn't speak English?"

"*Floero,*" he said. "That's vase in Spanish."

"I didn't know you speak Spanish."

"All my life we've had Hispanic employees. You pick up bits and pieces."

"What else can you say?"

"*Sus ojos brillan más brillante que las estrellas.*" Your eyes shine brighter than the stars.

She laughed. "That's more than bits and pieces."

He grinned. "I might have taken a year or two of Spanish in school."

"Which was it? A year, or two?"

"Four, actually. It was an easy A."

"So, what did you just say?"

"I said, I have to get back to work." He didn't want to, but he did. For the first time in a long time he didn't want a reason to stay inside.

"Liar."

He feigned an innocent look, and touched his chest. "Who me?"

"I'm not sure exactly what you said, but I know it had something to with stars and eyes."

He shot her a questioning look.

She just smiled. "I speak a little Spanish, too."

A month earlier, if someone had told her she would be living in Ben's house, totally dependent on him and actually enjoying it, she'd have laughed herself silly. But here she was, having a good time. It was true that it would all come to an end, but then she would have the baby to take care of and focus on and she probably would be too busy to miss Ben.

At least she hoped that was the case.

"You know that I consider you a friend?"

"I do, too," he said. "I wish things could always be this way, but after the baby is born…"

What? They would suddenly not be friends anymore? She got it. And she could see that he was trying to figure out a way to explain it that wouldn't hurt her feelings.

"I'll be leaving," she said. "I'll have my condo and you'll have your mansion and we won't see each other."

"It's not you, Tess."

No, it was the baby, which was even worse. But she understood. At least, she was trying to. "It's okay, Ben, I get it."

But it wasn't okay. It hurt. And there wasn't a thing she could do to change it. To make it better.

He stood there for a second, just looking at her.

He reached up and brushed the hair back from her face and tucked it behind her ear. Then he turned and walked away.

Tess couldn't sleep.

She lay in bed that night until after midnight, long past when she usually fell asleep, working the situation between her and Ben over and over in her head.

After their conversation that morning, they had both gone on to act as if nothing had changed. Business as usual.

Only, something *had* changed.

She knew Ben didn't want the baby, or more to the point, wouldn't let himself want it, but to actually hear him come right out and say it again. It just felt so…final.

It was difficult to not resent him, to not take him by the shoulders, give him a rough shake and demand to know what was wrong with him. But she already knew what was wrong. And she felt so helpless because there was no way to fix it. Ben had to work this one through himself. Only when he was ready would he face his past and move on.

The question was, could she wait that long? Did she even want to try?

She was already in over her head. Already cared for Ben more than she should. More than was safe.

It was time to put a lock around her heart and swallow the key.

She rolled over and looked at the clock. Twelve-fifteen and she was still wide awake. On top of that, she was feeling the sting of heartburn creep up her esophagus. Maybe warm milk would do the trick. That was what her mom used to drink when she couldn't sleep.

She climbed out of bed, slipped on her robe, and headed downstairs. The house was dark and quiet and full of shadows this time of night. A little creepy in fact, but she didn't want to turn on a bunch of lights and wake anyone.

She hadn't spent a whole lot of time in the kitchen so it took her several minutes to find a mug then figure out how to use the state-of-the-art microwave. When the milk was warm enough, but not too hot, she took a sip.

Oh, yack!

She screwed up her face. That was awful! She never imagined milk could taste so disgusting. A few heaping spoonfuls of cocoa mix would do the trick, but the last thing she needed was caffeine in her system.

She dumped the milk down the sink, rinsed her cup, then refilled it with apple juice instead.

She considered going back up to her room, but sometimes, when she couldn't sleep, music had a calming effect on her. And she knew for a fact that Ben had a copy of her favorite Van Morrison disk in the stereo cabinet.

She walked to the den, having to almost feel her way through the dark hall, stepped inside and eased the door shut. Rather than switch on the lights, she crossed the dark room and flicked the switch next to the mantle. The gas fireplace sparked to life, bathing the room in warm light.

Next she went to the CD player and, after a bit of fumbling with the millions of little dials and buttons, managed to put Van Morrison in and hit Play. An instant later the bluesy hum of a saxophone filled the room.

Yeah. This would do the trick.

Tess walked over to the fireplace sipping her juice. She wiggled her toes into the soft fur rug, wondering if it was real animal fur. Probably. When it came to decorating the house, Ben's wife hadn't exactly cut corners.

She closed her eyes and let the heat from the fire warm her, the earthy sounds surround her. She swayed to the music, felt her body relaxing, her mind settling. Dancing always did that for her.

She'd once had dreams of being a dancer. It didn't even matter what kind of dancing. She loved it all.

She'd started taking ballet and tap when she was four. She'd been so good that even when her mother couldn't afford to pay, Mrs. Engals, the dance instructor, gave her lessons for free. As she got older she'd worked as Mrs. Engals's assistant, and helped teach the little kids.

She began to view dancing as her ticket out of small town life. She fantasized about getting a full scholarship to Julliard, of performing at Radio City Music Hall in New York. It hadn't even been about the money, although she'd heard the best dancers made tons of it.

She just wanted to get away.

Then, when she was fourteen, she'd been in a car accident with her stepdad. He'd been drunk as usual and hit a tree. She'd been wearing her seatbelt, but as the front end of his crappy little car compressed, her ankle had been crushed by the impact. Three surgeries later she had enough mobility to walk, but her dancing days were over.

It was one more thing her stepdad had stolen from her.

But self-pity was counterproductive, so she swept the negative thoughts away and concentrated on the music, let it carry her away to a place that was peaceful and uncomplicated. Maybe what had attracted her to Ben that night was that he'd asked her to dance.

Well, technically, he hadn't even asked. He'd just locked eyes with her and walked over to where she'd been sitting chatting with the bartender. He'd held out his hand in a silent invitation and without even thinking, she'd taken it, and let him lead her to the dance floor. In her experience most men had two left feet. But Ben pulled her into his arms and they began to move, their bodies in perfect sync. She'd known that instant she would spend the night with him.

It seemed like such a long time ago. So much had changed since then.

Tess closed her eyes and let the music wrap around her. She spun in a circle, letting the thrill of movement wash over her. Her robe swirled around her legs, the orange light from the fire dancing across the silky fabric. She felt dizzy and silly and freer than she had in forever.

God she'd missed this.

The song ended and she heard applause. For a second she thought it was on the CD, then realized it was coming from the other side of the room.

She let out a squeal of surprise and gathered the robe to her chest, squinting into the darkness. "Who's there?"

She saw movement, just an outline at first, then he stepped into the light.

Ben walked slowly toward her wearing a loose pair of flannel pajama bottoms and a hungry smile.

Oh boy.

"You scared me," she said, tucking her robe tighter around her. She suddenly felt so naked, her body too big and ungraceful. "H-how long have you been standing there?"

He didn't answer. His eyes traveled very lazily up her body, from her bare toes all the way to her tousled hair.

Considering the look on his face, *too long*.

As he drew closer and the firelight reached out to grab him, she saw that his pajama bottoms were red. *Red.* He actually owned an article of clothing that wasn't black.

Something about it excited her.

"I'm sorry," she said. "Did I wake you?"

He shook his head, still walking very slowly

toward her. "I couldn't sleep. I was coming down to grab a book and I heard music."

The firelight poured over him, accentuating every inch of his beautifully defined chest, his wide solid shoulders and sinewy arms. Oh my gosh, she'd forgotten how amazing he looked naked.

Not that he was naked, not completely anyway. The rest was best left to her imagination. Although she doubted her memory did him the justice he deserved.

"I didn't know you could dance," he said, still coming closer.

"I don't. I mean, not anymore. I used to, a long time ago." Her back hit the mantle. Only then did she realize, as he was moving toward her, she'd been moving backward.

But her escape route had just disappeared and he was still coming, like an animal on the prowl.

The heat from the fire soaked through the filmy robe, warming her legs, making her feel hot and dizzy. Or maybe it was Ben doing that. She just didn't know anymore.

He closed the space between them, planting his hands against the mantle on either side of her, their bodies not quite touching, but close enough to share heat. And, oh, did he smell delicious. Clean and masculine.

He gazed down at her with penetrating dark eyes. "I promised myself I wouldn't kiss you again. Wouldn't touch you."

What a coincidence. She'd made the same promise to herself. And though a part of her wanted him to touch her and kiss her, another part knew what would happen if he did.

The rational part of her brain recognized what a mistake it would be. Unfortunately she was thinking with the louder, less rational side. The side telling her everything that had happened in the past month had been leading them to this exact moment. That it was fate. Even though she didn't believe in it. A person made their own destiny, determined their own future.

Of course that didn't mean a person wouldn't make a few careless mistakes in the process.

"Do you ever think about that night?" he asked, his eyes searching her face.

Only constantly. Like, what would have happened if she'd stayed? What if the condom hadn't failed?

What did it matter now?

Ben's eyes locked on hers, so full of desire and affection. She shivered with excitement and anticipation. She hadn't even realized until now just how badly she wanted him to kiss her.

"We shouldn't," he said, but he was already dipping his head, and she was rising up on her toes to meet him halfway.

"No, we shouldn't," she agreed. "But let's do it anyway."

Eight

It never ceased to amaze Tess how thrilling it could be kissing this man. When their lips met, she went weak all over.

It was hot and deep and passionate, as if they were making up for lost time. His hands cupped her face, guiding her head to the perfect angle, and she tangled hers in his hair. His bare chest felt hot and powerful through the thin cotton nightgown. His arms caging her, the way he assumed control, was as exciting as it was scary.

This wasn't just a kiss, this was a possession, and she could do little more than cling for dear life and enjoy the ride. At that moment he owned her, body, mind and soul, and like a fool she gave herself willingly.

When he finally broke the kiss, they were both flushed and breathing hard.

"We shouldn't be doing this," he said in a husky whisper, just before he captured her mouth and started all over again.

She felt reckless and irresponsible, and the worst part was, she liked it.

Then Ben was undressing her. Her robe went first, and as it fell to the floor he began kissing all the skin he'd exposed. Her shoulders and throat. The ridge of her collarbone.

He nibbled and licked his way back to her mouth while his hands continued their quest for bare flesh, tugging the straps of her gown down over her arms. In a few short seconds she was going to be naked.

"Mrs. Smith," she mumbled. "What if she—"

"The door is locked."

His housekeeper may have been as frigid as an iceberg, but she wasn't stupid. "If she wakes up, she's going to know exactly what we're doing."

He looked down at her, his eyes black with lust. "Do I look like I care?"

For reasons she didn't understand, the fact that he wasn't interested in hiding this, made her want him that much more. Besides, her brain was so fuzzy at this point it wasn't as if she could tell him to stop.

Ben tugged the gown down, somehow managing to be tender and commanding at the same time. He eased her against him and she shuddered when the sensitive tips of her breasts brushed his bare chest. Heat from the fire made her skin feel warm and tingly.

She didn't know if it was hormones or the fact that it had been so long, but she felt as if she were drowning, being sucked under by waves of arousal. And she let it happen.

"You taste like apples," he rasped against her lips, and kissed her deeper, as if he were trying to steal the flavor from her mouth.

Her panties were the next thing to go, then he just looked at her, his eyes roaming slowly and deliberately over her body. She wondered if her over-accentuated shape would turn him off, if seeing her bare belly would bother him.

If it had, he didn't let it show. And since she didn't want to be the only one naked, she took a great deal of satisfaction in liberating him from the pajama bottoms.

Ben eased her to the floor and they stretched out beside one another on the rug. There was more kissing and touching, slower this time. Sort of lazy and sweet, as if the urgency was gone. This was going to happen so there was no need to rush, no reason not to take their time relearning all the wonderful, sinfully erotic places they had discovered that first night. Her body had never responded so effortlessly, so fiercely to a man's touch. Something about this, about being with him, was so right.

And so very wrong—which made it that much more exciting.

"Talk to me," he said. "Tell me what you want."

"Anything," she said breathlessly. "Everything."

Eyes on her face, he slipped a hand between her thighs, teasing her with featherlight caresses. "Like this?"

"Yes." Exactly like that. But when she reached down to touch him, to stroke him just like he was stroking her, he brushed her hand aside.

"You'll get your turn later," he said. "Right now, I want to make you feel good."

"I want to make you feel good, too." She tried again but this time he caught her wrist in his hand and pinned her arm to the rug over her head.

"This does make me feel good." He lowered his head and sucked a nipple into his mouth. She felt the warm, wet pull of arousal, the zing of sensation travel all the way down between her thighs, to the place where his fingers explored and played, sinking deeper into the slippery folds of skin. She moaned and closed her eyes. "I wonder if you taste as good as you feel."

He began licking and nibbling his way down her body, pressing her thighs apart, and she knew he intended to find out. It seemed to take him *forever* to reach his destination, like he had all the time in the world. And by the time he took that first taste, when she felt the sweep of his tongue, she was wound so tightly her body arched up against his mouth. She didn't think it got any better than this...until he zeroed in on the little tangle of nerves. She cried out at the intense jolt of pleasure. Everything began to clench and almost instantly she was coming.

And coming…and coming.

"Wow," she breathed when it was over, her body as limp as a wet noodle. *"Wow."*

"As much as I'd love to take credit for that, I think it had more to do with hormones than skill." He kissed his way back up her body until they were lying side by side again.

"I've been wondering something, too," she said.

"What's that?"

"What *you* taste like."

He flashed her that sexy simmering grin as she pushed him onto his back, and tortured him in the same slow, lazy way he had her. Until the urge to make love to him, the need for him to be inside her was too great to resist.

As she straddled his hips and eased herself down, taking him deep inside of her, never had anything felt so right. So perfect. She lost all sense of time, all sense of herself. All that mattered was this moment. Making love to Ben was as simple as it was complex, as sweet as it was erotic.

She linked her hands through Ben's and pinned them on either side of his head, driving herself hard against him, over and over until he gasped and arched.

He looked up at her, his eyes glassy and unfocused and whispered her name, *"Tess,"* then the grip on her hands tightened and every part of him began to tense.

The sensation brought her to an entirely new level of ecstasy. She threw her head back and cried out as her body clenched tight around him, and for that brief moment everything in her world was painfully perfect. This was the way it should always be, this feeling of connection.

Ben pulled her into his arms and just held her. For several minutes they didn't speak. They just lay there quietly, arms and legs entwined, touching and stroking.

She snuggled against him, her head resting on his arm. "Say something to me in Spanish."

"Like what?"

"I don't know, anything."

"Su belleza elimina mi respiración," he said with perfect inflection.

She sighed contentedly. She didn't know what it was she found so sexy about him speaking a foreign language. "What does that mean?"

"My arm is falling asleep."

She laughed and poked him in the side. "No, it doesn't. I think *respiración* is respiration, and I'm pretty sure *belleza* is beauty. So what, I have beautiful lungs?"

"I said, your beauty takes my breath away." He rolled her onto her back and gazed down at her, searching her face. He kissed her forehead, the tip of her nose. "What are we doing, Tess?"

"I don't know, but we do it really well."

"We didn't use protection."

"It's not like I can get any more pregnant than I already am."

"Good point."

She looped her arms around his neck. God, she loved touching him. Being close to him. "Maybe this is just something we needed to do, you know, to get it out of our systems."

"Yeah, maybe."

"And if we do it a lot, by the time I have to leave, I'm sure we'll be completely sick of each other."

The corner of his mouth crept up. "How much is a lot?"

"As much as it takes, I guess." Although, she couldn't imagine herself getting tired of this. Getting tired of him. Ever. "What about Mrs. Smith?"

"She's really not my type."

Tess laughed. "What I mean is, unless we're extremely discreet, she's going to notice sooner or later."

"I told you earlier, I don't care if she notices. We're consenting adults. What we do is our business."

This had disaster written all over it. A pinkie bandage on a wound that required stitches—or amputation. But right now she was happy, and that was so rare these days that she was willing to hang on to the feeling, whatever the cost.

He was giving her that drowsy-eyed, hungry look again that made her feel warm and tingly all over. Looks like they were going to work on getting sick of each other right now.

She pulled him down for a kiss and their bodies settled together. Even with her tummy in the way, they were a perfect fit. Though she knew that soon enough she would be so big, lying this close in this position would be impossible. They would just have to find more imaginative ways to get close.

It was at that exact second that it happened. She felt a very distinct jolt dead center in her stomach. The baby's first kick.

She gasped with surprise and looked up at Ben. "Did you feel that?"

He'd felt it. She knew the instant she saw his face.

She wasn't sure what she'd been expecting. She knew excitement at feeling his baby move was a lot to ask for given the circumstances. Instead he looked like he might be sick.

And suddenly, she felt exactly the same way.

Until that moment it hadn't been truly clear to her, she hadn't been able to wrap her mind around the concept of just how much he didn't want this baby. And realizing that, seeing it for herself, sucked every bit of joy out of what should have been the happiest moment of her life.

Her arms dropped from around his neck and he rolled away, sitting up on the rug, his back to her. All she could do was curl into a ball and close her eyes against the bitter and acute pain in her heart.

His baby kicked, and rather than feeling happy, he was devastated.

"I'm sorry," he said.

She shivered. She suddenly felt so cold, all the way through her skin and deep down to the bone. Cold and vulnerable and rubbed raw.

She grabbed her robe from where it had dropped

on the floor and covered herself with it. It was hot from the fire, but even that didn't chase away the chill. She felt as if she might never be warm again.

"I should go," Ben said.

She couldn't answer, not without him hearing how completely torn up she felt inside.

He sat there for several seconds, then he got up, pulled on his pajamas and left.

She waited for the tears to come, for the grief to swallow her up, but she just felt numb. Cold and hollow and alone.

She would just have to get used to this, learn to live with it. At least as long as she was living in Ben's house, carrying his child.

Or maybe it would be this way for the rest of her life.

Ben stared out his office window, into the cold, rainy gloom, thinking that it was a perfect complement to his lousy mood.

He felt like such a jerk.

He shouldn't have left Tess alone, but there was no way he could sit there and pretend everything was okay, pretend that feeling his baby kick hadn't made him sick inside. It hadn't really hit him until then, hadn't truly been real until he'd felt it move, that it was his baby growing inside her. His flesh and blood.

It was so damned unfair. Why did this baby deserve to live when his son hadn't been given a chance? And why did his heart ache to love it when he knew that was impossible?

He didn't even have the guts to go talk to her. He had no idea what to say—how to explain. That feeble I'm sorry he'd left her with last night just wasn't going to cut it.

His office door opened and he turned to find Mrs. Smith standing there. When Tess hadn't eaten breakfast and didn't show up for lunch or dinner, he'd finally sent his housekeeper up to check on her.

"Is she awake?"

"She's still in bed. She said she's not feeling well, but that you shouldn't worry."

Like him, she probably hadn't slept last night. He'd tossed and turned, finally giving up and rolling out of bed with the sun. He turned back to the window. "Thank you."

"She looked as if she'd been crying," Mrs. Smith said, and Ben winced. He'd assumed she would be, but to know for sure, and to know it was his fault, was a million times more horrible.

"Would you like to talk about it?"

"Talk about what?"

"Whatever it is that's wrong."

What could he possibly say that Mrs. Smith would understand?

"Your mother called again this morning. She knows something is up. I'm running out of excuses. At some point you'll have to tell her what's going on."

"I will." When he was ready. When he was sure what was going on.

"You know," she said softly, "I lost a son, too."

He spun around to face her. "What? When?"

"He was a soldier in Vietnam. He was killed two days before his nineteenth birthday."

"I'm sorry," he said, not because he thought it would make her feel better. He just didn't know what else to say.

"Five years later my husband passed from cancer. That was the year I came to work for your family."

She looked so sad, and Ben could only stare at her, unable to comprehend what she was telling him. He hadn't even known she was married. Why hadn't he heard about this before?

She had a life, a history that he knew nothing about. It also explained why, as good as she was to him, he'd always felt as though she kept him at arm's length. He used to think it just her personality. Now he wasn't so sure. "Why didn't you ever tell me this?"

"To talk about it, would be acknowledging that it happened. That wouldn't bring them back. Would it?"

"So what, you just pretend they didn't exist?"

"The way Jeanette and your son no longer exist?"

She had no right to judge him. She had no clue what went on in his head. "Not a day goes by—not an hour—that I don't think about them. And miss them."

"Maybe that's your problem."

She wasn't making any sense. He was supposed to acknowledge them, but not think about them? Not miss them?

"You should go talk to Tess," Mrs. Smith said.

"I can't."

"You mean you won't." She shook her head sadly. "I hate to see you making the same mistakes I did."

He wasn't making a mistake. He was avoiding one.

He turned back to the window. He didn't think it was possible, but he felt even worse than he had before.

Nine

Tess gave herself a full day to wallow in self-pity. All Saturday she stayed in bed. And she must have looked pretty terrible, because even Mrs. Smith had been less snippy than usual. She'd come up to check on Tess and offered to bring her tea and toast to settle her stomach, when what Tess really needed was a gigantic bandage to slap over her chest. To seal the wound where Ben had reached in and ripped out her heart.

But by Sunday afternoon the self-indulgence was getting old and most likely induced by hormones more than anything else. The only thing she could do was get over it. She couldn't hide away any longer, and she had to stop feeling sorry for herself.

If she'd shut down every time something bad had happened to her, she would have stopped living a long time ago.

Maybe the real problem here was that she'd finally let herself admit something she'd been denying for months.

She loved Ben.

She'd fallen in love with him that night in the resort. Maybe not in the soul deep way that developed over time. But they had scratched the surface of something bigger. Something profound.

The question was, how could she love a man who would deny his own child? The baby they had created together. Maybe because in her heart and soul she knew he was a good person who had just been deeply hurt and hadn't yet bounced back.

At least, that was what she was trying to convince herself.

When she told him she considered him a friend, that had been a lie. Or at the very least a major understatement. What she felt for him went far beyond friendship. Far beyond anything she had ever experienced in a relationship. And in four months it would end.

Unless she could do something to change his mind.

It wasn't the first time her mind had entertained the thought. She'd been tiptoeing around the idea for days, not willing to let it take root. Because she knew that there was a very real possibility she would end up hurting and alone if it backfired.

She was just getting ready to venture downstairs

to find Ben when there was a knock at her door. It was probably Mrs. Smith, coming to get her lunch tray.

She swung the door open, but it was Ben standing in the hallway.

She could play this two ways. She could act indignant and try to make him feel badly for the way he had treated her, which would probably only make things more uncomfortable between them, or she could accept things for what they were, and make the best of the time they had together.

She smiled. "Hi."

"Hi." For a minute he just looked at her, probably trying to decide if she was mad at him. Then he asked, "Are you feeling better?"

She turned up the wattage on her smile. Even if she wanted to, she couldn't stay mad at him. He didn't mean to hurt her. He cared about her. She knew he did. She couldn't ask for more than he was able to give. More than he was capable of. "Much better, thanks."

He just stood there, hands in his pants pockets, and she realized, he was waiting to be invited in. She hoped this wasn't like the vampire books she used to read when she was a kid. Once you invited a vampire in, you were toast.

He was so dark and handsome, if she hadn't already seen him in the sun, she might have been worried. But Ben was as mortal as they came.

"Would you like to come in?" She opened the door wider and he stepped past her into the sitting room. The second she shut the door his arms were around her. He pulled her to him and just held her.

"I'm sorry," he said.

She sighed and pressed her cheek against his chest, breathed in the spicy scent of his cologne. He smelled warm and familiar. "Me, too."

He held her tighter. "I missed you."

She felt like laughing and crying all at once. "I missed you, too."

"Should we talk about it?"

That was the one thing that she *didn't* want to talk about, or even worse analyze to death. She just wanted to forget it had ever happened. "I understand the way things are. I just…it caught me by surprise, I guess."

He nodded. "Me, too."

"So if it happens again we'll be prepared."

"Exactly," he agreed. Then he smiled down at her and she could tell everything was going to be okay. They were past the awkwardness.

Then the baby kicked. Just like the other night. Plenty hard for Ben to feel it, too. She held her breath, waiting for him to back away.

He didn't.

"Does that happen a lot now?" he asked instead.

"Just since the other night."

"That night was the first time?"

"Yep."

He swore under his breath. "And I ruined it, didn't I?"

"It's not your fault."

He cupped her chin with his palm and lifted her face so he could meet her eyes. "Why do you put up with me?"

Because I love you, she was tempted to say. Instead she shrugged. "Beats me."

"Me, too." He studied her face, as if the answer was there somewhere. Then his eyes wandered down to her mouth and she knew exactly what he was thinking. He wanted to kiss her. And she wanted him to.

"You look tired," he said.

"I do?" She didn't *feel* tired. She'd practically slept all day yesterday. "I'm fine, really."

"No, really, you look exhausted." He flashed her that sizzling, seductive grin then leaned back and locked the door to her suite. "I think you need to take a nap."

Oh—a *nap*.

She could tell by his smile, this *nap* wouldn't involve sleep. "Come to think of it, I am a little drowsy. Maybe a quick nap wouldn't be a bad idea."

"I think a long nap would be better." He started walking backward toward the bedroom, pulling her along with him. "I'll tuck you in."

He led them into the bedroom, already working the buttons on her blouse. The drapes were drawn and the room had a hazy, dim look, like stepping into the middle of a dream.

He eased her shirt down her arms and let it drop to the floor then unhooked her bra. She'd never been terribly aggressive or confident when it came to sex, but Ben seemed to draw out the vixen in her. She tugged his shirt up over his head and flung it behind her, then went to work on his belt.

She didn't think anything could top making love on a rug in front of the fire, but just being with Ben, no matter where they were, felt special. It wasn't easy to forget all that they couldn't be together. Instead, as they caressed and kissed, loved each other in that sweet, effortless way, she felt as if she were exactly where she belonged. Even if that was only for five minutes, or an hour. Maybe, in the long run, all these little pieces of perfection would add up to something bigger. Something neither of them expected.

And if it didn't, the time that they did have together would just have to be enough.

They tumbled into bed together and snuggled up under the comforter. Ben stroked her skin, exploring every hill and crevice, his touch leisurely and sweet one minute, shockingly intimate the next. She loved the feeling of his hands exploring her, but she loved it even more when he used his mouth. He licked and nipped, here and there, as if she were his favorite snack and he didn't want to devour her too quickly. Somehow he managed to make every stroke, every touch feel as thrilling and new as the first time.

"I love the way you taste," he said, nibbling her throat, running his tongue lightly along the cleft between her breasts, making her whole body sizzle with desire. "What do you want Tess? Just tell me and I'll do it."

She didn't have to tell him. He was always able

to anticipate exactly what she craved, what she needed, but there was something erotic and forbidden about saying the words out loud. And she wouldn't dare deny him the pleasure of hearing them, not when he went far and above the call of duty to make her feel good. Gave her at least two orgasms to his one. Sometimes more.

So she told him, in very blatant, explicit language, exactly what she wanted, and how she wanted it.

"Damn," he said, shaking his head, but she could tell he loved it. "I'd love to, but are you sure I won't hurt you?"

"I'm sure," she said, and the next thing she knew, she was flat on her back, thighs pressed wide and Ben was burying himself deep inside her, just as hard and fast as she asked him to. She went from being aroused to…well, something she'd never felt before. Something bigger than herself, bigger than both of them together. It overwhelmed her body and when her skin could no longer contain all that sensation it radiated out, expanding and flexing and growing. She knew she was making noise, moaning and thrashing and digging her fingernails into his backside, raking them down his arms. Someone could have heard, but she was too far gone to care.

Ben hooked both of his arms behind her knees, easing them as far back as they would go and, eyes locked on her face, sank deep inside her. Deeper than any man had ever been. And with no warning at all, everything peaked and something inside her exploded. It filled her with a feeling, a sensation she couldn't even describe, something along the lines of ecstasy. Or nirvana.

As she slowly came back to herself, she looked up to find Ben gazing down at her, a perplexed look on his face.

"What was that?"

"I'm not sure," she said with a lazy smile, tangling her fingers in his hair and pulling him down for a kiss. "But give me a minute to catch my breath and we can do it again."

They *napped* for several hours on and off until dinner, which they ate naked in bed. In lieu of dessert they took another long nap, shared a shower, then lay in bed, their bodies tangled together, and just talked.

"Tell me about Jeanette," Tess said, rising up on one elbow to look at him, her belly pressed into the dip of his hip. "What was she like?"

"Colorful," Ben said, idly toying with a lock of her hair. "And spoiled, and complicated. But fun. And she was probably the most driven woman I've ever met. Her career meant everything to her. Come to think of it, she was a lot like my mother in that respect." He shifted on his side to face her. "What about you? Any significant romances? Besides the pool table kiss?"

"Not really. I have a gift for finding men who are bad for me. I think I inherited that from my mom."

"There must have been someone special."

"There was this boy in high school. David Fischer. He was a real sweetheart. But then I had to drop out of school and get a full time job, so that pretty much killed that."

"Why did you need a full-time job?"

"To pay rent. I couldn't stay in my stepdad's house any longer."

Ben frowned. "There was abuse?"

She shrugged. "The physical and emotional stuff. It was just a regular part of life. I was used to it. But then he started...*looking* at me."

His frown deepened. "Looking at you how?"

"With that look men get when they want something from you. I told my mom and she accused me of being selfish. I knew it was only a matter of time before he tried something, and I obviously wasn't going to get any help from her, so I packed up my stuff and left. She didn't even try to stop me. I've been on my own ever since."

That she'd been through something so horrible made Ben sick to his stomach. Her mother, the one person she should have been able to depend on, had let her down. It's a wonder she could trust at all.

"My parents might not have been around much, but they made sure I was well taken care of." He reached up and brushed the hair back from Tess's face, tucking it behind her ear. She was so pretty. So soft and gentle. But strong. Stronger than even he had realized. "Did your real dad know anything about this? Didn't he do anything?"

"This is a man who signed away all his parental rights so he could get out of paying child support. And it's not like he couldn't afford it. He didn't want anything to do with me."

Ben hated that she'd been through such hell, only to be rejected all over again by him. He hated that she accepted this kind of treatment as normal. Didn't she know that she deserved so much more?

She should be with someone who accepted her child. And maybe someday she would be. She was only twenty-five. She could meet a decent guy who would raise Ben's baby and be a good husband to Tess. He wanted that for her.

So why did the idea make his chest hurt? He couldn't be a father to this child. Not even if he wanted to. But he didn't want anyone else to be, either. He couldn't have it both ways.

It was as if there was some sort of barrier blocking the part of his heart that used to long for a family. Either that, or maybe it had just shriveled up and died.

And he knew the whole concept of sleeping together until they got sick of each other was just his way of justifying what they were doing. He wasn't going to get sick of her. If it weren't for the baby, he didn't doubt that he would eventually be down on one knee asking her to marry him.

He'd loved Jeanette. Their marriage had been good in a hectic, complicated way. But he and Tess had something different. Something easy and satisfying, and so deep they'd barely scratched the surface. Being with Tess had been like coming home. A safe, warm, comfortable place. A place where he could see himself putting down roots.

And because of him, they would never get the chance. He'd thought maybe, just maybe, he could make it work. Maybe he could get used to being around the baby. He'd been pretty much ignored by his parents as a child and he'd turned out okay.

The weird thing was, he couldn't do that. He wanted the baby to have everything he didn't. He wanted better for it. Two parents who loved and adored it, not one who merely tolerated its presence.

Besides, he knew Tess would never allow it. When it came to the baby, she didn't compromise. She expected better.

And she *deserved* it.

When Ben woke the following morning, he was still sprawled on Tess's bed. He reached over to find her, but the spot beside him was empty, the sheets cool. He hadn't meant to spend the night. They'd sat up late talking, and when Tess had drifted off to sleep, Ben just lay there watching her. Five more minutes, he kept telling himself. Five more minutes and he would go to his own room. He must have drifted off.

He couldn't help thinking that staying here had been a mistake. That Tess might get the wrong idea. He didn't want to mislead her into thinking anything had changed. Sleeping together was intimate enough, but to spend the night together?

He sat up in bed, stretching and rubbing the sleep from his eyes. He looked over at the digital clock and saw that it was eight-thirty. Much later than he usually slept in. From the vicinity of the bathroom he heard off-key humming. A second later Tess appeared, looking far too chipper and awake for someone who couldn't have gotten more than four or five hours of sleep.

When she saw him sitting there, she gave him one of those bright smiles. She looked so...*happy*. "Good morning."

"'Morning. You're up early."

"I would have slept in, but I have to go to the doctor."

"What's wrong?" he snapped, cringing when he realized how harshly the words had come out.

Tess was incredibly patient with him. "Nothing. It's just time for my monthly checkup. Six months already."

He shoved his hair back from his face. What was wrong with him that he automatically assumed the worst? He knew monthly visits were part of the routine. It's not as if he hadn't been through this before. And though he'd never written down her due date or kept track of her pregnancy, his internal calendar wouldn't let him forget.

"I'm sorry. I didn't mean to snap."

She just gave him that sweet, understanding smile. "It's okay. It'll just take time."

No, it wasn't okay. He had to stop overreacting, stop worrying so much.

She sat on the edge of the bed beside him. "I was kinda surprised that you were still here this morning."

"Yeah, me, too."

"In case you're wondering, I realize nothing has changed."

Leave it to Tess to come right out and say exactly what she was feeling. "That doesn't bother you?"

"If I had any expectation that this relationship had even a slim chance of surviving it might have, but I prefer to live in the real world."

If he really cared about her, he would end this right here, right now. He was only going to end up hurting her. And the longer they kept this up, the worse it would be for both of them. But he was selfish. He wanted her for as long as he could have her.

He wasn't ready to let go.

"I'm going to do some shopping after my appointment, so I probably won't be back for a while." She leaned over and kissed his cheek, as naturally as if they had been doing this for years. "See you later."

"Drive safe." He waited until she'd left, then fell back onto the bed.

How did people do it? How did couples who had lost a baby make it through subsequent pregnancies without going insane with worry?

Tess wasn't out of the woods yet. If something were to happen and she had the baby now, odds were likely it wouldn't survive, or if it did, it could be severely handicapped. Blind or mentally disabled.

Tess was wrong. Time wasn't going to fix this. If nothing else, it would only get worse.

Ten

Tess sat in the waiting room of the doctor's office, feeling confused and more than a little frustrated. Last night had been…incredible. She'd never felt so close to a man—to *anyone*. She'd never shared so many intimate secrets. She'd told him things about herself that she'd never told another living soul. She'd thought for sure that he would be gone in the morning. Then she'd opened her eyes and there he lay, sleeping soundly. Looking gorgeous of course.

And like an idiot, she'd almost let herself believe that it meant something. That something had changed.

Then he'd flipped out when she said she was going to the doctor and they were back to square one.

Back to the realization that this relationship was not long-term.

She should have ended it right there. She should have told him it would be best if they stopped while they were ahead and parted as friends. But she was selfish. She wanted as much time with him as she could get. Besides, there was always the chance that the longer she knew him, she would discover he had some annoying habit she couldn't stand to live with. Like, maybe he bit his nails—or even worse, his toenails. Or picked his teeth at the dinner table—or his nose.

It was a long shot.

Tess was called into the examining room, and the doctor sufficiently poked and prodded her belly, taking measurements and listening to the baby's heartbeat. Which was fast, meaning it may or may not be a girl…or a squid for all she knew. After receiving a clean bill of health, she dressed, then made her next month's appointment. But as she headed out to the car, she had the eerie sensation that someone was watching her. She stopped and scanned either side of the street, watching the people—mostly tourists—moving around her.

No one seemed to be paying attention to her, or even looked the least bit suspicious. She figured Ben's paranoia must have been rubbing off on her, and determined not to worry about it. But as she walked to her car later that afternoon, her arms filled with bags, she had that same sensation of being watched.

She dropped the bags in the trunk and climbed in the driver's seat, keeping an eye on the rearview mirror as she drove home, but if someone had followed her, they kept themselves well hidden.

When she got back she pulled into the garage and headed inside with her purchases, running into Mrs. Smith on her way through the kitchen. She sat in the breakfast nook, making a list on a yellow pad of paper. Her writing was small and neat, just what Tess would have expected from a woman like her.

"I'm going grocery shopping tomorrow," Mrs. Smith informed her. "Do you need anything while I'm out?"

Tess was so stunned by the offer she nearly swallowed her own tongue. Mrs. Smith had to have known Tess and Ben spent the night together. Tess had been anticipating hostility, not an offer to run errands.

For the life of her, she would never understand Mrs. Smith.

"I don't think so, but thanks for offering."

She gestured to the bags Tess was carrying. "Do you need help with those?"

Wow, now an offer to help? She gave the woman a scrutinizing look. "Who are you and what have you done with Mrs. Smith?"

She got a look of exasperation in return.

"I've got them, thanks. Do you know if Ben is in his office?"

"I believe he's upstairs in his suite."

Tess waited for a warning that he didn't want to

be bothered, or that Tess was forbidden to enter his private domain, but she just went back to her list.

Okay. She was really creeping Tess out.

As she walked to the stairs something else struck her as odd. Light. There was light and color everywhere. Someone had opened the curtains in the front room. She circled through the entire lower floor, going from room to room, finding each one flooded with sunshine, until she ended up back in the kitchen, still clutching all the bags.

Mrs. Smith gave her an odd look. "Are you lost?"

"No, I just...the curtains are all open."

She looked at Tess questioningly. "Yes?"

Like an explanation was too much to ask for? "Oh, never mind."

She headed up the stairs instead, to Ben's suite, bags in tow, and knocked on the door. When she didn't get an answer, she considered going back to her own room to wait for him, but she was too excited.

She knocked louder, and when he still didn't answer, she opened the door and peeked her head inside. Would he mind if she entered unannounced?

The sitting room was set up much like her own, only flopped the opposite way and decorated in darker, richer hues. Definitely more masculine, but without being too overpowering. It even smelled masculine. Ben's own unique scent. And surprisingly enough, the drapes were wide open, displaying the same breathtaking view of the garden as her room.

What was going on?

She hesitated on the threshold, still unsure of how he would feel about her being in his suite. Maybe that was a line in their relationship he wasn't willing to cross.

"Yoo-hoo!" she called. "Anybody here?"

"Come on in," she heard him answer. "I'm in the bedroom."

Or he wouldn't mind at all.

She pushed her way inside and shut the door behind her. She stepped into the bedroom just as Ben appeared from the closet, his hair wet and dripping, a dark blue towel riding low on his slim hips, his chest glistening with moisture.

"Hi," he said, shooting her a grin, not at all bothered by the fact that she had infiltrated his private space. He was also completely at ease being mostly naked in front of her. Not that he shouldn't be, especially after last night. She'd been up close and personal with just about every part of his body. And as many times as she'd seen it lately, it still took her breath away and made her knees feel gooey.

He gestured to her bags. "It looks as if someone had a successful shopping trip."

"It was. I got you a present. Actually, quite a few presents."

"You didn't have to buy me anything," he said, but the look on his face suggested it had been a long time since anyone had bought him a present and he was the teensiest bit curious as to what it could be.

"Now, I want you to keep an open mind," she said.

"Uh-oh. That's usually not a good sign."

"It's nothing bad, I promise." She walked over to the bed and dumped the contents of the bags out onto the comforter. "I was going to start you out slowly with a shirt or two, but there were some awesome clearance sales. I got a bit carried away."

"I guess," Ben said, staring at the clothes piled there. Colorful clothes.

Shirts and pants and even boxers. And not a single black item.

Ben picked up a polo shirt the same creamy beige as the carpet and looked at the tag on the collar. "Out of curiosity, how did you know what size to buy?"

"I peeked at the tags on your clothes yesterday."

He laid the shirt across the bed with the others. "So, you've been planning this, have you?"

"Just for a day or two." She'd worried he might be angry with her, that maybe this was crossing some invisible line in the sand that he'd drawn. Instead he looked almost…amused. "I know you like to wear black—"

"The truth is, I don't. It doesn't matter to me one way or the other. That just happens to be all I own."

She shot him a disbelieving look.

"See for yourself," he said and she followed him into his closet. And damned if he wasn't telling the truth. Row upon row of black.

"I have the fashion sense of a brick. I just wear

whatever is there. Jeanette pretty much did all my shopping, and she liked me in black. Then she didn't have to worry about me wearing clothes she considered mismatched or out of fashion. She was very much into appearances."

"Well, now you have colorful clothes," she said feeling relief and a tiny bit of pride. "Anything you don't like I can return."

"I'm sure I'll like it all," he said.

A corner of fabric peeking out from a partially open drawer caught her eye. Fabric that was not only not black, but also incredibly familiar.

She walked over to the drawer and yanked it open, then looked up at Ben who was grinning from ear to ear, and didn't seem to care that she was going through his things. Or more to the point, *her* things. "My clothes!"

They were all folded and tucked neatly away. She sorted through them and as far as she could tell everything was there. "You said you burned them."

Ben leaned in the doorway and folded his thick arms across that beautifully defined chest. He looked like a *Playgirl* centerfold. "No, *you* said I burned them. I just didn't tell you that you were wrong. I knew if you believed they were still recoverable, you never would have agreed to buy new clothes."

"Oh," she said, shaking her head. "You're evil."

He grinned. "Yeah, I am," he agreed, looking awfully proud of himself. "But it worked, didn't it?"

Yeah, it worked. "Just like you let me believe you were an alcoholic. Which I know now that you aren't."

"If I had told you I wasn't, would you have believed me?"

He was right. She probably wouldn't have.

"You were going to believe what you wanted to believe," he said. "And that's okay. I knew I would have to earn your trust. It wasn't a lot to ask."

"Just so we're clear, if you don't like the clothes I bought you, don't be afraid to say so. It won't hurt my feelings." At least, not too much.

"I love it all," he said.

"But you haven't even looked at most of it."

"Doesn't matter. It's from you."

That was one of the sweetest things anyone had ever said to her. Especially since technically, they were really from himself. He'd be paying the bill. She'd only picked them out.

"How did your appointment go?" he asked.

"I'm right on schedule." She could see that talking about it made him uncomfortable, so she left it at that. She gave him credit for even asking. No need to torture him with details he didn't want. "Do you have to work?"

"Not necessarily." Pushing off from the door frame he walked slowly toward her. "That shopping probably took a lot out of you, huh?"

"No, not really."

"I think it did. You look awfully tired."

Oh boy, he had that look. That sizzling preda-tory grin. They were going to play the nap game again.

A grin curled her mouth. "Yeah, you're right, I'm *completely* exhausted."

"I thought you were."

He dropped his towel and had her out of her clothes and under the covers in a minute flat. They made love most of the afternoon, had dinner, watched a movie, then had another *nap* in Ben's room before bed. She'd had more sex in the past couple of days than she had had in the last five years. They just couldn't seem to get enough of each other.

"Maybe I should go," she told Ben around midnight, when she was getting too sleepy to keep her eyes open. She didn't want him to be uncomfortable, or feel as if he had to let her stay because he had last night.

Instead of letting go, his arm closed tightly around her. "No. I want you to stay."

That was all she needed to hear. She burrowed under the covers, cuddling against him. If it ended tomorrow, at least they would have had this final night together. That was all they could do, live as if each day together might be their last.

Ben had a serious problem.

He'd realized it this morning when, like every morning for the past two weeks, he woke with Tess naked, soft and warm in his arms. It became clear the instant she looked up at him with a sleepy smile.

When he couldn't stop himself from touching her. When he didn't feel complete until he'd buried himself deep inside her.

He was falling in love with her.

A lazy, wistful, effortless kind of love that felt as natural to him as breathing. He wanted to marry her, and wake up with her every morning for the rest of his life. He knew it would be everything his first marriage hadn't been.

He'd loved Jeanette, but Tess was his soul mate.

But what he didn't want was her baby.

It didn't escape him what a complete bastard he was, what a horrible person he'd become for not wanting his own child. It wasn't even so much that he didn't *want* the baby or that he didn't *care*. He did care—too much—which is why he knew it would never work. His heart wouldn't let it happen.

"Have you got a minute?"

Ben turned to find Mrs. Smith standing in his office doorway. He'd grown accustomed to keeping it open. When he did shut it now, he felt closed off and isolated. Same with the windows. Where he used to prefer the darkness—the peace it brought him—now he craved the light. He'd even begun taking walks with Tess in the mornings and sometimes again in the evening. The days were longer now, the weather pleasantly warm.

"Sure, come on in."

Mrs. Smith walked into his office, a magazine clutched in her hand, looking very unsettled about something. "You have a problem."

Ben couldn't help laughing. He had more than one problem. He had a list as long as his arm. "Tell me something I didn't already know."

"I was in line at the grocery store when I saw this." She handed him the magazine. A gossip rag.

He read the cover and cursed under his breath—a harsh four letter word that would have earned him a mouth full of soap when he was a kid. "I guess I should have expected this."

"There's more inside."

He opened it, cringed and said, "Aw, hell."

"I take it you haven't looked out front."

"Not yet. Don't tell me…"

"There are at least twenty. Mostly local. A few cable. Word is going to spread fast."

Damn.

This was not something he had wanted to deal with. Not something he wanted Tess to have to deal with. "I should warn Tess."

He grabbed the magazine and pushed himself up from his chair. He left his office, stopping to peer out the front window—*damn*—then went off to look for Tess. He found her in the library curled up in the chaise by the window reading a book.

When she saw him, she gave him a bright smile. "Hi."

"Hey. We need to talk."

Worry crinkled her forehead. "Okay."

"We have a problem," he said.

No kidding, Tess thought. In fact, they had more than one.

Ben handed her a magazine.

"What's this?" Her heart sank as the headline screamed at her in bold letters, Millionaire Widower's Pregnant Mistress!

Underneath it was a photo of her coming out of the doctor's office, looking very pregnant and glancing around guiltily, as if she had something to hide.

So she'd been right. Someone had been following her.

"There's more inside," he said.

She opened the paper and there were more pictures. A few of her in town shopping and another of her driving up to Ben's house, the address clearly visible by the gate. Beside a column of type she was sure she would be better off not reading, there was a photo of Ben and his wife, a gorgeous Hollywood couple, and a shot of Ben in a dark suit getting out of a limo at what Tess could only assume was the funeral.

She shut the magazine. "Wonderful."

"There's more," Ben said.

"More?" How could this possibly get any worse?

"The press is camped out in front of the house."

Oh, yeah, that *was* worse. She muttered a curse under her breath.

"My sentiments exactly," Ben said. "By law they can't enter the property. Although that doesn't always stop them. And it doesn't stop them from using a telephoto lens."

"What should we do?"

He shrugged. "Not much we can do. Just wait it out. If you don't want to have to talk to them, or see your picture in the paper, I wouldn't plan on going anywhere for a while. That includes the garden. And don't get too close to any open windows at night."

"How long?"

"No way to tell. Probably until the next big scandal hits."

Swell. "I'm really sorry."

"How is this your fault? I'm the one who's sorry. I'm used to this kind of thing. You're not."

She sat on the love seat. Morbid curiosity got the best of her and she skimmed the article. Ben sat on the arm and read over her shoulder.

"The worst part is that nothing they printed is untrue. Not totally at least. I'm your mistress and I'm definitely pregnant."

"Tess, you and I both know that you are a hell of a lot more to me than a mistress."

She handed the magazine back to him. "I can't look at this anymore."

"What you need to understand," Ben said, "is that this will probably get a lot worse before it gets better."

Eleven

Ben had been right. It did get worse. For the next two days the phone rang off the hook. And rather than dispersing, the mob of media out front only grew in size. And as morbid as it was, she couldn't stop herself from sitting in front of the television watching the cable entertainment shows, seeing what new information they had dredged up about her. Or in some cases, fabricated.

By far the lowest, most humiliating point had been when she'd read that her own mother had accepted ten thousand dollars for an exclusive interview. She didn't doubt that her stepfather had fueled that fire. There was a photograph of them together, standing on the porch of their broken down shack of a house in Utah. The five years since she'd last seen them hadn't been a friend to either. Her stepdad was still a fat disgusting pig and her mother looked old, tired and used up. And sadly, ninety percent of the exclusive interview was based on lies and half truths. She hadn't been an angel in her youth, but they had painted her as a strung out sex-crazed juvenile delinquent.

"We could sue for slander," Ben suggested, but honestly, she didn't see the point. True or not true, the information was out there and there was no taking it back. Ever. A lawsuit wouldn't stop people from believing, and it's not as if they could get damages from a couple who had nothing. She wouldn't even want to.

And when she was sure they had reached the absolute rock bottom and things could not possibly get any worse, any more complicated, they did.

She and Ben were in the dining room eating dinner when the doorbell rang.

Ben was already at the end of his patience and struggling to hang on. "They have a lot of nerve coming to the door."

Mrs. Smith emerged from the kitchen. "Would you like me to take care of it?"

Ben threw his napkin down onto his plate. "No. I think it's time I gave them a piece of my mind."

Tess cringed, knowing this was all her fault. Her relationship with him, the existence of the baby, was the only thing they were interested in.

Ben got up and headed for the foyer. She could hear the angry thud of his footsteps on the marble floor, the squeak of the hinges as he flung the front door open.

She waited for the shouting and the cursing, but what she heard was a long pause, then a baffled sounding, "*Mom,* what are you doing here?"

Oh boy, could this get any messier? Ben's mother had flown all the way from Europe, probably to drive Tess away. As any good mother would considering what the press had been reporting.

Tess stood at the far end of the foyer, trying to make herself invisible. Ben just looked stunned.

"Oh my goodness, what a dreadful mess!" his mother chirped, waving a hand dramatically in her face. She had no idea how true that was. "Now I remember why I got out of the entertainment business. Nasty people those reporters."

"Mom, what are you doing here? I told you it isn't a good time."

She gave him a patient smile. "It looks to me as though this is the perfect time."

As much as Tess would have liked to be able to tell herself Ben's mom looked like a normal everyday person, she didn't. She looked young and gorgeous and glamorous—like the movie star she'd been. And Tess felt like an ugly duckling.

Then Mrs. Adams looked around, her eyes screeching to a halt on Tess, as though she'd just realized someone else was standing there with them.

"Is this her?" she asked Ben.

"Mom, this is Tess. Tess, this is my mom."

Mrs. Adams swept across the foyer, gliding with

such smooth grace, Tess could swear her feet never hit the ground. She took Tess by the shoulders and looked her up and down. Tess waited for her to shove her away in disgust or possibly spit on her shoes. Instead, tears welled in her eyes and she yanked Tess, very unladylike, into a crushing hug.

Tess was so shocked that for a minute she forgot to breathe, and when she finally did, a cloud of flowery perfume filled her lungs. Over her shoulder, Tess saw Ben cringe.

"Oh, Benji, she's *adorable!*"

Benji? Tess mouthed the nickname back to him and Ben rolled his eyes.

Mrs. Adams held her at arm's length again, the tears hovering just inside her lids, as if they knew better than to spill over and mar her perfectly applied makeup.

Tess felt like a new family pet, a fuzzy little puppy they could housebreak and teach tricks. And she didn't get it. The tabloids had painted her as some moneygrubbing harlot. Mrs. Adams was acting as if she were happy to meet Tess.

"When are you due, sweetheart?" Mrs. Adams asked her, her grip on her arms not loosening.

It had been so long since anyone actually asked about the pregnancy, it took a minute for Tess to realize she meant her due date. "September nineteenth."

She let out a gasp. "Mine is the thirtieth! Maybe it will be born then!"

Eleven days late? God, she hoped not. She already felt like an elephant.

She turned to her son. "Benji, why didn't you tell us. Didn't you think we would want to know about our grandchild?"

"I planned to," Ben said, but Tess had the feeling it was a lie. He didn't want his parents to know about the baby. He didn't want them to get attached.

"Mom, why don't we get you settled in, then we'll talk?"

"That's a wonderful idea," his mother said, gently touching her shellacked hair. "I must look a fright after the long trip. Mrs. Smith, could you please have my bags taken to the guest suite?"

Mrs. Smith shot Ben a questioning look.

"I'm sorry, Mom, but the guest suite is occupied. You'll have to take a spare bedroom."

"Who's staying in the guest suite?" she asked.

"Tess is," Ben said, bracing for the questions that would follow.

He didn't have to wait long.

"Why on earth is she staying in the guest suite?"

This was going to be tough for her to understand. His mom, the hopeless romantic, would undoubtedly be very disappointed in him.

"We'll talk later," he told her. He would explain everything the minute he'd decided what to say.

He opened the front door to get the bags from the porch, and found five *enormous* cases sitting there. His mom tended to overpack, but this was ridiculous. "Um, how long were you planning on staying?"

"Well, until the baby is born, of course! Did you think I would miss the birth of my first grandchild?"

Ben cringed. This was worse than he'd thought. "What about Dad? Doesn't he mind you being gone so long?"

She waved a hand at him. "Oh, you know your father."

What was that supposed to mean?

"If I'd known you were coming, I could have prepared." As in he would have told her to stay in Europe.

"Didn't Mrs. Smith tell you I was coming?" his mom asked.

Mrs. Smith had talked to her? He looked over to his housekeeper who was trying hard not to look guilty. Peculiar that he was only hearing about this now.

"It must have slipped my mind," she said.

That was a lie, and he knew it. She had a mind like a steel trap. She never forgot anything.

He turned to his mom. "We'll get you settled in, then we'll talk. Mrs. Smith, when my mom has everything she needs, please come see me in my office."

She nodded, then led Mrs. Adams up the stairs.

"I get the feeling someone is in big trouble," Tess said from behind him.

"Yes," he agreed, turning to her. "Someone certainly is. I can't believe Mrs. Smith didn't warn me she was coming."

"This is bad, huh?"

"It's not the end of the world, but it is going to complicate things."

"If she asks me what's going on, what should I tell her?"

He didn't want Tess telling her anything, not until he'd decided exactly how much he wanted his parents to know. Besides, it wasn't fair to dump any of this on her. It was his responsibility. "You don't have to tell her anything. Just leave the explanations to me."

"You wanted to see me?"

Ben looked up to find Mrs. Smith standing in his office doorway. "Come in and shut the door."

She shut the door and walked stiffly to his desk. She had to know he would be furious with her for this.

"What has gotten into you? Why didn't you tell me the minute she called? I could have smoothed this over. You know how I felt about her coming here."

She gave him her usual belligerent, down-the-nose stare. "I was only thinking of your best interests."

"How is this my *best interests?*"

"That baby is her grandchild. She deserves to know it. Besides I can see how happy you are when you're with Tess. Even if you're too stubborn to admit it."

"How I feel about Tess is completely beside the point." He rubbed his eyes with the heels of his palms. "I have to figure out a way to explain why they can't be a part of the baby's life."

"There's no reason they can't be grandparents to this child."

"There's one damned good reason," he said hotly.

"How will they explain it once he's older? Why it's okay to see his grandparents, but not his own father?"

"If you feel as though you've done nothing wrong, and your actions are justified, why would you care what the child thinks?"

He hated when she cornered him with logic. She always had this way of making him question himself, when he knew deep down he was making the right decision.

"Maybe this is something you should have considered before," she said.

"Before what? Before I accidentally got her pregnant? Despite what you believe, this was not an easy decision for me to make."

"I only want what's best for you, Ben."

"Which means what?"

"It means Tess is best for you. You need her, and you need this baby. You need them almost as much as they need you."

He shook his head. "I can't go through that again."

"You don't have a choice. It's done. That girl is having your baby and there is nothing you can do to change that."

"Everyone has a choice, and I've made mine." He stood. "Now if you'll excuse me, I need to go speak with my mother. I have to figure out a way to fix this mess. To get her back on a plane and out of California."

"You can't run forever," she said.

"Oh, yeah. Watch me."

Twelve

"**Y**ou should have told me," Ben's mom said, after he spent twenty humiliating minutes explaining the situation. It was bad enough having to admit to his mother that he had had a one night stand. But when she started in on him about the virtues of safe sex, he'd had to explain that they had practiced safe sex. Unfortunately there had been a condom malfunction.

"Why do I get the impression you weren't going to tell me at all?" she asked.

"No," he admitted. "If the press hadn't gotten a hold of the story, I probably wouldn't have."

He could see she was disappointed, and he was sorry for that, but that was just life. He had spent most of his childhood feeling disappointment of one form or another. He owed her a little bit of misery.

She shook her head sadly. "I raised you better than this."

"*You* raised me? Are you kidding?" It was probably due to the stress from the media coverage, but all the bottled up disappointment and feelings of indignant anger he'd buried during his childhood welled to the surface. "*You* didn't raise me at all. Mrs. Smith did. You were too busy being a star to give a damn about what was happening to me."

He hadn't meant to be cruel, but the words just sort of flew out. Maybe he'd needed to say them for a long time.

Too long.

She didn't even have the decency to look wounded. "Well then, don't make the same mistakes I did. Be there for your child."

Her words stung. And the fact that she didn't bother to deny it surprised him.

"This baby will be well taken care of. He'll have the best of everything."

"That obviously wasn't good enough for you, was it?"

Ouch. Direct hit. But this was different.

"Do you think he won't notice that he doesn't have a father?"

He'd thought about that, and he hated it, but there was nothing he could do about it. "Maybe it would be best if you just go home."

"I'm not leaving, Ben. I may have been a lousy mother, but I'm going to be the best damned grandma you'll ever meet. So you might as well get used to the idea."

"And what about Dad?"

"What about him?"

"How does he feel about you being gone for three months?"

"To tell you the truth, I don't think he cares."

Ben gave his mom a disbelieving look. His father had an ego as wide and deep as the Grand Canyon. He lived to be doted on and pampered. It would only be a matter of time before he demanded she come home and pay attention to him.

"I didn't want to bother you with this, but you should probably know that your father and I are getting divorced."

She said it so calmly, it took a second for the meaning of the words to hit home. "*Divorced?* What happened?"

"He's trading me in for a younger model. Literally. She was on the cover of the swimsuit issue last year. Thirty-eight years younger than him. The poor thing doesn't know what she's getting into."

His world felt as if it had been flipped upside down and dropped on its head. He wasn't naive. He'd heard rumors that his dad had flings with his costars. Ben had never asked if it was true, and neither his mom nor his dad had ever brought it up. And thank God for that, because frankly, he didn't want to know.

But his parents had been together for almost thirty-five years. How could his dad just up and leave her?

And why didn't she seem all that disturbed by it. He would have thought she'd be devastated.

"When did this happen?"

"After Christmas."

"That was months ago! Why didn't you tell me?"

"That isn't something you tell someone over the phone."

Aw hell, now it made sense. Now he understood why his mom kept calling and asking to visit. She'd needed to talk to him, and probably just plain needed him, and he kept blowing her off.

"I'm sorry."

She patted his shoulder. "So, as you can imagine, your father most definitely does not need me, meaning I'm in no rush to get back. In fact, I may never go back. I may just stay here with you in California. You have the room."

That had to be a joke. For thirty-two years she all but ignores him, now she wants to move into his house? And what was he supposed to do? Ask her to leave. Tell her he didn't want her around. He may have had a lot of pent-up hostility toward her, but he didn't want to hurt her feelings. Especially after what his father had done to her.

This was nuts.

"Now shoo," she said. "I have to unpack and fix my face. Then I'd like a tour of this lovely house."

The best Ben could do, as his mother shoved him

out the door and into the hall, was smile and pretend like everything was normal. When he had the distinct feeling life would never be *normal* again.

Tess walked slowly through the garden, stopping here and there to inhale a bloom, the sun warming her skin. She tried to convince herself she was just out there enjoying the weather—even if that meant getting caught on film by some elusive photographer's telephoto lens—when the truth was, she was hiding. She didn't want to run into Ben's mom, and possibly have to explain her side of the story.

She didn't have a clue what to say. Her face was plastered on every gossip rag, her entire life—complete with juicy lies for added flavor—printed in black and white for the world to read.

Although she couldn't help being curious about what Ben had told his mom, and how she felt about him not wanting the baby.

"Tess!"

Tess turned to see Mrs. Adams gliding toward her down the path, arm waving wildly. Tess cursed under her breath. She couldn't exactly outrun her. She had no choice but to stop and wait.

"Mrs. Smith said I would probably find you out here," she said breathlessly as she caught up.

Tess would have to remember to thank Mrs. Smith. Maybe a garter snake in her bed.

"It is okay if I call you Tess, dear?"

"Of course," Tess told her. She was surprised she

would even ask. She would have expected something a bit more colorful, like Harlot or Tramp.

"Phew!" Mrs. Adams waved a hand in front of her face. "It is warm out here, isn't it?" If she was over-heated, it didn't show. She looked cool and dry in her rose colored blouse and white slacks. Tess doubted people like Ben's mom even had sweat glands.

"It is warm," Tess agreed, knowing she probably hadn't come out here to talk about the weather. There was more coming.

Just smile and make nice and agree with every-thing she says. Grovel if necessary.

They walked slowly, side by side. Well, Tess waddled and Mrs. Adams glided.

"I recall being hot all the time when I was pregnant with Benji. And sick, right up until the day he was born. That's why I never had more children." She waved her hand, as if she could swat the unpleas-ant thought away like a pesky bug. "I think that's why Benji always wanted a family so badly. Because he felt lonely growing up. His father and I were gone far too much."

Ben had wanted a family. She'd just come along a little too late.

That shouldn't have hurt so much. She shouldn't have felt so cheated. But she did. Somewhere deep down, as often as she denied it, she still wanted the fairy tale. The happily ever after.

"I only hope that you don't hold this against him. He's a good man, Tess."

"I know he is." If she didn't know any better, she would think Ben's mom wanted him and Tess together.

"It's been terribly difficult for him since he lost Jeanette," she went on. "You might not realize this, but your being here has helped him."

Tess swallowed hard. "I take it you two have… talked."

"Yes, we've talked. He explained the situation. He's quite convinced he's doing the right thing."

"You don't agree?"

She laughed. "Heavens, no! I think he's being an ass. That's my grandbaby you're carrying. That makes you a part of this family."

Tears burned behind Tess' eyes. She'd never expected Ben's mom to accept her into their family. "I guess I thought…well, the things that you probably read about me…"

She stopped abruptly and took Tess firmly by the shoulders. "Dear, let's get something straight. I was in the entertainment business a long time. Long enough to know that ninety-nine percent of what you read in the tabloids is fabrication, and the other one percent is usually only half-right." She let out a long, exasperated sigh, laying a hand gently across Tess's belly. "If I live to be two hundred, I will never understand men and their egos. My son tells me I can never see my grandchild and thinks I'm just going to nod and agree. He's like his father in that respect. He left me, you know. My husband. For a twenty-year-old supermodel."

Holy—why was she telling Tess this? "I'm so sorry." She didn't know what else *to* say.

"I'm better off without him," she said bravely, then her lips began to quiver.

Uh-oh.

She dragged in a shaky breath and forced a smile.

"Are you okay?"

"I'm fine," she said. "Just fine." Then buried her face in her hands and dissolved into tears.

For a second, Tess was too stunned to react. What had happened to the larger-than-life, confident superstar? And what was she supposed to do? Stand there and watch while the woman fell apart?

She did the only thing she could, what she would want someone to do if she were having an emotional melt down, she wrapped her arms around Ben's mom and hugged her.

"I'm sorry," Ben's mom said, the words drowned out by a sob.

"It's okay," Tess said, patting her back. She led Ben's mom to a bench and sat beside her. She dug a clean tissue out of her pocket and pushed it into her hand.

Mrs. Adams sniffled daintily and dabbed her eyes. "I'm not naive. I knew he'd had flings over the years. But I loved him so much I pretended not to notice, even though it broke my heart every time he came home smelling like another woman's perfume. But he did come home. No matter who he was sleeping with, he was still mine at the end of the day."

"I'm so sorry," Tess said, rubbing her shoulder.

She couldn't imagine loving someone so much she would tolerate infidelity. Ben's mom was gorgeous and famous. Why would she put up with that if she could probably have any other man in the world?

Because she was human, Tess realized. Not a larger-than-life icon. Today she was just a lonely and confused woman who needed a shoulder to cry on.

"On top of everything else I'm going through menopause," she said, fresh tears rolling down her cheeks. "Anyone who tells you it's not that horrible is full of bunk. I feel so *old*."

"You don't look old. And I have no idea how you can cry without your makeup running. Mine would be all over my face."

"Waterproof mascara. One hundred and twenty bucks a tube and worth every penny." With a wistful sigh, she reached up and touched Tess's cheek. It was such a gentle, motherly gesture, Tess felt her heart swell. "Just look at that gorgeous skin. I used to have skin like that. So youthful. I don't dare go without makeup these days. I look ghastly without my face on."

"You're beautiful," Tess said.

"My plastic surgeon thanks you." At Tess's surprised look she said, "It's no secret that I've had work done, for all the good it's done me. I should have just let myself grow old gracefully. You think you're turning the biological clock off, then you realize you've really only hit the snooze button. But enough about me. Tell me about your pregnancy."

"What would you like to know?"

Excitement sparked in her youthful eyes. *"Everything."*

It was Tess's turn to get weepy. It was stupid, but besides her doctor, not a single person had asked her about her pregnancy. She'd been dying to tell someone. *Anyone.*

She told Ben's mom *everything,* down to the last little detail. They sat outside in the garden for hours, talking as if they'd been acquainted for years. Despite being from opposite ends of the social spectrum, they bonded out there among the flowers. They became friends.

She knew, without a doubt, even if she couldn't rely on Ben to be there for her and the baby, his mom would never let her down. It made her feel a little less lonely.

Things got very weird after his mom arrived. Or maybe things were normal, which for Ben was unusual.

They coexisted together like a happy family, which, ironically, is exactly what he'd told Tess wouldn't happen. Unfortunately he wasn't the one calling the shots anymore. His mom had come in and completely taken over.

He'd seen more of her in the past two months than he had the last twenty years. She and Tess were practically attached at the hip. They took long walks and went shopping together, and his mom even went with Tess for her seventh and eighth month checkups. She planned to be there for the birth, so they began taking Lamaze classes together once a week.

Sometimes the two of them would sit for hours and just talk. Not only could he not imagine what they could possibly have in common, but he was also sure they would have eventually run out of things to talk about.

His mom had even managed to defuse the situation with the press. They had accosted her and Tess in town. Someone shoved a microphone in his mom's face and asked, "How do you feel about becoming a grandmother?"

His mom slipped her arm through Tess's and gave the camera crews a bright, genuine smile. "My husband and I couldn't be more thrilled. We adore Tess. Now if you gentlemen will excuse us, we have shopping to do."

She always had been great at working a crowd.

Ben gave up trying to stop it. In part because he could see that it was useless, and another part of him was actually enjoying having his mom around. Enjoying, for the first time in his life—and probably the last—the feeling of close family.

Although sometimes he could swear his mom liked Tess more than him.

But it couldn't last. After the baby was born, which was a mere three weeks away now, they couldn't pretend to be a happy family anymore. Although he had the sneaking suspicion that when the time came, he was going to be the odd man out.

He would be alone and Tess would have his family. Even Mrs. Smith was making noises like she might stay with Tess for a few months until she got settled into her new condo.

He might have been angry, or even hurt, but Tess was so happy lately. One evening after they had made love, she told him that for the first time in her life, she felt loved. She thanked him for sharing his mom with her.

He'd begun having those thoughts again, like maybe there was a way to make this work.

Then the other shoe fell. In fact, they *both* did. Ben was in his office working when his mother burst through the door, her face white as death.

"Tess fell!"

He died a thousand deaths in the three seconds it took him to jump from his chair and follow her to the base of the stairs where Tess was sitting on the marble floor clutching her left ankle. Mrs. Smith crouched beside her.

There was no blood, she wasn't unconscious. Nothing looked broken. She was okay.

His heart was hammering so hard and he felt so light-headed with relief he nearly joined her on the floor. "What happened?"

"My bad ankle," Tess said. "It gave out on me when I was walking down the stairs."

"You should be more careful," he snapped. He didn't mean to. He *never* meant to get mad at her when what she really needed was comfort. He just did.

Suddenly everyone was looking at him like he was an ogre.

It wasn't an unfair assessment.

"Gee, Ben, you think?" Tess snapped back. But she looked more hurt than angry. "It's probably the extra weight and water retention irritating it. There's not much I can do about that."

"Do you think you can walk?" Mrs. Smith asked.

"I think s—" She gasped and folded in half. "Oh!"

Ben went from relieved to petrified in an instant. "What's wrong?"

"Pain in my stomach," she gasped. "You want to blame that on me too?"

He'd definitely deserved that.

Ben's mom shot him a distressed look. Even Mrs. Smith looked worried.

It passed after a few seconds. She sat up and said, "That was weird."

"Are you all right?" his mom asked.

She nodded. "I think so."

"Let's get you up off the floor." His mom shot him a look, but he just stood there. He knew he should help, but he couldn't move.

This was all his fault. He should have never let her climb the stairs alone. He should have insisted she use the service elevator behind the kitchen. If she lost the baby because of his carelessness...

She wasn't going to lose the baby. He was just overreacting again. She was fine.

The women helped Tess to her feet and Ben saw her wince when she put weight on her ankle.

"Can you walk on it?" Mrs. Smith asked.

"I think so." She started to take a step then let out a startled gasp and doubled over again, clutching her belly. "Ow! That hurts!"

She couldn't possibly be in labor. It was too early. She still had three weeks to go.

"Maybe we should take you to the doctor," Ben said, waiting for the women to say not to worry, Tess was fine. Random stomach pain was completely normal.

It's what he desperately *needed* to hear.

Instead, when Tess looked up at him, there was fear in her eyes. "That might not be a bad idea."

Thirteen

Tess lay in bed, the television on, flipping mindlessly through the channels. There were a million of them, and not a damned thing on she wanted to watch.

She didn't know how much more of this she could take.

After her fall, the doctor had confined her to bed. Her ankle was only twisted, but her blood pressure had been elevated, so she was ordered to stay off her feet for the duration of her pregnancy. Two weeks later she had a serious case of cabin fever.

Ben's mom stayed with her most of the time, and some evenings Mrs. Smith came in and played cards with them, or watched a movie. Sometimes they just sat around—or in Tess's case lay around—talking.

Ben's mom never ran out of stories to tell. She could always make Tess smile.

Ben was another story altogether. Tess knew that her accident would be a defining moment in their relationship. He would either be so relieved she and the baby were okay, he would realize what a fool he'd been and they would live happily ever after, or this would freak him out to the point that he shut her out completely.

Unfortunately, it was the latter.

Ben hadn't been in to see her the entire two weeks she'd been off her feet. He wouldn't even go into the examining room with her at the hospital while the doctor saw her. It was as if she didn't exist anymore.

As hard as she had tried not to, she'd let herself believe there was a chance with Ben. Things had been going so well that she'd had hope. How many times had she told herself she expected no more than he was willing to give? Only now, when she was faced with the limitation of that, did she realize it had been a lie. She wanted it all.

She probably should have been hurt and rejected, but the truth was, she just felt numb. And foolish.

Foolish for letting herself fall in love.

At least she still had Ben's mom to keep her company. She was Tess's family now. The mother that Tess had never had.

There was a soft knock at the bedroom door and Ben's mom popped her head in. "Are you awake?"

"I'm awake," Tess said, shutting off the television and tossing the remote aside. She wished she could sleep more. She wished she could drift off and wake up when the baby was due. "Awake and in danger of dying from boredom."

"I brought your lunch," she said, stepping in the room holding a tray.

"I'm not very hungry." She was never hungry anymore. She felt tired all the time, too, but couldn't seem to sleep for more than a couple of hours at a time. She was probably depressed, and just too numb to realize it.

Ben's mom set the tray on the nightstand. "How are you feeling?"

Tess shrugged. "My back is still bothering me, but otherwise I'm okay I guess."

"I wanted to talk to you about something." Ben's mom sat on the edge of the bed. "My husband called me last night."

"Really?" Tess sat up. "What did he say?"

"He said he made a terrible mistake and he wants me to come home. The thing with the model only lasted a few weeks but he's been too ashamed to call. He says he's been miserable without me."

As hard as she tried to hide how much she missed Ben's dad, Tess knew deep down she was miserable, too. "What do you think?"

"I think he sounds like he means it. Or maybe I just want to think that. I told him that before I would even consider reconciling with him, a lot of things would have to change. The infidelity would have to stop for one thing. I deserve better."

"Good for you." She was right, she did deserve better. And so did Tess—better than what Ben could offer her. Only problem was, she didn't think she could find anyone better for her, anyone she could love more than Ben. She didn't even feel like trying. Maybe she would feel differently later, after the baby was born and she got her life back together.

"He booked us rooms at a resort in Acapulco, so we can spend some time alone and sort things out. He wants me to meet him there tomorrow."

"Are you going to go?"

"I told him I'd think about it and call him back today. He seems genuinely sorry, but I hate the thought of leaving you. You need me here."

The thought of Ben's mom leaving broke Tess's heart, but her marriage was at stake. That was definitely more important.

She forced a smile. "I think you should go. I'll be fine."

"If I did go, I would make sure I was back a few days before the baby is due. I promised to be there with you, and I won't let you down."

What if something happened and she didn't make it back in time? Tess would have to go through it alone. The idea made her sick inside, but she wouldn't let it show. She couldn't be selfish. This was something Ben's mom needed to do. "I know you won't."

"I tried to talk to him again," Ben's mom said, and by *him* Tess knew she meant Ben. "He just won't listen."

Well, if nothing else, Ben was consistent. "Thanks for trying."

"Maybe he'll come around. Maybe after the baby is born—"

"I can't let myself believe that. If I do, and he doesn't…" A knot of emotion settled in her throat and wouldn't let the rest of the words out.

Ben's mom put her arms around Tess and hugged her. "I just don't understand it. I know he loves you."

The worst part was, she did, too. But sometimes love just wasn't enough.

Ben stared blindly at his computer screen, at the game of solitaire he wasn't really playing. He couldn't sleep. Just like last night. And the night before that, and the night before that. He hadn't had a decent night's sleep in two weeks, since the day Tess fell. And he felt as though he might never again.

He hated what he must have been doing to her. If she felt even half as tortured and sick inside as he did, she had to be miserable. It was like losing his family all over again. He had tried a million times to walk down the hall to her suite, but he could never make it all the way to the door. Every time something stopped him.

"Ben?"

Tess's voice. She was standing in his office doorway. He looked at the clock and saw that it was after midnight.

The doctor had told her to stay off her feet. She shouldn't even be out of bed.

"What are you doing down here?" He didn't mean to sound angry, but he couldn't seem to stop himself. He had to hold on to his anger and grief, or he would wind up pulling her into his arms and holding her. And that wouldn't be fair to Tess.

"Would you mind calling me a cab?" she asked, her voice sounding small and strained.

"What for?"

"I need to go to the hospital." She stepped into his office, and as she drew nearer, into the lamplight, he could see her skin was pale and her forehead damp with perspiration.

"What's wrong?"

"Nothing is wrong. I'm in labor."

"You can't be, you're not due for another week." He realized how dumb that sounded the second the words left his mouth.

"I thought so, too," she said. "Apparently the baby is ready now."

"Are you sure?"

"Incredibly sure."

He just stood there. He couldn't seem to make his feet move. He knew this day was going to come. But why did it have to be today? He wasn't ready for this.

Though he didn't think standing here like an idiot was going to stop it.

She clutched her belly. "Unless you want to deliver this baby yourself, I would call now."

"How close together are your contractions?"

"Every three or four minutes."

That got his attention. *"Three minutes?* How long have you been in labor?"

"I guess since this morning."

"This morning?" She couldn't be serious. "Why didn't you say something sooner?"

"It was all in my back, but I've had a backache for weeks. I didn't actually figure out that it was labor, until about ten minutes ago when my water broke."

His stomach dropped out. "Jesus, your water broke, too?"

"Would you please stop yelling at me!" she shouted, then her eyes went wide and she gasped a breath, clutching the edge of his desk. "Oh boy, here comes another one."

Tess gritted her teeth and tried to remember to breathe as the contraction hit her with the force and velocity of an express train. The pain just kept building and building until she didn't think she could stand it anymore, until tears were leaking out of her eyes. They said it would hurt, but never in her worst nightmare had she dreamed it would be this painful.

After what felt like hours, the pain finally began to ease. This was *so* not fun. This kid could just forget about natural birth. She wanted drugs. Lots and lots of drugs. And siblings were completely out of the question.

She looked up and saw that Ben was just standing there. His baffled expression might have been amusing in any other situation, but right now all she wanted to do was reach inside him, yank his spine out, stomp on it a couple million times and then set it on fire. Maybe then he would have at least a clue how damned much this hurt.

"I really need that cab," she said through gritted teeth.

"Somehow I don't think you have time to wait for a cab. Where is your bag?"

"By the stairs."

"I'll help you to the car."

He probably thought she did this on purpose, so he would have to drive her.

"Maybe Mrs. Smith could drive me."

"She doesn't drive at night." He led her to the garage, grabbing her bag as they passed the stairs.

"I'm sorry."

"Sorry for what?" he asked.

"That you have to do this."

He didn't answer, but she knew that he was sorry, too. He didn't want to go through this. But he would because he knew she needed him. He got her into the car just as the next contraction hit. They were coming even closer now, and she was beginning to feel pressure where the baby's head was coming down.

"Drive fast," she told him as he climbed in.

He started his car, peeled out of the garage and roared through the gates to the street. This was not the way she'd imagined this happening. She was supposed to have more time. Ben's mom was supposed to be here. Suddenly she couldn't remember a single thing she'd learned in class.

She felt so useless. Her body was doing all these off-the-wall things and she had no control. What if something went wrong? What if something happened to the baby?

She needed someone to tell her what to do.

"I can't do this," she told Ben. "I changed my mind. I don't want to have a baby."

"I think it's a little late for that, sweetheart."

"I'm scared."

He took her hand and squeezed it. "Everything is going to be okay."

But it wouldn't be. Not everything. They'd reached the end of the road. *Everything* would never be okay again.

The drive to the hospital was nothing but a blur of pain. Every bump they hit in the road, every turn he took, rocked through her body like a catastrophic earthquake. Her entire midsection, front to back, felt like a gigantic exposed nerve. It was so all-encompassing that she couldn't even determine the point of origin anymore. It just hurt, sharp and stinging, and it hurt *everywhere.*

Her only comfort was the reassuring squeeze of Ben's hand.

He drove *way* too fast, with only one hand on the wheel, and she was pretty sure he ran two or three red lights. Thank God it was the middle of the night and no one was on the road, and the hospital was only ten minutes away.

"You can just drop me off here," she told him when they pulled up to the emergency room doors. An orderly met them at the car with a wheelchair. She had just managed to slide into it when another contraction hit swift and intense. Every time she thought it couldn't possibly get any worse, it somehow managed to. It made sense now why she was an only child. How could a second pregnancy be anything but an accident? Who would want to go through this *twice?*

She could hear people talking around her, but through a haze of pain she couldn't focus on the words. She thought this one was just going to last forever, but it finally began to ease when they reached the elevator. Only then did it register that someone was holding her hand, and she looked up to see Ben standing beside her. "You're still here?"

"I'm still here."

And he wasn't leaving. Ben had no idea what he was doing, he only knew that he wasn't enough of a bastard to make her do this alone. He didn't let himself think about the repercussions. All he knew was that he loved her too much to leave her. It would probably be the hardest thing he'd ever had to do in his life, but he owed her that much.

The grip on his hand snapped like a vise, and he knew she was having another contraction. He stroked her hair and talked to her in a low, soothing voice. He remembered enough from his classes with Jeanette to remind her to focus and breathe.

He had a bad feeling that if they didn't get her to a room soon she was going to have this kid in the elevator. How long did it take to ride up four floors for God's sake?

Finally the bell tinged and the doors dragged slowly open. The orderly led them down the hall to Labor and Delivery. Next came the nurses, and a million questions he should have known the answers to. Everyone was calling him *Dad* and acting as if he was supposed to be there and he played along because it was the only thing he could do.

They barely had time to get her to a room, into a gown and prepped. In the whirlwind of activity, he stayed right beside her, talking her through it.

"I want drugs," Tess told the nurse who was taking her blood pressure. Then she turned to Ben and begged, "Tell them to give me drugs."

Ben looked at the doctor but she shook her head. "No time. She's fully effaced and dilated and the baby is coming down. Whenever you're ready, Tess, start pushing."

After a couple of false starts, Tess seemed to get the hang of it. Ben helped her sit up and counted out the seconds while she pushed, finally feeling as if he were doing some good.

Considering the force of her contractions, he expected the baby to shoot out like a bullet but it was slow going. He wiped the sweat from her forehead, fed her ice chips when she rested, watched in awe as she worked diligently to push the baby out. In his life he'd never loved or respected a woman more than he did Tess.

"The baby is crowning," the doctor said after forty minutes or so.

Ben didn't even stop to think about what he was doing. He just peered down to look and saw the top of the baby's head, covered with what looked like a lot of dark hair. It was the most amazing thing he had ever seen. "Oh my God. Tess, I can see the baby."

"One more big push," the doctor told her.

"I can't," Tess gasped. "I'm too tired."

"Look at me," Ben said, and she looked up at him, her eyes glassy. Two hours ago, he couldn't have been less ready for this baby to be born, now it was all he wanted. "You can do this. One more push and it will be all over."

She took a deep breath and he could see her gathering all her strength, giving it everything she had. Eyes closed in concentration, she bore down one last time and the baby popped out, slippery and squirmy with a full head of dark hair. Just like his.

"It's a girl." The doctor rolled her onto Tess's stomach and suctioned out her mouth.

A girl. A daughter.

He and Tess had a daughter.

She was small and pink and already exercising her lungs. And more beautiful that anything he had ever laid his eyes on.

Tess touched her. Her tiny little arms and legs, her fingers and toes. "Look at her, Ben. She's perfect."

The baby stopped crying and turned her head toward the sound of Tess's voice. She looked up at them both with bright, curious blue eyes. Intelligent eyes.

Ben fell instantly and completely in love with her.

It was so ridiculous to him that he had actually thought he could stop himself from loving her. The second she came screaming into the world she was his. Totally and absolutely a part of him.

He hadn't cried since the third grade, not even when he lost his son, but he could feel actual tears burning in his eyes.

"I am so sorry," he told Tess. "I don't know what I was thinking. How could I have not known how much I would love her?"

She reached up and wiped the tears from his cheeks.

"I love you, Tess."

"I love you, too."

The nurse took the baby away long enough to weigh, measure and clean her up—which felt like an eternity to Tess—then she wrapped her in a pink receiving blanket and brought her back. Gradually the room cleared until it was just Tess and Ben and the baby.

Their baby.

She was going to grow up happy, with a mommy and a daddy and grandparents to love her. A real family. She would never know just how lucky she was, and that was exactly the way Tess intended to keep it.

Ben sat on the bed beside her, gazing down at the little bundle in his arms. Tess had nursed her for a while, and Ben had been holding her ever since. And as much as Tess wanted a turn, she knew Ben needed her more right now. They had years and years to share her. To watch her grow and change.

"She looks just like you," he said, playing with her tiny little fingers.

"Your mom will be so disappointed she missed this."

He shrugged. "So she'll be here for the next one."

She shot him a questioning look.

"I know I don't deserve a second chance, but if you let me, I swear I'll make it up to you."

She just smiled. "You already have."

All this time she'd been wrong. Fairy tales could be real—if you just had faith. And in her story, the dark, enchanted castle was now filled with light and laughter and new life. And the prince had been set free from his curse by the love of a maiden.

The miniature one snuggled in his arms.

* * * * *

REFLECTED
PLEASURES
by
Linda Conrad

LINDA CONRAD

Award-winning author Linda Conrad was first inspired by her mother, who gave her a deep love of storytelling. "Actually, Mum told me I was the best liar she ever knew. And that's saying something for a woman with an Irish storyteller's background," Linda says. In her past life Linda was a stockbroker and certified financial planner, but she has been writing contemporary romances for six years now. Linda's passions are her husband, her cat named Sam and finding time to read cosy mysteries and emotional love stories. She says, "Living with passion makes everything worthwhile." Visit Linda's website at www.LindaConrad.com or write to her at PO Box 9269, Tavernier, FL 33070, USA.

· Prologue ·

"**T**ake it," the old gypsy, Passionata Chagari, demanded. "The mirror is meant for no one else."

She narrowed her eyes and watched as Tyson Steele glanced over his shoulder at the empty French Market square behind him. Passionata snickered as he looked for the cameras that would mean this was some kind of practical joke. She knew nothing but darkness would meet his gaze at this late hour.

The gypsy sensed Tyson setting his shoulders with determined skepticism. This young Steele heir had appeared tall and strong-willed as he'd swaggered to her corner. She was well aware that an hour ago he'd been at a meeting with his cousin, Nicholas Scoville, who'd claimed he had been given a gift of an antique book from a strange gypsy earlier in the evening at this very place.

She chuckled, knowing that pure curiosity was what had brought the young Texas native out into the quiet New Orleans night. This heir to the gypsy magic would not be so easily won over as was his cousin. But she knew her duty.

On her father's deathbed, she had given her word.

"I'm not accepting anything from you until I know the scam," Tyson Steele told her with a scowl.

"I want nothing. I bring your legacy."

"Legacy? I'm not in the mood for games. What the hell are you talking about?"

The gypsy spread her lips in an enigmatic smile. "I know the reason for your somber mood, young man. You spent the better part of the day at your great-aunt Lucille's funeral. And you have already been told that you were not mentioned in her will."

"That doesn't matter," he insisted. "I don't need her money now. She gave me everything I needed years ago, when it mattered the most. I could never have repaid that debt in a thousand lifetimes."

"This gift comes not from Lucille Steele," Passionata told him sharply. "But it is because of her kindnesses that you have been so honored by the wise and powerful gypsy king who was also in her debt."

"Excuse me?" Tyson backed up and put his hands in his pockets, trying fruitlessly to keep her from placing the golden mirror into his hands. "What king?"

"My father, Karl Chagari, king of the gypsies, master tinker and magician." She lowered her voice and took the proper deferential tone. "He has at long last gone ahead to the ancestors…as has Lucille. But he charged me with settling his debts."

Tyson eyed the antique mirror in her hands and she could hear him wondering to himself if it was stolen property. "Sorry about your father, ma'am. But uh... I don't think so. Thanks anyway.

"I shouldn't have come here," he argued. "But my cousin Nick said something so ridiculous that I just had to see for myself."

"It *is* magic, Tyson Steele," the gypsy hissed. "And it is your legacy...designed just for you. It will take you to your heart's desire."

"The only thing I desire is someone to fill the vacant fund-raising assistant's position at my charitable foundation," Tyson muttered. "And it isn't likely that a 'magic' hand mirror will be helping me with an applicant."

Passionata knew that at the exclusive personnel office where Tyson Steele had met his cousin earlier this evening, the young heir hadn't been able to find anyone who would agree to relocate to his remote town in deep south Texas. Tyson was frustrated. She'd planned it that way.

The gypsy shoved the mirror in his direction and concentrated her efforts on making him want a better look.

At last Tyson reached out and took the mirror from her hands, turned it over and inspected the back. Passionata saw his amazement when he spotted his name engraved in the gold-leaf scrollwork, adorning the sides and back.

"What the devil...?" he stammered.

"You see? It belongs to you, and you alone."

Tyson flipped it over to inspect the mirror's front side, and Passionata nearly laughed aloud.

"I don't see my image," he complained. "This isn't a mirror. It's simple glass. I don't understand."

"The true nature of that which you seek will be reflected in the depths of the glass when the time is right," she said. "It's made to reveal the truth, no more."

Passionata took the easy opportunity to slip out of sight while Tyson Steele stared at the mirror and tried to comprehend what he held. When he finally glanced up with more questions, he was all alone.

"That's just creepy," he mumbled to himself. "So far, I haven't managed to get any answers for my cousin. I haven't been able to locate an assistant fund-raiser. And now I have to worry about some old gypsy's magic mirror, too?"

Passionata nodded as she watched him in her crystal. "Just until you accept the gift of sight and use the magic, young Steele."

One

Serve his coffee? Sheesh. *Served her right.*

Merri Davis clamped down on her smart mouth, turned around and stalked out of the office to go get her new boss his cup of coffee. Tyson Steele had only been back from his New Orleans trip for a couple of hours and already in the first few minutes of their acquaintance the two of them were testing each other.

He apparently wanted to see how far he could push her—she was a fund-raising assistant, not a gopher after all. And *she* wanted to find out if he was truly the macho chauvinist that he appeared to be. Well, duh. The coffee request put him right there in the proper category.

She'd initially been wary of Mr. Tyson Steele anyway, wondering if he would recognize her from the tabloids. But her model's training had apparently worked a miracle in the disguise-makeup department. Good enough, so that he never really used those startling blue eyes to look at her twice.

She swallowed hard at her silent slip of the tongue about his eyes. Merri Davis was not interested in men's eyes. Startling or otherwise. That was simply not her mission or her concern.

At least not since Merrill Davis-Ross, high-fashion and jet-setting model, had effectively become Merri Davis, quiet and plain-looking fund-raiser's assistant.

Now she could only pray that the tabloid reporters, who normally snooped on her every move, would not be able to pick up the scent of where she had disappeared to this time.

So far, so good, she congratulated herself. This nowhere hick town in Texas should be the perfect hiding place. And the perfect place to find the simple life she had always dreamed of too.

But Merri cautioned herself to keep walking on eggshells around her new boss and to save any of her regular snappy comebacks. If she was going to maintain the charade, he would have to believe she was just the person she was now claiming to be.

Tyson's attorney, Franklin Jarvis, might suspect the truth, or at least a version of the truth. But he'd gotten her this job as a favor to *his* old friend—her own attorney from back in L.A.

To keep Mr. Jarvis from asking too many questions, she'd made up a story about who she was with her attorney and had vowed to keep her mouth shut and stick to the story. Part of her story was that she was a shy, quiet woman who would be happy living and working in this small town.

Actually, that wasn't too far from the truth. Despite what the tabloids wrote about her. She *was* shy and had been desperate to live in this small town. Her parents had sheltered her and, no matter where in the world they were living at the time, they surrounded her with bodyguards.

Merri had hated every minute of it. The last couple of years, since she'd been out of college and had worked on a few modeling jobs in Paris, were also not indicative of the person she really was deep inside— or who she wanted to be. She wasn't the person they wrote about in all those tabloid articles.

The reporters had taken the place of most of the bodyguards, and they were much more difficult to deal with. So…she would get Tyson Steele's damn coffee and run his errands if that's what it took to stay hidden in her brand-new world.

Drawing on all her old drama classes, Merri straightened the tight bun of mousey brown hair on the top of her head and headed back to her new boss's office with a mug full of dark sludge that would have to pass as coffee.

She had to play the part exactly right if she was going to turn this new life into her own.

"Thanks," he said absently when she placed the mug on the corner of his desk. "Sit." He waved her toward one of the vacant metal fold-up chairs next to his desk.

Damned man couldn't even bother to ask? Merri backed up and sat down as ordered, waiting for him to finish his phone conversation. As she sat, she took the pose of supposedly inspecting her unpolished finger-nails. But she was surreptitiously studying her new boss from behind her thick, fake glasses.

And he was definitely the picture of masculinity, she could see that quite clearly. Tight, well-worn jeans, sleeves rolled halfway up muscular arms and intelligent but slightly dangerous blue eyes. Whew. A smidgen of heat budded deep in her gut, but she tried to ignore it.

She'd been in his office many times without him over the last two days, learning the surroundings of her new job and getting accustomed to the names on the Foundation's many donor files. That part of her job would be easy enough.

But his attorney had also asked for her special help "civilizing" Tyson Steele. She hadn't originally thought that would be a big part of her job—Steele was a well-known billionaire after all. However, Mr. Jarvis was convinced that his client needed some major polish.

He'd said that since Merri came from sophisticated L.A. and seemed professional, perhaps she could encourage Ty to drop some of his Texas cowboy image. Apparently, Merri would never entirely be rid of her damned boarding school background—no matter how hard she'd tried to disguise herself.

She had reluctantly agreed to Mr. Jarvis's sugges-tion, thinking her new boss must be some kind of ogre. But now all of a sudden Tyson Steele was here in the flesh. And instead of trying to think of how to change him, his presence made her feel too warm and the room suddenly felt too closed-in to breathe.

He hung up the phone and reached for the coffee mug. "Mmm. Steaming and strong." He took a swig and made a face. "Yeah, just like always. Strong enough to stand by itself and hot enough to melt the plastic off the cup. Those are the only good things about the coffee here."

"Maybe you should enter the twenty-first century and buy a decent coffeemaker?" Damn. She'd managed to make a smart remark after all. *Keep your mouth shut, Merri.*

Tyson Steele narrowed his eyes at her, but he made no comment. He set the mug back down on the desk and picked up a stack of papers. "Now then, Miss…" Hesitating over her name, he glanced up and pinned her with another hard glare.

Oh, man. She didn't like her body noticing what he did to the atmosphere in the room. What was up with that? She'd thought that it had been steamy in here before he turned those piercing blue eyes her way.

"Davis," she supplied quickly to fill up the dangerous silence. "But please call me Merri, Mr. Steele." Feeling the sweat beginning to form at her temples, she ran a hand over her hair and tried to breathe quietly through her nose.

Merri didn't want to give her true self away. If she either told him to shove it—or did what her body wanted and flirted with him—he might figure out her charade.

And if he caught her in the lie, she had no doubt he wouldn't hesitate a second to pick up the phone and give her whereabouts over to the tabloids. A shiver ran down her spine at just the thought of having to face those horrible paparazzi bastards right now. Then not only would her own new life be ruined, but she would never be able to help Steele's orphans or his foundation at all.

"Merri, then," he said casually. "And you can call me Ty. Most everyone does. Except maybe my aunt Jewel, who always uses Tyson...unless she's mad enough to call me by my full name, Tyson Adams Steele. That's when I know it's time to disappear."

His face relaxed into a wide grin and Merri felt her whole body jump in response. Sonofa... She'd been hit on and propositioned by some of the wealthiest and most beautiful men in the universe. And she hadn't been interested or tempted by any of them.

So why was it that gruff Tyson Steele had been just a rather interesting man—right up until he laid that smile on her?

She'd been doing a credible job of ignoring his long, lean body encased in jeans and beat-up work boots. But there was no way to ignore that grin. It ran electric currents along her skin and shot hot, wet bullets of sensitivity down her spine.

"Your aunt is Jewel Adams?" Merri managed to sound steady and more in charge of her senses than she felt. "She's my new landlady."

Ty cocked his head and studied her for the first time. "You rented that old broken-down cottage on Jackson Street from Jewel? She was my mother's sister and she raised me after my parents were killed."

"You're an orphan?" Her heart had taken a little detour all of a sudden.

"I don't think of it that way anymore," he growled. "You may have noticed that I'm all grown up now."

His face held a scowl but his eyes were laughing at her. Oh, man.

He had to know the effect he was having on her. With eyes that startling periwinkle blue color, women just had to fall all over themselves to get him to pay attention—even if his outward clothing left something to be desired.

It wouldn't be possible for him not to know what that sexy look could do—was doing—to her. She had to find some steady ground here. Her whole future in this town depended on it.

"The house might be old but it's not really broken-down," Merri told him with a croaky voice. "Someone has recently remodeled the inside. It's quite cozy." There. Didn't she sound just like she was in charge of the situation and in control of her own bodily responses?

"Jewel painted it and refinished the wood floors," he agreed. "But the roof still leaks, the plumbing is shaky and the electric needs a total overhaul. I was going to help her out with the heavy work, but I haven't had time."

"Oh. I'm sure it will be fine. It's all I could afford until I can save up some money from this job," she lied. Money was not a problem. But she wanted desperately to make her own way for once, and make it in a small and completely plain way at that.

"I've already put in a few personal touches," she added. "It's beginning to feel like home." Well, maybe not exactly like any of her parents' many homes. Thirty-room mansions didn't usually qualify as cozy. And not one of them had ever felt like her home.

But Merri was determined to start a new life without any of the pretensions of all that wealth. She was ready for a home to call her own and for honest contacts with real live human beings. She'd turned her back for good on fictional family life and plastic feelings.

So why did she have to be drooling over the one man who could end it all with just one phone call? Why was he so different?

Okay, so he was probably the most real man she'd ever come across in her whole life. There was not one single thing about Tyson Steele that was plastic or phony. But she simply had to remember that the man was her boss, and she had no business thinking about him in any other way.

"Yeah?" he said with a half smile. "Well, it won't seem so homey when the rain starts falling into the kitchen or the septic tank backs up." Ty stood and stepped away from his desk. "Tell you what. If you can honestly help take the responsibility of fund-raising off my shoulders, I'll spend the extra time fixing up that old cottage."

"You wouldn't hire it done? I mean, you'd do it yourself…with real hammers and tools and stuff? Don't you have other businesses to run?"

He really chuckled this time and moved to the credenza. "Yes, I'd do it with real tools and *stuff*. Most of my other ventures run quite well without me now. I have excellent help. I only need to check up on them occasionally. That's why I've had the time to devote to getting this charitable foundation up and running."

Hesitating, he picked up a stack of pre-opened letters before he continued. "Fixing up old properties for resale was the way I made my first million. And I still like to be pretty hands-on when it comes to residential real estate. It relaxes me. Besides, I promised my aunt I'd help."

Ty frowned down at the letters in his hand. "But as good as I am with tools and *stuff,* I'm absolutely terrible at acknowledging donations."

He looked up then, staring at her as if trying to judge her capabilities. "The Lost Children Foundation is one of the most important things in my life, Merri. I've made more money in real estate and oil than fifty people could spend over a lifetime, but it will all be a waste if I can't make a difference in abused or exploited children's lives."

She saw the honesty shining in his eyes, and suddenly noticed something else that looked a lot like pain buried deep within them, too. And her heart skipped another beat.

"Your foundation has already saved children…made a difference," she said softly. "Mr. Jarvis, your attorney, explained it all when he hired me. What you've done, all that you've built for children. It's quite impressive."

Ty continued to stare at her for a moment, then nodded once and shoved the thick stack of letters into her hands. "Yes, well… Frank Jarvis told *me* you had some experience in nonprofit development. I hope that means you know how to send out thank-you letters, because a few of these donation letters date from six months ago."

"Donors don't feel appreciated when their generosity isn't acknowledged," she said with a disdainful frown. "How did you manage to fall so far behind?"

The smile that spread across his face this time was a wry one. "You aren't the first person I've hired to fill this position."

He raised an eyebrow and sighed in a self-deprecating way. "You're the fourth...no fifth...young woman who has agreed to be my assistant. I was hoping one of them would eventually work into the Director of Development position I've been wanting to create. And take the burden of the everyday administration off my shoulders.

"Unfortunately, none of them lasted more than a few weeks—as you can probably tell by the state of things around here."

"But why didn't they last? The pay is fair and these offices are really plush. What made them all quit so fast?"

He started to shrug a shoulder but stopped midway and scowled. "I thought it was because this town is so out of the way and...backward. I mean, the nearest fashion mall is a three-hour drive away."

Running a hand through his hair, Ty looked as if he was frustrated and confused. "But the last woman left screaming something about never again being taken in by such a handsome ogre. I guess that means she thought I was something I'm not. Or maybe the job was more than she bargained for.

"I don't know for sure," he added, finishing his shrug. "But I have always tried to be completely honest with everyone, and I expect that in return."

Ty turned to retrieve his cowboy hat from its hanger on the wall behind the door. "I have an appointment now with my attorney and a new donor. I'll be back in a few hours to check up on you and see that you get a lunch break."

Honest. He would have had to say something like that. "Take your time," she gulped. "I have plenty to do and I'll be fine."

He walked out with a quick nod but his words had made Merri nervous. She had to lie to him, to everyone, if she wanted to keep her freedom and her hard-won reality.

Two

There was a lot more to the unusual assistant than her outward appearance. Ty felt it in his gut. As he drove his Jeep down the block toward his attorney's office, he went over what was bothering him about Merri.

It had seemed miraculous that he'd come back from New Orleans, discouraged at not being able to locate a new assistant, only to find that his attorney, Frank, had hired one right out of the blue.

And what an assistant this one was. All the other women—and it had always been women—who'd accepted the position had been stunning beauties with little knowledge of charitable organizations.

He'd wondered about that each time. In the first place, why would any single woman want to relocate to tiny out-of-the-way Stanville, Texas, and dedicate her life to helping a children's charity? It hadn't made any sense, even though he'd always hoped they would stay.

But this woman was…different from the others. Merri was businesslike and professional-looking, with her black pantsuit and sensible, low-heeled pumps. And she seemed genuinely interested in living in this two-bit town.

Stanville was his home. He loved it here and was truly grateful that he could leave the big cities behind, except for short visits, and come back to settle in the one place that had always felt welcoming. Ty had enough money to live wherever he wanted. And he wanted to be here.

But he still couldn't get his head around why a nice young woman would want to bury herself here.

His thoughts went back to his new assistant. Her skin was fair and creamy, and she looked like she should be a natural blonde. But instead of highlighting whatever she had been born with, the hair that she'd pulled up in a tiny bun on the top of her head was dull and the color of an unattractive wood table. Brown. Just brown.

He'd never met any woman that seemed so unconcerned with her appearance. She didn't wear any makeup or jewelry, which shouldn't have seemed so out of place, but on her it did. She was tall and her body appeared to be as skinny as a toothpick. Though it was hard to really judge what her body looked like under the heavy suit jacket and pants.

It was her eyes that had most captured his attention. Hidden behind inch-thick, black-rimmed glasses, those deep-set windows to her soul were an incredible shade of green. They sparked as she controlled her displeasure with him and the unfamiliar surroundings, and sizzled when she studied him from under her ultra-thick lashes.

Emeralds. Yes, perhaps those eyes could be called the color of emeralds. Expensive and exclusive.

In total, there was something off about the picture Merri Davis presented to the world. He couldn't quite say what yet. But given enough time, he would figure it out.

Ty parked, went into the attorney's office and was ushered immediately into Frank's conference room. The new donor they were expecting was a rich farmer from the panhandle and hadn't arrived at the office just yet. But Frank was waiting for Ty, sitting at the far end of a conference table that was big enough to seat twenty.

Frank stood and shook his hand. "Sorry about your great-aunt Lucille Steele, Ty. But she was rather advanced in age, wasn't she?"

Ty nodded and took a seat. "Yeah. And she died peacefully in her sleep. We should all be so lucky to go that way.

"But I do wish I could've talked to her one last time," Ty continued. "I had an interesting experience with a gypsy while I was there and I would've loved to ask Lucille what she knew of her. Now I guess I'll never know."

"Interesting? You want to talk about it?" Frank sat down in his chair again and leaned back.

"Not much to say. She was a strange old lady who

gave my cousin a book and gave me a mirror…then she just disappeared. I don't know her reasons, but it feels wrong."

"You want me to have a private investigator do a little digging? Maybe try to find her?"

"I guess so. I can give you the very few things I know about her later. But it really doesn't seem terribly urgent now that I'm home. At the moment, I want to talk about the new assistant for fund-raising you hired while I was gone."

"Merri? I think she's the answer to all your problems. We were really lucky to get her."

"That's just it, Frank. How *did* we get her? I hadn't been able to get so much as a nibble on anyone who was qualified and would also be willing to relocate this far out in the sticks. I was about to give up."

Frank smiled. "Between us, we have now come up with five different women to take that job. And none of the first four worked out due to circumstances beyond our control. I was talking to…"

"Just a minute. It sounds like you might know why the other assistants quit. Do you?"

"I have a good idea," Frank admitted. "In a couple of the cases I managed to conduct cursory exit interviews and checked with outside sources."

He studied Ty for a minute, then continued. "It seems that most, if not all, those women had marriage and not employment in mind when they agreed to take the job."

"Marriage?" It suddenly hit him what Frank must mean. "You mean to me?"

"Well, your picture has been in several of the state-wide Texas magazines as an eligible bachelor. Think about it. You're filthy rich. Single. Good-looking…in a rough-and-tumble sort of way. Why wouldn't a woman want to take her best shot at that?"

It took Ty a minute to get enough of his powers of speech back to make it clear why not. "I never gave any of those women…or anyone else for that matter, the impression that I was looking for a wife. I'm not."

He fought to bring his voice under his command. "I have no intention of getting married. Not now. Not ever."

Frank raised his eyebrows. "Never? That sounds like a broken heart talking. You want to tell me the story?"

"No." It had been ten years since he'd given a single thought to his old college flame, Diane, and to what a fiasco becoming engaged to her had been. And he didn't want to think about it now, either.

Instead he shifted the conversation back to the original question he'd had when he walked in the door. "I want you to explain why and how we found Merri Davis…and I want you to assure me that she won't be like all the others. I want to know absolutely that she intends to stay in Stanville and doesn't have designs on me."

"I think you can tell by looking at her that she isn't like all the others," Frank said with a smile. "She's refined and all business. You would do well to take some lessons from her in how to behave around donors. I believe she's got the sophistication and the congeniality you lack. Try to absorb some of it, will you?"

Yeah, maybe. But there was still something about her that didn't sit right….

"Anyway," Frank continued, "I had been telling my old friend Jason Taylor—you remember the Taylor family from here? He's been my best friend since grade school, even though he's a hotshot attorney out in L.A. now."

"Yes, I know of him. His mother and Jewel were best friends when they were girls. But what does he have to do with…?"

"Jason and I still talk a couple times a month. I've been keeping him up on local goings-on. Over the last year or so, I've told him of our utter frustration at not being able to hire a responsible…and qualified…person for the fund-raising position.

"Then a few days ago, Jason called and said he had the perfect applicant for the job and she would be willing to start immediately. I waited until she actually arrived and settled in before I called you about her."

"Yes, yes. I don't mind that you hired her without consulting me first. That she's right for the job and is prepared to stick with it is all I care about." Ty shifted and rested one of his booted feet against the other knee. "So tell me her background."

"Jason told me he's known her family since he moved to L.A. They must've been neighbors or something. He says he's known Merri since she was a kid, and that she is a very serious and sober young woman who has experience with fund-raising. She took nonprofit management courses in college and has decided she wants to have a career in development. Her main ambition is to help those less fortunate."

"Does she come from money?" Ty knew the suit and the shoes she wore looked expensive, but she still seemed so wrong in those clothes that he'd imagined she must've bought them at a consignment shop.

"I don't think so. I believe Jason would've mentioned it. What he did say was that she didn't *care* about the money. All she needed for a salary was enough to get by—which, as you are well aware, is not all that much in Stanville."

Ty nodded in agreement. "Right. So again, I have to ask, why would a single young woman be willing to give up her friends and her family in order to come to a backwater town with almost no social life to speak of?"

"Who knows?" Frank shrugged and grinned. "I got the impression that she didn't have much of a social life back in L.A. Maybe our friendly town will be all the high life she needs or wants."

Ty didn't think so, but finding out her true motivation was fast becoming a challenge. It was what made him push her and test her this morning, he knew. But he tried not to think of his own true motivations.

The woman simply fascinated him, and he refused to consider how dangerous that might really be.

"I always liked your great-aunt Lucille," Jewel told Ty as she wiped down her kitchen counters. "Ever since she gave you the money to go to college and then to buy your first piece of property, I thought she was special, even though she wasn't blood kin to me. I'm sorry she's gone. So, her funeral was well attended?"

Ty opened Jewel's refrigerator door and stood absently inspecting the contents the same way he had ever since he'd been a five-year-old kid. "The funeral was huge. I never realized my father's side of the family had so many relatives. I guess I'm just used to you being the only one on my mother's side."

He bent to check the bottom shelves. "It seems that Lucille had some strange friends. I ran into a weird gypsy who gave me what she said was a magic mirror."

"What? Was it a joke?" Jewel walked over, reached around him and pulled out the milk carton. "Is this what you're looking for?"

Beaming, he took the carton from her and popped it open. "I'm not sure about the joke. I thought so at first. I mean, the mirror looks like an antique, but it has my name engraved in the gold leaf. And the actual mirror is nothing but plain glass. Frank's checking it out for…"

"Hold it, mister," Jewel interrupted as she kicked the refrigerator door closed and handed him a glass. "You can drink straight out of the carton at your own house when I'm not around…if you must. But I taught you better manners than that."

Ty grimaced and poured the milk into the glass. "You sound like Frank. He says I need polish. Hell, I've got more money than ninety-five percent of the world, why do I need polish, too?" He tried to hold back a grin as his aunt scowled. "Besides, there's nothing fit to eat or drink at my ranch."

"And whose fault is that? You're an adult. Go to the grocery store." Jewel went to the teakettle on the stove and poured herself a cup.

Man, he really loved Jewel. It would never occur to her to suggest that either one of them hire servants to do the work—no matter how much money he had in the bank.

Ty ignored her remark, just like he ignored having to shop for food. He'd been too busy to do anything lately, what with trying to get the Nuevo Dias Children's Home and the Lost Children Foundation off the ground and also overseeing his oil and real estate businesses.

And then that last-minute trip to Lucille's funeral had really thrown him for a loop. He hated to think what might actually be growing in his refrigerator.

"I met Merri Davis this morning," he said with an effort to change the subject. "She's hard at work in the Foundation office as we speak."

"What did you think of her?" Jewel asked. "I thought she was just adorable."

"Adorable?" With that severe bun, those thick glasses and sensible shoes? All he'd seen was a practical and shy woman whose ugly thick glasses had been hiding sexy green eyes. But he had enough sense to keep his mouth shut.

Jewel clucked her tongue at him anyway. "Merri Davis may not be a raving beauty, but she has other charms that make her very special. I swear, Tyson, you only seem to take notice of people's outward appearance. Just like that horrible Diane person you were engaged to in college. I would've thought that experience had taught you a lesson."

She shook her head. "You are not really that shallow. No one I love can be that superficial."

He groaned and swiped his mouth with the back of his hand—which earned him another cluck from his aunt's tongue, along with a paper towel.

"I thought you were happy when I asked Diane to

marry me in college," he said without challenging Jewel's shallow remark. God. He hadn't thought about that terrible lying witch, Diane, in years. And now he'd been faced with the disastrous memories twice in one day.

"No, I was glad *for you* when you seemed to be so happy for once." Jewel walked over and put her hand on his arm. "I know the pain of losing your parents is always there, right behind that wicked smile of yours. I see it, son. Even if you won't admit it."

Now she was about to hit on something he absolutely refused to dwell on. "I don't know what you're talking about. Mom and Dad's accident was a long time ago. There's no pain left after twenty-five years. You did a good job of raising me. I'm a happy man."

"All right. We won't talk about it if you don't want to." She released his arm and sighed. "I do want you to find someone to love, though. But I didn't believe that Diane was the one to make you really happy. And it turned out I was right. She was all frosting and no cake."

Ty pitched the towel in the trash and set the glass down so he could wrap his arms around Jewel. "From now on, you tell me what you think, okay? I trust your judgment." And he would've given just about anything not to have had his heart ripped out by Diane. "But I don't imagine I'll be finding love with anyone but you. I frankly just don't have the time. I hardly have enough time to eat."

Jewel turned in his arms. "Is that a hint? Are you hungry?"

He kissed her on the top of the head and released her. "Naw. I need to get back to the Foundation office. I promised I'd go back to check on Merri's work and make sure she took a lunch break. I'm a little late."

"Lunch? Tyson Adams Steele, it's nearly two o'clock. You are not allowed to starve my new renter. Not when she's paid me two months in advance."

He chuckled at the stern look on his aunt's face. "And that's another thing. I thought we decided you wouldn't rent out that old cottage I gave you until I had a chance to make sure it was habitable."

"That's your opinion, Tyson. I think it's fine. The few things left to do can be done when you have the time. And there really wasn't anywhere else for Merri to live in town. You know the nearest apartment complex is miles away in Edinburg."

Jewel pointed to a kitchen chair. "Now sit a minute. I'll make a few sandwiches and put some potato salad in containers. You take them back to the office so both you and Merri can have a decent break."

She opened the refrigerator door. "You can nag at me about the cottage while I'm working if you must. But I'll warn you that I won't be too remorseful. I've told you I can hire someone to finish the restoration if you're too busy.

"Merri needed a place to live and I needed to make some rent money to pay for the new appliances," Jewel continued. "And on top of that, she's a lovely person with terrific manners. You would do well to listen to Frank and take some pointers."

* * *

Merri licked the flap on the last envelope and pressed it down to seal. She sat back in Ty's chair and inspected her work.

Not bad, if she did say so herself.

All the training on writing thank-you notes that her mother's housekeeper had given her when she was a child had finally come to good use. At the time, her mother had complained it was useless information for a Davis-Ross to have and berated both Merri and the housekeeper. *Their kind* simply did not need to dirty their hands with such mundane occupations.

Even for the meager few semesters Merri had spent in college, her mother had insisted that she live in a penthouse apartment near campus and not dirty her hands in a dorm with other students. Of course, Mother claimed it had to be that way for safety. Threats of kidnaping were always a worry.

So Merri had allowed the bodyguards to follow her to classes. But she'd tried hard…and failed…to avoid having a full staff of house servants there. In the end, she felt so distant from the rest of the university kids that it was too much and she'd quit college altogether.

During her modeling career, on the other hand, she'd been determined to have a regular life. But with all the paparazzi hounding her every move, it had been impossible. She'd finally understood that the only way to escape from all the trappings of wealth was to become someone else.

Merri was having to find out about a lot of mundane occupations for the first time now. She was living on her own in a wonderful cottage and actually working at a real job. Thrilled at every newly mastered daily task, she cursed her "kind" every time some simple chore turned into a challenge.

Slipping off the ugly, squat heels, Merri curled her legs up under her body. Ty's huge desk chair was much more comfortable than that old computer chair where she would do most of her work. She sighed and thought about buying a new seat cushion for herself...and a hot plate to boil water for tea in the office.

It looked like maybe she was going to get the hang of this new life after all.

The door opened, startling her. She blinked at the interruption, then quickly straightened up when she realized it was Ty coming back, carrying a huge paper sack.

"Good afternoon, Merri. How'd your day go?"

"Uh, just fine, sir." She used her toes to feel around, trying to find her shoes so she could stand and move out of his chair. But she'd apparently kicked the darn things way under his desk.

He scowled down at her and set the sack on his desk. "None of that 'sir' stuff. It's Ty, remember? Come give me a hand with this food."

"Food?"

"Lunch. Jewel sent it over with instructions that both you and I take a proper break and eat every bite."

Darn those shoes. "That was very nice of your aunt. But I'm really not hungry. I don't usually eat lunch." When she'd been at the top of her game in the modeling biz, she'd rarely allowed herself to eat anything at all. Old habits didn't just disappear with a new life.

"Maybe you should start. You look as if a strong

breeze could knock you right over. It's fine to have beautiful eyes and all, but you need good food and exercise to stay healthy."

She stopped fidgeting and forgot about her shoes. "You think I have beautiful eyes?"

She'd worked hard to find a way to play down all her features. But she had chosen not to change her eye color with contacts so as not to irritate her eyes. They had a tendency toward allergies.

These damn thick glasses should be doing the disguise trick. "You can't."

"I can't?" He laughed and put a hand on his hip. "No one has ever told you before that you have pretty eyes? You must have lived a very secluded life…or else all the men around you must've been blind."

Shut up! The man was one gorgeous hunk when he smiled. She resisted the urge to rip off the glasses and bat her eyelashes at him.

It suddenly hit her that she wasn't the only one to think of flirting. Tyson Steele was coming on to her—in his own backward way.

But he couldn't. That was the very thing she'd been trying to avoid. On top of the fact that he was her boss, he was also one of the filthy rich and appeared periodically in regional magazine spreads. If even a hint of her presence in this town got out, or if she was photographed and it leaked to the national press, her wonderful new life here would be finished.

No. That he was interested in her was flattering. And she was most definitely interested in him. But she simply could not allow herself to get that close.

She gave up and ducked under his desk to find the damn shoes.

"What's going on down there?"

"Nothing. I was just…" She captured her shoes and twisted around to back out of the desk's cubbyhole. But instead of being able to escape with a little grace, she found herself face-to-face with her new boss.

"Oh…" Merri gulped and tried a weak smile, but he was so close that she could barely breathe. "My shoes. I was trying to find my shoes."

"You lost your shoes under my desk? Do you always disrobe when you work?" He reached up and absently pushed a stray piece of hair back behind her ear. Then pulled his hand back as if he'd been burned. "Uh…"

Ohmigod. His touch had sent shivers down her back, but they were forced to compete with the sweat that was beginning to pool at the base of her spine.

This was not working at all the way she'd hoped. "Excuse me. But will you let me out, please?"

"Sorry. Sure." He stood and held out a hand to help her up. "Your clothes got kind of dusty down there. I guess the clean-up crew hasn't mopped under that desk for a while. I suppose I should reprimand them."

She stretched her legs and brushed at her jacket. "It's my own fault for taking off my shoes. And I'll speak to the crew, you needn't worry about it. My duties will include being office manager since there is no one else." Bending to slip on her shoes, she felt his hand brush against the back of her leg.

The shock of him touching her again caused her to stand up without giving a thought to how close behind her he must be. She heard a crack as the top of her head connected with the bottom of his chin, and the blow knocked them both off balance.

He wrapped his arms around her shoulders and twisted his body so he went down with her on top. Luckily his backside landed right in his own chair. Unluckily, she was sprawled out on his lap.

"Uff. Sorry," she said with a gasp.

Not half as sorry as he was, Ty mused. "It's my own fault for trying to help. I just thought I'd give you a hand dusting off. As usual, no good deed goes unpunished."

She turned in his lap and made a face. "That's a terrible cliché, and not true at all. It was an accident."

Mercy. But he was being punished—every time she shifted against his groin. The non-sexy assistant had suddenly become a hot siren in his lap. And in a second, she was going to realize what it was doing to him.

Ty fitted his hands around her waist and lifted her to her feet in as smooth a move as he could manage. "Shoes all in place now?"

He waited to let go until he was sure she was steady. Then he backed off as fast as possible. He might need a little training in manners, but he certainly knew better than to be accused of sexual harassment.

"Um. Everything's fine." She straightened her jacket.

But it was too late for him. He'd already felt the truth of what lay underneath that drab black business suit.

She was thin all right. Thin and curvy. Rounded bottom and tiny waist. It made him wonder about the rest.

Ty had a feeling that from now on his attention was going to be focused exactly where she apparently didn't want it. He'd wondered all along what she would look like in something besides those heavy clothes.

It was no longer an idle thought. Now he would make it his mission to keep her around long enough to find out.

Three

Ty sat back and watched Merri pick at her potato salad. He didn't know whether she normally ate next to nothing or if she was still embarrassed over the fiasco with the shoes. He knew he might never get "over" it.

"Did you get a start on those thank-you letters?" he asked, trying to put the lap dance out of his head for the moment. Anything would be better than standing here with his tongue hanging out while he stared at those magical eyes.

"They're done." She pointed to a stack of envelopes all sealed and stamped and ready to post. "The copies are there in that folder, waiting for your approval before we put them in the mail. I signed the letters with the title of 'Assistant for Development,' if that's okay with you."

"You finished them all?" That was more work for one morning than any of the other assistants had managed in two weeks time. Dang. Sexy and competent, too. Whew!

He opened the manilla folder and flipped through the letters. "Very nice. You said something about each person's individual gift. The letters aren't all the same."

"Each of those people spent their own individual time and money to help your children. The least we can do is send them a unique thank-you."

She stood and soberly began to pick up the remnants of their lunch. "Actually, I was thinking that you should consider having a reception to honor all the donors. People like it when they're shown public appreciation."

"Good idea." *But couldn't you just smile once?* "This is the first year that we've had enough response to our fund-raising efforts to warrant spending money on appreciation."

Merri gave him one quick shake of her head. "Wrong way around. You have to spend money to make money."

"Well, I know that's true in business, but I didn't believe..."

The outside office door opened and the flash of sunlight signaled that someone was on the way in. Ty quit speaking and stood to greet whomever it was.

Jewel walked across the threshold with her usual jaunty stride. A young fifty-five, and slim and petite, this afternoon she'd changed into a knit turquoise dress with a print blouse and scarf. He supposed it wasn't at all fashionable, but to him she always looked beautiful.

She was the mother of his heart, and had been since his own mother had left him in her care for one last time those many years ago. Jewel was a classic—and at the moment she appeared to be annoyed.

"Jewel," he said as he went to her side to kiss her cheek. "I didn't know you planned to visit the office. You haven't come all the way down here for your food containers? I told you I'd…"

Jewel narrowed her eyes and gave his chest a weak nudge. "Don't be silly. I don't care about those…" She moved to the desk and picked up a half-eaten ham sandwich. "Someone didn't finish their lunch."

Turning to Merri, Jewel's whole face softened. "Weren't you hungry? Or would you care for something else?"

Ty was amazed to see Merri's face soften, too. He was beginning to believe the woman didn't know how to let go and really smile. Hmm. Maybe it was just him that couldn't make her give up a smile.

"Oh, no, Mrs. Adams. The sandwich and salad were wonderful. I wasn't very hungry, that's all."

"You probably waited too late to eat. That's my nephew's fault." Jewel turned back to Ty. "I won't have this, Tyson. You will see to it that Merri eats at regular hours. She's too thin as it is."

He turned to Merri, rolled his eyes and grinned as if to say, "See? Someone else agrees with me."

"If you don't care about your containers, why have you come in to town, Jewel?" He thought he would change the subject and give Merri a break from his aunt's scrutiny, knowing how uncomfortable that position could be.

"I'm attending a garden club meeting this evening, but we've had to call an emergency board meeting first."

"An emergency…at your garden club?" Merri asked.

Ty chuckled. "That club does a lot more than just work on gardens. They're the backbone of this community. Without the money they've raised for local charities, we wouldn't have been able to take care of the Nuevo Dias Children's Home for all those years before the Foundation got off the ground."

"That's the problem," Jewel began, in explanation to Merri's surprised look. "We usually have two big fund-raisers during the year. One in early February, that we call our Spring In the Air drive, and the other in early October that's our Fall Spectacular.

"The fall fund-raiser is the easiest," she continued. "We always have a bazaar then, including a festival with children's rides. People are thinking about Christmas presents by that time, and we make things to sell all year long. We've done that fund-raiser so many times that everyone knows their jobs by now."

She'd gotten Merri's full attention. Talking about fund-raising was a lot safer than talking about her model thin figure—or having Tyson Steele roll his eyes at her.

Jewel took a breath and turned back to Ty. "It's the spring drive that gives us fits every year. We've tried different things to raise money. Some have worked better than others. Last year's pancake breakfast and plant sale, for instance, was a disaster when it rained."

"I tried to warn you," Ty said with a frown. He turned

back to Merri and winked. "That wasn't my favorite idea."

"Well, I wonder if…" Merri began.

"We were going to have a casino night this year," Jewel interrupted. "But the one woman who knew how to pull it off has gone to Dallas in a family emergency. Her daughter is seven months pregnant and the doctor confined her to bed for the duration. The mother went to care for her two grandchildren while the daughter rests.

"Which leaves the garden club in a mess," Jewel ended with a scowl.

Jewel looked so frustrated that Merri opened her mouth without thinking. "Have you tried a mother-daughter luncheon and modeling show in the past?" What was the matter with her? That was the last thing she should've suggested. She simply had to learn to keep her mouth shut.

Shaking her head, Jewel looked thoughtful. "No… We didn't have anyone that would know how to run such a thing."

"Well…" Merri never should've mentioned modeling.

"We can organize a luncheon. That's not a problem," Jewel said, studying her. "Merri, have you ever put this kind of thing together? Or have you perhaps attended one of those modeling luncheons while your were living in L.A.? I understand they're quite popular in big cities."

"Did you?" Ty cocked his head and asked Merri.

"Well, yes, but…" She hesitated, not wishing to lie to them. But not wanting to step into something she'd been trying to avoid, either.

Unfortunately, she waited too long to finish. Just like she hadn't waited long enough before suggesting it.

Ty jumped in. "Great. Merri has so far proven to me that she's a fantastic administrator, Jewel. She seems to be a 'take the bull by the horns' kind of person. I'm sure she can whip this whole modeling deal into shape in time to save the fund-raiser."

At his words of praise, Merri could feel the sting of embarrassment riding up her neck. "Thanks. But I…"

"If you're worried about your job here, don't," Ty broke in. "You can spend mornings in the Foundation office while you learn the ropes. And your afternoons can be spent working on the luncheon. That way, you'll get to meet and work with a bunch of the women volunteers, who are also some of our biggest contributors."

"It's not that," Merri hedged, hoping she would think of something else—fast. "I don't know enough people in the town to choose models."

Ty casually shrugged a shoulder. "I understand you probably don't know the first thing about modeling. But if you've been to a few of these shows, I'm sure you can take care of the behind-the-scenes stuff. I saw a show in a movie once. Someone had to get stores to donate the clothes and then coordinate the outfits with the words and the music. I'm positive you could do that.

"And Jewel and her friends can help you locate the women with daughters to be the models," he said with a grin.

Merri bit down on her tongue to keep the smart remarks to herself. She'd wanted people to think she was capable, hadn't she?

So maybe she'd done her job a little too well.

"I suppose I could help," she mumbled at last. She knew every last detail about how to pull off a show. It was how to keep her ego out of the way and stay in the background that was really bothering her.

That and how to maintain a professional distance from the dangerous man that she suddenly wanted more than anything to impress.

Merri carried her teacup into her tiny new living room. Setting it down on the antique side table she'd found yesterday in that cute Main Street shop, she relaxed back into the floral print overstuffed chair and sighed with pleasure.

Her mother would be mortified if she ever caught her doing such things—having such things in her home. Hmm. Perhaps "mortified" was the wrong word to use about a woman who only cared about superficial things. Mother was not one to be humiliated by anything. No indeed.

Arlene Davis-Ross looked more like Merri's sister than her mother. Though she had good genes and took care of herself, her big secret was that she'd also had more plastic surgery than any human being should be allowed. And it was highly unlikely that Arlene would even notice what Merri was doing if she was standing right in her living room.

Merri didn't seem to matter one way or the other in either of her parents' lives as long as she kept up their idea of appearances. But she'd always hungered for a life that mattered to someone.

There had been a time, many years ago, when Merri

had wished for a mother who would care. She'd seen other girls at boarding school whose mothers were like that. They sent birthday cards and rushed to pick up their daughters from school on holiday breaks.

Merri's mother always seemed to be irritated when her daughter arrived at one of the family homes for school vacations and someone had to be found to look after her. Eventually, Merri gave up her empty dreams of a family who cared. That was when she'd set out to find reality. She knew it had to be out there somewhere.

Maybe it was right here in Stanville, Texas. She had finally found a spot where the flashbulbs didn't explode in her face at every turn. More, it was a place where people found satisfaction in having a simple cup of tea and in helping others who were less fortunate than themselves.

She'd come up with this desperate plan to both get away from the ravages of the paparazzi and to step into life in a very real way. Leaving modeling was no hardship. She'd hated the life they'd expected her to maintain. And leaving the lifestyle of her parents had been a longtime dream.

This opportunity that her lawyer had uncovered, the chance to do something for the Lost Children Foundation, was going to be her break from that former vapid existence. It was her opportunity to do something real…be someone…with real thoughts and feelings.

This evening she'd met with Jewel's garden club and agreed to help them give their modeling show and luncheon. Fortunately, Tally Washburn was more than willing to oversee the luncheon details. Now *there* was a real administrator—or maybe a commandant would be a better description.

And Ty's aunt Jewel had browbeaten a couple of the women into rounding up suspects for the mother-daughter modeling positions. This whole fashion show idea was going to work out all right. They had six weeks to pull it off.

It was just her relationship to Ty that Merri was having trouble dealing with. When she'd first come to this town and rented the cottage, the only thing she'd wanted was to be alone.

Well, to do her job the best she could, and to be alone. Far away from the runways, nightspots and microphones. Far away from the phonies of the world.

So…as much as Merri hated lying to Ty and having to hide out, she was willing to do anything for her one chance at a new life. And that included ignoring the sensual sensations she'd felt whenever he looked in her direction.

Okay. Maybe she could do that. But how on earth was she going to teach him to become less brash and uncivilized as his attorney had suggested? That was one job that might be a lot tougher than even she could handle.

Relationships, any kind of real relationships, were out of her experience. But *phony* ones—now there was a place where she excelled.

She smiled to herself when she thought of her recently broken *engagement*. Poor Brad. The tabloids were no doubt having a field day at his expense…and hers.

At first, she'd been more than willing to let herself

become his tabloid girlfriend in order to throw the paparazzi off the trail of his real relationship. Brad was a good guy and she'd never minded lying to reporters—until the paparazzi caught him with his boyfriend.

But lying was exactly her problem. Eventually, her whole life had become one big, pixiedust-filled lie. Nothing but fluff. When another model she'd thought of as a friend taunted that she wouldn't recognize real human beings if she fell over them, Merri decided that it was time to get out of her old life and find a new one.

The phone rang and broke the silence that she'd been enjoying. She blinked and wondered if it was one of the women volunteers she'd met earlier. She'd deliberately left her cell phone behind in L.A. It was too easy to trace.

Maybe tomorrow she would go to the discount store and buy an answering machine so she could monitor her calls. Heaven forbid if a reporter found her phone number and dialed her up to check.

When she did answer, a familiar voice was on the other end. "Did you manage to eat dinner, or did the garden club keep you tied up all night?"

Tyson Steele. That low, masculine voice was impossible to forget. It ran shivers over her skin and set fire to a tiny bubble of warmth low in her groin that threatened to explode at any moment. But she hadn't expected him to call.

"Don't you say hello before you begin your conversations? You're not my mother, just my boss."

Oops, that sounded a little too smart-mouthed for something that Merri Davis would say. He *was* her boss and she needed to try to remember it. Maybe the low, sensual sound of his voice had pulled a plug in her mind and her brain had drained.

"I'm sorry," she apologized, before he could say another word. "But you took me by surprise. I wasn't expecting you to call after working hours."

After a moment of silence, Ty cleared his throat and began again. "Hello, Miss Davis. Good evening. I understand from my aunt that you were late coming home from the garden club meeting. I was concerned that you might've had to miss your dinner."

"No, Mr. Steele, I did not miss dinner. I fixed myself something when I got home."

Another moment's silence dragged along on the other end of the line. "Could we go back to Ty and Merri?" he finally asked. "I didn't mean to sound so brusque, but my aunt was worried."

"Your aunt?"

"All right. *I* was worried, too. I promised Jewel I'd see to your welfare, and I intend to keep that promise."

She smiled, charmed by his concern, but glad he couldn't see her to know it. "Don't think you need to take me on as some kind of mission. I'm an adult."

This time the quiet went on so long Merri was worried that the connection had been lost. "Did you have something else on your mind?"

"Uh. Yes. Tomorrow morning I have to be at a meeting concerning my oil businesses in Corpus Christi. I know you can handle the office without me, but I just figured I'd better tell you I won't be in."

"No problem. I thought I might work on the donor reception idea tomorrow, if that's all right with you."

"Good idea. But won't that be too much for you to

take on, since you've agreed to help the garden club with their fund-raiser?"

"Not at all. If there's one thing I know how to do, it's how to hold a party."

"Really? Why's that?"

Hell, she'd said too much again. "My…uh…family was in the hospitality business." Well, that was a version of the truth, if not all of it. Her father's family did own chains of hotels and restaurants. But the party-giving was something she'd picked up from her mother—without ever being taught.

"Okay. Why don't you consider scheduling the reception for early April?" he proposed. "We could hold it on my ranch. The weather should be nice enough then to set it up outside under the trees."

"That would be lovely. I'll begin working on it right away." She hesitated and wondered what else was left to be said.

Finally, Ty cleared his throat and told her what was on his mind. "I plan to be back in town by midafternoon tomorrow. I thought, if you weren't scheduled for a meeting at the garden club, that you might like to go out to the original Nuevo Dias Children's Ranch and see what kind of things our foundation supports."

"Nuevo Dias? The New Day. I'd like that, yes. Thank you."

"Good. And while you're in the mood for saying yes, I'll ask if you'll let me take you to dinner afterward. I have to keep my word to Aunt Jewel, you know."

She could hear the chuckle in his voice and tried to keep the smile out of hers. "That wouldn't be like a date, would it? Because I don't think it's a good idea for a boss and employee to date."

"No. It wouldn't be like a date." His laughter hummed over her skin and set her blood on fire. "It would be like a boss making sure his employee took care of herself."

Yeah, right. But she remembered her promise to his attorney. Maybe outside of business hours were the best times to find a way to mention his appearance and manners.

On top of that, there was something terribly compelling about Tyson Steele. She decided to put her terrific opportunity for a new life in jeopardy in order to spend more time with him.

"I think you might be telling just a tiny fib with that one," she said with a sigh. "But…"

"I never lie," he interjected in a sober tone.

"Okay, then." She took a deep breath. "I'll go to dinner with you tomorrow night after we visit the children's home. But don't think that means I'm giving you permission to watch over me. I can take care of myself."

"Yes, ma'am," he said in his deep, sexy voice. "Good night, Merri. I'll look forward to seeing you tomorrow."

After he'd hung up the phone, she sat for a long time, still holding the receiver in her hand. What had she done?

She really couldn't let Tyson Steele get that close. They shouldn't be seen out together.

But, well…he was just so tempting. And he'd actually flirted with her, even though she hadn't worn her usual tons of makeup and fancy clothes. Ty seemed to like the plain Merri Davis just fine.

All she could do now was pray that her wonderful new life would not be ruined by getting too close to someone who was so earthy…and so very real.

Ty's gaze moved past the giggling little girls in the lounge and landed on the fascinating woman who sat cross-legged on the floor amongst them. The whole time he'd been outside, playing ball with the older boys of Nuevo Dias Ranch, he hadn't been able to think of anything else but the green of her eyes behind those glasses. And the tiny beauty mark at the side of her mouth that he'd spotted while in the car on the way out here.

He leaned back against the doorjamb and folded his arms to watch her interact with the children. She had her back to him, but he had a clear view of what she was doing.

She'd removed the restrictive navy jacket that was part of the dress suit she'd worn today so she could play with the girls. The crisp white shirt she'd had on under it shouldn't have looked sexy at all.

But it did.

Letting his eyes wander where they would, he started his perusal at the back of her long slim neck above the shirt's collar. A few soft tendrils of hair had escaped the bun and they trickled across her flesh at the hairline. He wondered how she would react if he replaced those strands of hair with his lips and kissed the tender skin there.

Would she yelp and reprimand him? Or would she giggle and go all soft and warm? It was another sensual image of hearing her moan with pleasure that drove him, at last, to move his gaze past her collar and on down her back.

The new view wasn't a whole lot better for his libido. As she reached out to brush a little girl's hair, the white shirt stretched across her back and he got a good look at the outline of the underwear she had on beneath it.

And underwear was the best word he could come up with. She wasn't wearing a bra, that much he could easily see. There was no obvious horizontal strap line like a bra.

This gizmo had shoulder straps, but it didn't have a back strap. Instead, the flimsy material captured his attention and drove his gaze lower as it went down her back and disappeared under her waistband.

Mercy.

Ty straightened up and shook his head to clear it. This would never do. He needed to get her alone so they could *talk*—get to know each other better. There was something she was hiding and he just couldn't get a handle on what it might be. He shouldn't be having these thoughts about what was hiding under her blouse.

He walked closer to the group on the floor and was amazed to see Merri helping a couple of twelve-year-olds as they applied a light shade of lipstick to their pouty young lips. What the heck would she know about putting on makeup? She didn't wear a drop of it herself.

"It's best if you can use a lip liner first," she told one cute little girl with long blond braids. "Maybe I'll bring a few out the next time I come."

"Are you coming back?" the blonde asked.

"Sure." Merri's eyes softened and she gently cupped the girl's cheek. "I live in this town now. I'll come out as often as I can. I promise."

He cleared his throat to announce his presence. Six sets of various shades of brown and blue eyes turned to stare up at him. But it was the emerald green eyes, swimming in tears behind thick glasses, that made his knees go weak.

"I've been told to announce that dinner is ready," he managed with a rasp. "Everyone should go wash up now."

"So soon?" a brown-eyed girl complained with a whine.

Merri sniffed once and laughed, throwing her arm over the girl's shoulder. "You need to eat so you can grow straight and tall." She looked up at Ty and continued with a grin. "We all need to eat to keep up our strength."

He reached out his hand to help her up. "You look beautiful when you laugh that way, Merri," he said as she stood up beside him. "You should do it more often."

"I do laugh," she told him with a frown.

Rolling his eyes with exasperation, Ty shook his head. "But not around me. Is that right?"

She chuckled, and the sound wound around his nerves and settled deep in the pit of his gut. The sweat broke out on his forehead.

"Do you want to wash up before you eat?" he gulped.

"Where are we having dinner?"

"I know of a wonderful place. They serve lots of vegetables and salads. You'll probably love it."

"I haven't heard of a place like that around town. Where would that be?"

"Here. In the main dining room."

Her eyes lit up like he'd just given her a present. "Can we stay? Really?"

Oh, God. She was adorable. Aunt Jewel had been right in her original assessment.

Now he was noticing everything about her—and way too often. Dang it all.

Four

"**A**re you tired?" Ty asked as he turned out of the Nuevo Dias Ranch road and onto the main highway.

"A little," Merri replied with a sigh. "But it's a good tired."

Though it wasn't terribly late, the sky was black and the air smelled of rain. She leaned her head back against the passenger seat of his huge pickup truck and breathed in the scent of ozone mixed with mesquite.

"I'm glad you got a chance to see the ranch," Ty said without taking his eyes off the road. "The kids sure enjoyed your visit."

"I enjoyed meeting them, too. They're all so…" She hesitated over the words, remembering what one of the women in charge of the kids had told her about Ty.

"Uh…" she began again. "Can I ask you something?"

"Sure. Shoot."

"Someone told me that the reason you've taken on a charity for abused and abandoned children is that you were abandoned as a child. Is that true?"

He raked a hand through his dark chestnut hair, but didn't turn to look at her. "No. Not at all. Jewel was babysitting for me when my parents were killed in a car accident. She raised me. I was never abandoned."

The words made sense, but Merri noticed that his tone of voice seemed to suggest something else. It appeared to be a real sore spot for him. So she let him change the subject.

"Back before dinner, when you were playing with the girls on the lounge floor..." he began. "Were those tears in your eyes?"

Ah. He'd managed to hit on one of her own sore spots. Well, she would tell him the truth of this one. No sense lying about something that she considered to be nonsense.

"Yes. Silly, huh?" She fidgeted under her seat belt but kept her eyes trained out the windshield. "Those little girls were so sweet to me...so needy. They actually wanted me to stay with them."

She turned her head away from Ty in order to stare out of her side window and lowered her voice to a whisper. "No one's ever really wanted me that much before."

"No one?"

She shook her head, but didn't imagine that he would be able to see her in the darkness.

"*I* want you, Merri," he said in his own whispered voice.

Whipping her head around, she caught the hungry

look in his eyes before he turned to face front again. "Oh, sure you do," she said on a strangled gurgle. "You want me to do a good job of fund-raising."

"Yes. That too. But…"

She could hear the desire—slow, silky and sensuous in his voice. It threw her, set her soul aflame. In self-defense she slipped into her mother's spoiled-diva persona.

"Don't tell me we're going to have the talk about you taking me to bed? If that's the kind of wanting you mean, rein it back in, please. It can't happen."

Through the darkness of the truck cab she saw him set his jaw and narrow his eyes. "Not at all," he began in a low and dangerous tone she'd not heard from him before. "I know you've felt the electricity between us…just like I have. But I have no intention of jumping your bones. I may be an ogre to work with, but I don't force myself on employees—Miss Davis."

She was more flustered than she could ever remember being. Her stomach was doing little backflips. She could imagine the two of them together, taking pleasure in each other's bodies and finding that special high peak that had always eluded her in the past.

But the reality of the situation drove her mind back around to face the chilly night and the raindrops that had begun to fall on the windshield. She thought about running away from her feelings—and from him.

However, this place had been her last resort. She'd already run away once—from the press and her old life. This time she had to stay and fight for what she wanted. Even if it meant fighting her own desires.

Ty didn't wait for her to deny or agree with his statement. "What I meant by needing you was...I need a friend," he said in a quieter tone. "I've told you before that helping the kids means everything to me. It's the one thing I can really do to give back.

"I have—had—a great-aunt who just passed away," he continued sadly. "Lucille gave me a hand up when I was down on my luck. She paid for my college and gave me the money to buy my first fixer-upper properties...because she believed in me. But there was never anything I could give her—or any way to adequately thank her. And now there never will be."

Merri could hear his voice crack under the strain of grief. Damn, but this guy could get under her skin—in so many different ways. She'd never met anyone like him.

Embarrassed at her own stupidity, Merri squirmed in her seat and bit her tongue. What an idiot she was.

He took a deep breath. "I thought raising money for a charity would be easy. But it isn't. At least, not for me. And my foundation can't do it all.

"Frank suggested to me that you might be willing..." he continued hesitantly. "Well, to give me a few pointers on how to do it better. Say the right things. Dress more like—I don't know—a banker maybe. Learn to ask for what I need...and not simply demand."

Her mouth opened before she thought it through—again. "Are we in need of one of those extreme make-over reality shows here?" she asked with a wry grin. But then in the glow of oncoming headlights she saw the smile fade from his lips. And she felt like kicking herself. Why couldn't she just keep quiet?

"Ty..." Merri began again as she gently touched his

arm. "You're a decent man, with all the right instincts. Believe me, there are tons of slick fund-raisers out there who couldn't care less about their charity or the suffering behind it. You do care, that's easy for anyone to tell.

"All you need is a little polish," she added. "I'm not sure I should be the one to help you...but..."

Before she realized his intention, he took one hand off the wheel and tenderly captured her hand within his own. "I can handle it if you can. I fully intend to keep my promise to Jewel about seeing to your welfare. You're in a new place with strangers around you. If you can stand me reminding you to take care of yourself, then I can take whatever stuff you've got to throw at me."

The heat from his touch was frying her brain. Merri was half afraid that she would *give* anything—*take* anything he ever wanted to dish out, if only he would touch her more often. But even wanting his touch so badly, there was nothing she wanted more than to be his friend, to listen to all his secrets and to share all of hers in return.

Unfortunately, *her* secrets had to remain buried. Ty had said, many times, that he didn't care for liars. And that's exactly what she was.

Merri sighed and gritted her teeth. She wanted her new life badly enough to keep on lying to him, too. And she intended to force these new erotic urges deep into her subconscious, to be forever buried there.

But... She also wanted very badly to find a way to help Ty, and befriend him. What a confusing predicament this was.

"I came here for a new start," she began as her brain raced for excuses and answers. "And I thought I needed to do that all by myself. But if you need a friend then I..."

"A new start?" he interrupted. "Is there someone you're running away from? A husband? Or a boy-friend?"

He'd just supplied her with a great excuse to keep them from being anything but friends. Maybe she could fudge a little on this one and not come out and really lie to him. It was just so important for her to find a way to keep the two of them at a proper distance. Before it was too late.

"I broke my engagement a few weeks ago," she told him. "I'm not terribly shook up over it, but I do need some time to heal." See? Not a lie. Not exactly the truth, either, but it was good enough.

"Hmm. You don't seem all that heartbroken to me."

"Enough that I don't want to get involved with any-one right now," she said with her fingers crossed at her side. "But I *do* think we can try being friends—try helping each other out. Maybe we should just leave our relationship at that for now."

"Merri, I told you that I don't take advantage of..."

Just then the heavens decided they had played around long enough. A bolt of lightning crashed across the night sky and, with a tremendous whoosh, huge raindrops obliterated everything in sight out of the windshield.

"Uh-oh," Ty said as he slowed the truck.

"What's wrong?"

"The heavy rain is not good news."

"Why? The roads won't flood, will they? And we're almost home anyway."

Ty turned off the highway and made a second turn down her street. "It's a good thing we're nearly to the cottage, all right. We're going to have a lot of work to do tonight."

"Why? Doing what?" She couldn't imagine what he was talking about. Once she was back in her cozy little cottage everything would be just fine.

Ty didn't bother to answer her. He roared down her street and literally slid his way down her gravel driveway.

"How many buckets do you own?" he yelled as he flipped open his seat belt and opened his door.

"Buckets? One, I guess. Why?"

"Out!" he hollered as he stepped outside into the drenching rain. "Find that bucket and meet me in the kitchen."

Merri gritted her teeth against the downpour and stepped out of the truck. She tried to find her footing on the sloshy grass. But finally she decided to pull off her shoes and make a run for it.

She unlocked her front door, dropped her shoes and purse just inside, and dashed toward the utility room. She was sure she'd seen a bucket in there.

Finally finding the bucket stashed behind some cleaning supplies in a cupboard, she turned and flipped on the kitchen light. The light blinked off and on a couple of times. But when at last it stayed on, it illuminated the full view of a soggy disaster.

Water dripped from the ceiling onto her brand-new kitchen floor. Lots of drips. From lots of places.

Ty ran into the kitchen. "Put the bucket under a drip."

"Which one?"

"Any of them," he said with a sharp rasp. "Then use pots and pans. Anything you have handy. I found a ladder out in the shed. I'm going up on the roof to see what I can do."

"Now? In the dark?"

He flashed her a quick grin. "Worried about me? Don't be. I'll be fine. I'm not sure I can help, but I've got to try." With that he dashed out the back door and into the blinding and blowing rain.

It took Merri a minute to decide where the bucket would be of most use. She put it down and then cursed herself for taking so much time. The water was already fully covering the kitchen floor. Another few minutes and it would be an inch deep.

She dragged out every pan and placed them under the worst of the drips. But it wasn't enough. Next she pulled out the big mixing bowls and tried them. Finally, in desperation, she sought out the two glass vases from the living room.

While fussing over the rearrangement of the bowls, she almost missed a loud crashing sound from outside. Ty?

Ohmigod. He must've fallen off the ladder.

Merri flew out the back door, dreading what she would find in her backyard. Barreling around the corner of the house, she slipped on the wet grass and went down. Face first in the muddy grass.

Strong hands grabbed her shoulders and pulled her up to her feet. "Are you okay? What did you think you were doing?" Ty roared through the noise of the rain.

She couldn't see a thing. Couldn't speak. Mud caked her glasses and she had enough grass in her mouth for a salad.

"I…" she sputtered and spit the grass out. "Thought you were hurt."

Ty dragged her up into his arms and headed for the cottage's back door. After he'd kicked open the door and set her on her feet inside, he tried to clean her up with his hands.

As he removed the glasses and picked tiny sticks and grass out of her hair, it was all he could do not to crack a smile at the picture she'd made as she went down. "Hold still. I'll get a paper towel."

He was back in an instant. Though he too was dripping wet, he tried dabbing at the caked mud on her face. She tipped her face up to his and let him dry her off.

It was a temptation, gently stroking her cheek and focusing on the full, thick lips so close to his own. A temptation he fought to set aside.

But he couldn't concentrate on his promises to just be her friend. Not now. All he could think of was how beautiful she looked without the glasses. And of how intense they would be together during long, slow kisses and hot, passion filled nights.

He'd said he wouldn't push…he needed Merri's friendship. But suddenly the fact that he hadn't so much as kissed a woman in over six months became a truth he just had to change. Instead of thinking it through, he leaned in and covered her mouth with his own.

She tasted not unpleasantly of wet grass, sort of earthy and much like the freedom to be found in childhood. But there was nothing at all about the kiss that seemed like his boyhood. The heat of her body next to his chest filled him with sizzling needs and growing sensual images. Her kiss was like no one else's in his memory.

Merri made a strangled noise deep in her throat and melted into his arms. When he nudged her lips, she opened up to take his tongue into her mouth. Their two tongues danced in perfect harmony. As if each one had always known the other.

They stood there, dripping wet, while the world around them disappeared. Her sweet taste and feminine warmth was wrapping them both in a blanket of heat and need.

Oh, my darlin' one, he thought dimly. I do want you. More than I want to admit. Maybe more than you'll ever know.

Instantly hard, for a second Ty thought about stripping them both and dragging her into the shower. Images came of slick, soapy bodies, sliding under the cascading water, learning each other's needs—giving pleasure—wringing every sensual sensation from desperate souls....

Whew, babe. The sensations and blinding images were all too strong, too fast. He'd promised her he wouldn't—

Lifting his head, Ty fought his body's demands and stepped back. "I...uh...have to go."

What was the matter with him? Go where? He was here to help her clean up the mess and make sure the roof had stopped leaking. But standing this close made it impossible for him to think. Impossible to concentrate.

Lord have mercy, but such things had never happened to him before. Never.

"I mean, I should go back out and make sure the tar paper I nailed on the roof is holding in the wind. Are you okay enough now to start mopping up right away?"

"Mopping?" She looked up at him with confusion in her eyes. He noticed her kiss-swollen lips and erotic flushed face and it made him want to reach for her all over again.

Instead he took another step toward the door. "Yeah, mopping. Like with the mop…on the floor."

"Oh," she said in a tiny voice. "I…guess."

She'd said the words as if she was cold…numbed by what had happened between them. But he wasn't so sure that was true. The kiss had been hot, but he'd felt her holding back. Not nearly as desperate for him as he'd been for her.

"Okay, then," he wheezed. "Good. You start cleaning up and I'll be back to help you in a few minutes."

He started out the door but caught himself midstride. He had to say something. Something about the kiss. But it was still a jumble in his head.

When he turned, thoughts racing to catch up, he saw her reach out to steady herself with the counter. "Merri?" He took a step back toward her again.

She raised her hand, palm out to stop him from coming any closer. "No, Ty." Closing her eyes, she took a deep breath and stared down at the wood plank floor. "I'm fine. But we can't ever do that again. I can't just kiss you and go on as if nothing happened. Not if I'm going to work for you…not if we're going to be friends."

He'd never had a woman tell him no before. It stunned him. Plastered his feet to the floor.

Before he could gather his thoughts enough to speak, Merri silently turned her back and walked out of the room. She hadn't stopped to look at him, hadn't even raised her chin.

But she'd seemed so soft and vulnerable, walking away with her shoulders slumped and her hair all wet and falling down around her shoulders. The last thing he'd seen as she disappeared through the doorway was the mousy brown nest tumbling out of its binds on the top of her head, and dripping cascading water rivulets down her back.

It took everything he had to finally move.

Driving a hand through his own dipping hair, Ty felt the pain of being alone worse than he had in years. He forced his feet to carry him back outside and onwards toward the ladder to the roof. But he barely noticed that the rains had already slowed.

He stood, with one foot on the bottom rung of the ladder and rain dripping down his neck, wondering if he'd just let the most important thing in his life slip through his fingers. But in his soul that idea felt ridiculous.

What did they really know about each other? One kiss and a strong sensation in the vicinity of his groin, did not make for a lasting relationship.

The last time he'd felt something similar was in college, and that woman had damned near stolen his integrity, along with his heart, with her lies and her cheating. He should've known better even then. Lies came too easily for some women.

But he truly didn't believe Merri had any reason to lie to him, she was just shy and a little introverted. That had to be why she didn't seem to mind coming to live in this backwater town and living alone without family.

He would definitely love to bring out the passion in her that he knew lay right below the shy surface. But Ty didn't need entanglements at this stage in his life. He only needed a friend.

Just a friend…dammit.

Five

*M*opping? What the heck did a mop look like anyway?

Merri stood, staring into the broom closet and trying to settle her nerves. Her lips were still tingling, her breasts still tender as they rubbed against her starched blouse right through the thin material of her teddy.

She blew out the breath she'd been holding and leaned back to steady herself against the door. Closing her eyes and counting the beats of her pounding heart, Merri wondered if she was going crazy.

All she could think about was the look in Ty's eyes when he'd turned back to check on her. The passion had still been flaming in those beautiful blues, that was for sure. And she was real familiar with that lust herself. She'd also been beyond hot and bothered.

But deeper, below the heat, she'd seen confusion and desperation in his eyes. Again, the very same emotions she had been struggling to conquer in herself.

That need, that desperate need having nothing to do with lust, was what had gotten to her the most. It made her want to wrap her arms around him and cuddle through a long night. To smooth back the strands of hair from his forehead and soothe away the frown lines that seemed so much a perpetual part of him. It would be so easy to listen to his passionate secrets in the dead of the night, and to be that special someone who would be there to understand.

Secrets? Hell. She had to get a grip here.

It wasn't Ty who had secrets. *He* wasn't the one who was deliberately misleading everyone. *He* wasn't the one who had gone to huge lengths to change his looks so he wouldn't be recognized. And that was why she had pushed him away and forced herself to keep a distance between them.

Merri breathed in a lungful of air and did get a grip. She gripped the plastic handle of what she was sure must be a mop and turned back to the urgent job of getting the water off the kitchen floor.

It took a few minutes for her to understand that the mop wasn't going to pick up any water until it was damp. But after a few inept attempts, she finally managed to fall into the natural rhythm of this mopping thing.

Almost pleasantly monotonous, the push-swipe-wring felt so good she caught herself smiling. This was exactly the kind of thing she had longed to experience.

No pedicures, breakfasts served on the terrace, or

massages before bed for her anymore—no pampering at all. The things Merri wanted in her life now were alarm clocks, boxed cereal and discount store sales— the real world. And that included floor mops.

"Hey!" Ty's voice as he entered the kitchen interrupted her thoughts. "You've got a great wave action going there, but I don't think you're making much headway." He grinned and looked down as the water she'd just pushed in his direction covered his boots.

"Let me grab some towels and I'll help. They're still kept in the hall closet, aren't they?"

"Yes, but…" She started to say that she'd rather finish the cleanup job herself, but he disappeared down the hall before she could get it out.

In thirty seconds he was back, carrying an armful of bath towels. "Here." He threw her a towel before he went down on his hands and knees with a couple of towels himself. "See? The towels pick up a lot more water than the mop."

Merri froze and stared, scarcely believing her own eyes. The man was rumored to have earned over a billion dollars before he turned thirty. He owned real estate in ten states and oil wells all over the world. His charitable foundation was destined to be a multi-million dollar project.

And here he was, on his hands and knees, using towels to sop up rainwater from her kitchen floor. Well…she'd wanted real, hadn't she?

She dropped to her knees and ran the towel over the puddles on the floor. Following Ty's lead, she soaked up water with the towel and then wrung it out over the bucket. Within a few minutes every muscle in her body hurt.

What had happened to the muscles she'd thought she'd toned in all those upper-body workouts at the gym?

Maybe this was a little too real. Just like Ty.

It struck her all of sudden—she was lying to everyone in order to experience the truth of a real life. How screwed up could she possibly be?

How on earth could she keep on lying to Ty and still expect to be his friend? But she had to…she just had to. One false move and the paparazzi would descend on them like ants on sugar.

There hadn't been much of a life for her before she came to Texas. But if the tabloids found her and ran stories on her sudden appearance in a small town after that fast disappearing act when her phony engagement went bad… Well, she could just imagine how horrible her existence would be from then on.

And now—she had involved Ty and Jewel in her deception, too. The reporters would never believe they had no knowledge of who she really was.

Her family would disown her permanently and forever. Though that wouldn't make too much of a difference in her sham of a life, it would also mean that her few new fragile friendships here would be broken forever, too.

But could she really keep these lies going long enough to establish herself as a neighbor and true friend? And long enough so that the paparazzi lost interest and moved on to the next "hottie" celebrity?

Sighing, Merri ticked off all the things that could go wrong with her plan.

Her new life could be ruined. Ty could see through

her disguise completely and would hate her. She wouldn't get a chance to live in a real-life world. Ty would hate her. She might never have another opportunity to find real friendship.

And, oh my God, Ty would hate her.

A tiny reminder that eventually she would have to own up to her deception and tell Ty the truth came into her conscious mind. But she pushed it aside.

She simply could not bear for that to happen. No way would she ever *let* that happen. No damn way.

After two days of finding excuses to stay away from the Foundation office—and Merri—Ty gave in to the urge to see her again. He was tired of fighting it. Tired from not sleeping—and tired of arguing with himself about her.

For a half-dozen reasons, he needed to get over it and get on with becoming her friend. Her roof was in need of more permanent repair. The Foundation needed her help with new donations. Jewel was constantly bugging him about Merri's welfare.

Dang. He stood in front of the full-length mirror in his walk-in closet and studied his appearance the way he had never done before in his life. Was this chambray work shirt the right thing to wear? Maybe he should change out of his work jeans into something nicer.

Eyeing his still-wet work boots that were standing in the corner, Ty knew for certain those soggy old things wouldn't work for Merri today. Hell. He never hesitated or fussed over his clothes, and as long as he'd been the boss of his own companies it had never mattered. Bank presidents, oil sheiks. Shoot, even senators and governors. None of them ever once mentioned his looks or so much as cared one way or the other.

But now it mattered—a lot.

As he flipped through his shirts to find something more suitable, Ty's thoughts turned to Merri once again. Her clothes didn't seem exactly right for her, either.

Okay, they were probably right for a shy office assistant with impeccable manners. But after that kiss they'd shared the other night, he'd become absolutely convinced that Merri could be so much more than that. *Was* so much more.

He remembered thinking years ago that his former fiancée, Diane, was so much *less* underneath her sexy clothes and outgoing personality. Merri was just the opposite.

That kiss was driving him totally insane.

Finally, he found a long-sleeved shirt and dress jeans that seemed to match. Today he had an appointment with a donor that wouldn't care about his looks. But he wanted to please Merri.

He just had to get closer to her. Business associate. Friend. Lover. Hell. He would take whatever she would give.

Of course, it didn't mean he could forget to keep the gates up on his heart. That was nonnegotiable. But he wasn't above testing Merri, trying to find out what was really behind the gates she had erected around herself.

In less than half an hour, Ty pulled his pickup into the Foundation office's lot and parked. After stepping out of the truck, he tucked in the shirt at the back of his waistband and straightened his collar. He even rubbed the toes of his new boots against the backs of his jeans-covered calves to make sure they were free of dust before he allowed himself to open the office door.

"Hey, there," he said when he spotted her at the computer. "How's your day going?"

She looked up at him with an irritated glimmer in her wide emerald eyes and his knees wobbled. It took a minute for him to realize she wasn't wearing her glasses. The sight nearly took his breath away.

"I've had better days," she finally admitted with a scowl. "The computer keeps going blue screen. And on top of that, Jewel called a while ago to say she's made an appointment for me to meet with a retail clothing buyer who's a friend of hers for four o'clock this afternoon.

"Apparently this woman is willing to donate clothes for the modeling show, but that will mean I have to drive to some town named McAllen and find the department store where the meeting is to take place. Waste of an afternoon, if you ask me."

"Juanita Ramirez."

"Excuse me?"

"Jewel's friend, the buyer. Her name is Juanita Ramirez and she grew up near here. Jewel taught Sunday school for years and Juanita was one of her star pupils."

"Oh? Yes, well…" Merri's scowl changed to a half smile. "I'm sure she's a lovely person. But still…"

"Let me try to make your day better if I can," he interrupted with as much charm as he could manage. "I'm on my way to see an old friend who lives on a ranch about an hour out of McAllen. I wanted to invite you to come with me since he's about to become one of the Foundation's biggest donors.

"So…why don't we make a day of it?" he continued as he placed both hands flat on her desk and leaned closer. "I'll call the computer tech, who may yet be able to make it out here to the office late this afternoon. Then you and I can go pick up a check from my friend before we swing by and visit with Juanita on the way home."

Merri blinked a couple of times and looked as if she was considering all the possibilities—including the fact that the two of them would be spending most of the day together riding around in his truck. But Ty wasn't about to mention any such thing. Not until he got her to agree.

"I don't think…"

"Your eyes are the most fascinating color of green," he told her, trying for distraction until he could make her say yes to his proposal for the day. "Do you absolutely have to wear those glasses all the time? I mean, in the last few minutes I've counted at least three different shades your eyes have turned as the emotions rolled across your face. It occurs to me that it must be a real pain having to wear glasses unless you're positively forced to."

"What?" She looked stricken as she fumbled on her desk for her glasses. "No…I mean…yes. I have to wear the glasses. Uh…except to work on the computer."

Ty found the glasses and handed them over. She flipped them on her face and took a breath. Interesting reaction. Maybe he was having an effect on her, after all.

"What do you say?" He was determined to push her as far as possible without being rude. "It's turning into a great day. The sun is finally out and things are drying up from that last rainstorm. We can do all our chores at one time and when we return, the computer should be up and you'll be back in business tomorrow."

"I suppose so…"

Gotcha. "Terrific. Grab your things while I make the call, and then we can lock up. The tech has a key to let himself in."

He watched Merri slowly stand up and begin to straighten her work in order to move it out of the way for the computer technician. She was dressed in something softer today. Her long-sleeved dress was still prim, but not nearly as severe as the last couple of things he'd seen her wear.

And it was in an icy jade color. Just the exact shade her eyes had become when he'd seen her considering being alone with him for the afternoon.

Uh-oh. He'd never noticed such things before in his entire life. He just might be in a world of trouble here.

Great day, Merri mumbled to herself. Right. Sure it was great—if a person liked ninety-degree temperatures and humidity high enough to frizz hair and make clothes feel all limp and sticky.

The sun looked like a burner on an electric stove set at "high." But it was hanging out in the cerulean sky overhead and beating down through the windshield as if it were determined to ruin any chance that the pickup's struggling air conditioner would be able to make things comfortable.

Ty hadn't said much while they drove for an hour and a half down winding farm-to-market roads. A minute ago they'd bumped over a grate in the road, then jostled under a twenty-foot sign indicating this was the Double S ranch.

"Ouch," she complained when the truck dipped into a pothole the size of Orange County, California, and knocked her sideways into the door handle. "I thought your friend must have money if he's going to make such a big donation. Can't he afford to pave the driveway to his house? Or does he just like gravel roads?"

"This isn't gravel. It's caliche," Ty told her without turning to face her. "And Miguel Santos could afford to pave over the entire state of Texas if he wanted to. But part of his empire includes the largest caliche pit in the world. You might want to refrain from bringing up the subject of paving."

"Ah. I see. Well, caliche is nice, I guess."

She half turned to look at Ty and found herself noticing how he absently drove his fingers through his hair and then straightened his collar as he kept his eyes trained on the road ahead. This *great* day would have a long way to go in a competition with Ty on who looked the best in the sunshine.

Obviously, he'd made an effort to dress a little nicer than usual in order to make a good impression on the new donor. His royal blue shirt brought out the deeper blue in his eyes. The jeans he wore looked brand-new and she was sure his boots had never been worn before today.

It warmed her heart to see him trying to change his appearance.

Merri wondered how long she would have to know him in order for her to feel comfortable taking him on a shopping trip. She could just picture him in an expensive, designer suit and tie. Yum.

Within a few minutes, they'd parked the car and were being ushered into a rambling house that seemed to stretch out into the next county. Miguel—Mike—Santos met them halfway down a Saltillo-tiled hall. He was a short man with salt-and-pepper hair and a twinkle in his dark brown eyes. Even though he was an inch shorter than Merri, his regal presence made him seem like a giant.

And…he wore dirty, torn blue jeans and boots that looked like they hadn't been polished once in their whole existence. Merri smiled at her own naive stupidity. Clothes did not always make the man.

Ty clasped the man's hand and her boss's expression said it all. He genuinely liked Mike Santos. And he couldn't care less about the way that either of them were dressed.

Maybe she had a lot more to learn about real life than she'd ever imagined.

For the next hour, over cold drinks and tamales, she listened to Mike as he reminisced about his late wife and showed them pictures of his grandchildren. He had been born right here on this ranch, which had come to his family as a Mexican land grant over two hundred years ago.

But his wife had come from a poor immigrant family and had lost her parents when they crossed into the United States. Hers was a sad story, filled with struggle and hardship. And it made Merri feel more than a little uncomfortable with her own spoiled upbringing.

At last Mike stood, but he signaled for her and Ty

to stay in their seats. "You have been very gracious to listen to an old man's story, Merri. I feel that I could tell you anything. *Gracias.*"

Mike turned to Ty and put a hand on his shoulder. "I planned to donate a nice sum to your children's foundation, *amigo*. Without your backing when I needed it most, I might not have saved the ranch.

"But now…" he continued hesitantly. "Seeing Merri and talking to her about my Maria's childhood has made me ashamed that I have not done more for your lost children. If you will excuse me for a few minutes, I will remedy that situation by tearing up the original check and writing a new one. I think perhaps Maria, looking down from heaven, would not be pleased unless I gave twice the amount that you and I discussed."

With that, Mike turned and smiled at Merri. "You are quite a lady, senorita. I hope Tyson appreciates the outstanding gem he has in you."

Mercy. Tyson did in fact appreciate the gift he had been given in Merri. More every minute. He'd watched her as she charmed his old friend. He had been enthralled with her genuine interest in Mike's tales and by the kind way she had urged him to tell only what he could manage without becoming too morbid.

Merri whispered her thanks and Mike disappeared into his study.

"I've never heard that story about Maria," Ty told Merri when they were alone. "You completely captivated him. I think with a little more encouragement you might've had him confessing every sin he'd ever committed. You are amazing with people, darlin'."

She blushed a delightful shade of pink and shook her

head. "I like Mike. It was easy to listen to his stories. But he's giving to the Foundation because of you and the respect he has for what you are trying to accomplish…it has nothing to do with me."

Ty wasn't so sure about that. He knew that, if asked, *he* would gladly give her anything—everything.

He had to find a way to make sure she stayed with him—uh—with the Foundation. In fact, he'd found himself giving serious consideration to making her the head of the entire charity instead of just the head of Development. She was so much better at this charm business than he was.

Maybe she should become the public face for the Lost Children's Foundation? Yeah, her face was bound to be better suited for that sort of thing than his was.

Hmm. Not a bad idea at all.

Six

The old gypsy woman narrowed her eyes and scowled down at her crystal ball. Fool!

It was hard to believe Tyson Steele was smart enough to have made so much money in his life. He certainly seemed too stupid to be descended from a great lady like Lucille Steele. Bah!

The gypsy steepled her gnarled fingers and sat back in her chair. Her father had been clear enough with his last instructions. The needy members of Lucille's family were to receive the magic gifts made specifically for them. Tyson Steele's gift had been the magic vision.

Twisting her fingers through the silver strands of hair that poked out from under her favorite scarlet scarf, she shook her head and scowled. What was she to do with such an idiot? She had placed the magic in his

hands, hadn't she? She'd even told him how to use it.
All he had to do was pick up the glass and look.

But so far, he'd only managed to wade ever deeper
into a fog of hazy confusion. With his heart's desire near
enough for him to reach out and grasp, he ignored the
magic. Even now he considered moving ahead on a
very dangerous course instead of following her advice.

There was nothing the gypsy could do to make him
see. Her hands were tied. She was not allowed to interfere. The magic only worked if he used it of his own vo-
lition.

Sighing, the old woman shook her head again and
raised her eyes. Could it be possible that the man would
never see? That he would let his stubborn disbelief
cause him to lose his one chance?

Stupid. Stupid. She would continue to observe him
in her crystal, but she wondered if she could stand
watching Tyson Steele lose everything. It would be the
ultimate disrespect for the memory of Lucille Steele.

The young fool!

Walking across the steaming asphalt parking lot,
Merri felt as if she were wilting. Could this really be
just early spring? What would the weather be like in the
heat of the summer?

"I think you're going to like Juanita," Ty said casually as they strolled toward the department store for her
appointment.

The man didn't seem fazed by the heat. He was still
as cool and crisp in his long-sleeved shirt and jeans as
he had been hours ago when he'd first walked into the
office.

But riding around the countryside with him and being so close was driving Merri crazy—and making her body temperature rise higher than ever.

She would've thought that being sweaty would cool any erotic longings she might have. But no. If anything, having perspiration inch its way down between her breasts was causing her mind to automatically form images of tangled bodies and blazing hot passion.

But those kinds of thoughts would never do. She and Ty were on the verge of forming a true friendship. There were hardly any strained silences between them anymore.

Hopefully, he had put their one kiss out of his mind. She only wished she could've done the same. But just when she was laughing at some joke he'd told—or whenever they were quietly discussing his plans for the future of the Foundation. That's the time when the memory of his arms around her, taking her lips and making her blood sing, came back to haunt her—and make her long for more.

As Ty would say, *Shoot. And dang it all.*

"I hope Juanita will be able to help us with clothes donations," Merri managed to say, trying hard not to think of kissing him again.

"I'm sure she will," Ty said with a smile. "Juanita is a big shot in the fashion industry. She's headquartered in New York and is the national sales manager for some huge design firm. She comes back to Texas a couple of times a quarter to check on sales here. I'd guess she knows lots about modeling shows."

"Oh?" *Uh-oh.*

They entered the department store and asked for

Juanita. A nice clerk called to some office and then directed them to the second-floor specialty boutique.

Merri had a bad feeling about this. Even in the cold blast of air-conditioning that had felt so good at first, the sweat broke out on her forehead. There probably weren't two people in high positions in the New York fashion world that she didn't know—and most she knew very well.

Her mind was racing, first trying to place a Juanita that she might know from the New York scene. And second, trying to figure some way out of her appointment altogether.

"There she is," Ty said as they stepped off the escalator. "Hey, Janie!" he called, trying to capture a woman's attention on the other side of the floor.

Janie? Oh my God. No. Not Janie Ramirez. It couldn't be.

"Janie?" she asked with trepidation. "I thought her name was Juanita."

"Oh, sure. Janie is a nickname. 'Round here she goes by both, but in New York I understand they only know her by Janie."

It was too late for Merri to run and there was nowhere for her to hide. Was this going to be the end to her true-life Odyssey?

As they walked closer, Merri dropped her chin and hung back, hoping that she could keep most of her body hidden behind Ty's. Though her mind was racing, there didn't seem to be any way of avoiding catastrophe.

"Good to see you, Juanita," Ty said as he greeted the other woman with a smile in his voice. "I'd like for you to meet my new assistant and Jewel's new renter, Merri Davis." He stepped aside so that the two women could face each other.

Merri kept her eyes down, took a deep breath and stretched out a hand. "How do you do, Ms. Ramirez."

"Merri? Why...I..." Janie said with obvious confusion in her voice. But she took Merri's hand and clung to it.

"Yes," Merri broke in. "The name is Merri Davis. Jewel has told me so much about you. It's a pleasure to meet you."

Merri took a chance and glanced up through the top of her glasses to watch the other woman's expression. Not good. Janie was studying Merri's dress and shoes, all the while shaking her head in disbelief.

Merri decided to take another big risk and pray that the woman would take pity on her and keep her mouth closed.

Turning to Ty, she said, "Thanks so much for bringing me here for the appointment. But I'm sure our discussion about modeling clothes will be terribly boring. Maybe you could wander around the store for a little while and give us girls a chance to get acquainted." She was desperate for a chance to talk to Janie—alone.

He frowned, but then checked with Janie. "If you need me, just call my cell phone. I should get decent reception while inside the store. And I've got a couple of calls to make in the meantime."

Janie nodded to him, but she couldn't manage a smile.

Ty turned to Merri with a grin. "Maybe I'll swing by the men's department. What do you think?"

"That's a good idea. But…ask for a clerk's help, okay?"

He laughed. "Yes, ma'am. I know where my talents lie…and where they don't."

Despite being a hairsbreadth away from total ruin, Merri's brain took her on a fantasy ride of imagining what other talents Ty might just have—and to imagining where exactly on her body she would like for them to lie.

Ty touched her arm lightly and broke into her dreams. Then he nodded once, turned and walked away. When he was out of earshot, Merri swallowed back the inappropriate lust and turned to face the storm.

And it came instantly. "Merrill Davis-Ross, what in heaven's name do you think you're doing?" Janie hissed, and grabbed her arm. "This had better not be another one of your bad jokes or some game of dare…or else I swear…"

"Please, will you just listen while I explain?"

The other woman nodded, grabbed her elbow and stormed the two of them off in the direction of the private offices.

When they were secure in a tiny office with one small desk and two chairs, Janie let go of her arm and turned to face her. "This had better be good. You're messing with a couple of people who mean the world to me and I won't stand by and let you hurt them."

"Wait a minute," Merri said with a huff. "If Jewel and Ty mean so much to you, why didn't you just give me up back there? Why not tell Ty who I was the minute you spotted me?"

Janie narrowed her eyes and shook her head. "At

first you surprised me so much with the disguise that I couldn't speak. But then…"

"What? You and I have never been that close. I mean, I like you, and I liked working with you, but…"

"It has nothing to do with you," Janie told her. "And everything to do with the look on Ty's face when he introduced you. The man's seriously goofy about you, and I made a quick decision to go slow until I found out the situation. So now…you tell me the situation."

"Goofy?" Merri asked with a laugh. "Tyson Steele—about me? I don't think so."

"No question about it," Janie said. "And unless I miss my guess, you've got it bad for him, too."

She plopped down on one of the chairs and motioned for Merri to take the other one. "I want the truth and I want it now. The last I heard about you, the tabloid headlines were screaming that you were a fake. Something about you deserting your gay boyfriend, wasn't it?"

"What?" Merri sank down in the chair and closed her eyes. "I knew it. That is so not the way it was. Let me explain what really happened."

She told Janie the whole story of how she'd agreed to become Brad's make-believe girlfriend in order to throw the paparazzi off his trail. Merri had been trying to be a friend to Brad. But when that photographer caught him coming out of his boyfriend's house and the whole thing blew up in their faces, Brad's publicist asked her to take a vacation for a while.

She'd readily agreed. The "wronged" woman was not a role she had any intention of playing out in front of the entire world. Especially when it wasn't true.

"Okay, I understand why you needed to start a new life," Janie began. "And I certainly accept that you had to change your looks in order to escape the paparazzi. It's true your face is recognizable all over the world, and they would've made your life a miserable hell. They're hot on your trail as we speak, as a matter of fact.

"But what I don't understand is why in Stanville, Texas?" she continued. "Why involve decent people like Ty and Jewel in your deception?" Janie lifted her head with a thoughtful scowl. "They don't know, do they?"

"No," Merri said sadly. "They don't know. I came here to do something worthwhile with my life. I really wanted to help raise funds for Ty's foundation. And before I met them I was afraid they would give me away if they knew the truth."

Merri squirmed in her seat and continued. "I don't expect you to believe this, but I also wanted to live a normal life. For once in my life, I wanted to know what it would be like for people to think I'm just a regular person. To maybe make a friend who didn't want something from me or my family."

Janie sat back in her chair and studied Merri's face. "You did a damn good makeup job there, honey. If I hadn't seen you just a few weeks ago before a show without your makeup, I might've missed the connection altogether.

"And I can almost understand your motivations," Janie went on. "But…none of it excuses you from taking the chance of hurting Ty and Jewel. Why don't you simply tell them the truth? I'd be willing to bet they'd keep up the charade for you."

Merri shook her head. "Maybe it wouldn't bother Jewel, but Ty would hate me. He can't stand liars of any sort. It's too late for me to go back now."

Janie cocked her head and frowned. "Mmm. You can't keep this up indefinitely, you know. You will have to tell him the truth someday."

Merri dropped her chin. "Yeah, I know. But I thought if I could get by for a few more months…just until the paparazzi lose interest in me…that by that time Ty and Jewel would've grown to like me for who I really am. Then maybe they wouldn't hate me so much when they find out the truth."

Janie thought that over for a few seconds. "Well… It's against my better judgment. I think that the longer you go on lying to Ty, the worse it will be when he learns the truth."

"Please," Merri begged. "Let me do it my way. I'm trying to walk a fine line with Ty—a line between becoming his friend and letting him get too close. Give me a few more months. And besides, I think I'm really beginning to make a difference for his kids. I just need a little more time."

"All right," Janie agreed grudgingly. "Making a better life for those abandoned and abused kids will give you a second chance with Ty, I know. But be careful. If you hurt him, I will hunt you down and ruin your life. This whole thing could go wrong at any turn."

"I know," Merri whispered. "Believe me, I know."

A couple of hours later Ty strolled across the main floor of the department store and stepped onto the escalator. He hefted the packages in his arms and caught himself as he began to whistle an old Willie Nelson love song.

Whistling? Ty hadn't whistled in years. Interesting that he was finding himself doing things he would not have contemplated doing only a few short weeks ago.

It must be Merri's influence that was changing his lifestyle. He knew for certain that she'd been having an effect on his libido. The closer they became, the more he wanted her in his bed.

Well, he would just have to do something toward making that happen. And soon.

He rounded the corner and spotted the two women off in the distance in the children's department. Heading in their direction, he studied the differences in the two.

Merri was easy to spot. Tall and slender, she stood talking to Janie with an almost regal bearing. In fact, she looked rather statuesque from this distance. It was strange that he hadn't noticed that about her before. She'd always seemed so shy and vulnerable to him. Today she stood like a queen.

Tiny Juanita standing beside her looked lost, though her jet-black hair was shiny and smooth compared to Merri's dull brown wisps. And Juanita's suit seemed sophisticated but flashy in a spring green shade, making Merri's plain dress and clunky shoes look ever more homely. But none of that changed the fact that it was Merri who drew his attention.

It was almost as if she had a spotlight shining on her from above.

"Hey there, ladies," he said when he got close enough to capture their attention. "Did you miss me?"

Two sets of eyes turned in his direction. Juanita's dark eyes smiled when she saw him coming. On the other hand, Merri's greens carried a fleeting look of panic behind the thick lens as she spotted him walking down the aisle. Instantly, she slouched back into the shy stance that he had thought defined her, but her face brightened and she tried for a weak smile.

"We've been too busy to think of you, Ty," Merri told him with a sarcastic chuckle. "Janie and I have picked out some lovely mother-daughter dresses for the models. Janie has agreed to furnish all the clothes for the show. Isn't that nice of her?"

He turned to Juanita and let the easy grin cover his face. "It sure is. I can't thank you enough, Juanita. Are you sure it won't be too much? Jewel would kill me if you got in trouble over my foundation's need. Maybe I should offer to pay for the dresses out of my own pocket?"

Juanita rolled her eyes. "Don't be silly. It will be worth a ton in publicity for the company. They always try to do their part for worthwhile charities. And I consider yours to be extremely worthwhile."

She tilted her head and looked at the packages in his arms. "It looks like you bought out the store while Merri and I were busy. Trying to change your whole wardrobe?"

"Yes," Merri chimed in with a smile. "Are you trying to do a complete makeover in one trip to the store?"

"No ma'am," he said with a laugh. "But that wouldn't be so bad, would it? My so-called wardrobe could stand making over."

"What did you buy?" Merri asked. She looked horrified that he might buy all the wrong things without her along to advise him.

"This and that," he said with a wink.

When Merri scowled and narrowed her eyes, he decided to tell them both what was on his mind. "Actually, this isn't everything I bought. I bought a suit and a tux, too, but they're being altered."

"A tux? What on earth for?"

"Well, now, darlin', I'm glad you asked. I spoke to Frank on the phone a while ago and he reminded me that tomorrow night is the governor's annual charity ball.

"The governor throws these shindigs to honor all the charities that operate in the state, and this year the Lost Children's Foundation has been invited to attend," he explained. "It's quite an honor and great publicity for the charities, but I wasn't planning on going originally. Didn't think it suited my personality."

"So what changed?" Juanita asked.

"My wardrobe, for one," he joked. "For another, I now have Merri to go along and advise me on the proper etiquette."

Ty took Merri's hand before she could shake her head. "You will go with me, won't you? It's important for the Foundation…for the children."

Damn man, Merri thought. He could be just too charming for words sometimes. But emotional blackmail didn't seem like his normal style.

"Sorry," she said and pulled her hand free. "You'll have to attend the party with someone else. I don't have anything to wear to such a thing." It was the best excuse she could come up with on such short notice but she knew it was pretty lame.

He looked stricken. As if her refusal had wounded him personally.

"Hello-o-o," Janie spoke up. "Remember me? Clothes are my business. You need something to wear to a ball, I'm your man…so to speak."

"Oh, no," Merri exploded. "I mean, I couldn't. I mean, I can't afford…"

"What a really kind thing for you to offer to do, Juanita," Ty broke in with a smile. "And of course, you can bill me. The Foundation needs Merri to be there. And so do I. Do you want her to try on a few things while we're here? We won't have much time to have alterations done. The ball is tomorrow night."

"But…" Merri began, before she was interrupted.

"Not at all," Janie said, waving Ty's suggestion away. "I know exactly what size she— I mean, I can tell just by looking what will fit her. Not to worry. I'll pick out something and have it delivered tomorrow when they bring out your alterations."

"Thanks," Ty said. Then he seemed to think of something else. "Could you pick out something really special? Something in red, maybe?"

"No!" Both women exclaimed in unison.

Janie shot her a quick look and Merri tried to surreptitiously let her know how mad she was about the whole stupid suggestion of a dress.

"Something sedate would be more appropriate for a charitable function." Merri told them both through gritted teeth. "I'd rather it not be terribly *flashy*." It was too late and she was too outnumbered to keep from going to the ball now. She was stuck.

The other woman appeared to agree wholeheartedly

with the sedate suggestion. At least she remembered part of her promise to keep Merri's secret.

"Yes, dark blue or black would perhaps be a better choice for Merri's coloring," Janie told Ty with a straight face. "Trust me to make the right choice."

"All right," he said reluctantly. "If you say so. I do appreciate you taking care of the dress for us. I'd just as soon take Merri home now, anyhow. This shopping takes a lot out of you. It's getting late."

Oh, man, Merri thought with chagrin. You have no idea how really late it is. She was only just now finding out the truth of that herself. It was way too late for her to tell him the truth and manage to keep their relationship intact through it.

Sheesh. Heaven help her.

They were almost back home when Ty shifted his weight in the driver's seat and spoke for the first time in over an hour. "Who are you really, Merri?"

Her head came up and her whole body shuddered in panic. "What do you mean?"

"I don't know anything about you. What your family is like. Where you went to school. How you ended up engaged to some guy you didn't really care about." Ty breathed deeply. "I want to get to know more about you. You know where I come from...who I am. My background is an open book.

"I want to know the real Merri Davis," he added.

"The real Merri Davis *is* the person you know," she told him. "The one that dreams of a quiet life in a small town and the opportunity to do something good for those less fortunate."

Ty shook his head but didn't turn to look at her. "There's something else. I don't know exactly what, but…" He hesitated then went on. "Did you attend boarding schools when you were a kid? Sometimes you sound European. And then there's the way you stand. It seems almost like you might've gone to modeling school—or maybe charm school somewhere."

"Uh…" Her mind was blank and her breathing had become shallow. "Yes, I went to boarding schools. Some of them were in Europe. That's probably why I sound funny on occasion." The truth. And hopefully a diversion from questions about modeling.

The man was beginning to ask insightful questions she didn't want to answer. Couldn't answer if she wanted to stay as truthful as possible.

No wonder he was a young self-made billionaire. Obviously, he had good instincts and was more than a little savvy. She would hate to have to face him from across a negotiation table.

She held her breath and wondered what on earth would be coming next.

Seven

"So your parents are rich?" Ty asked. He gave a slight nod of his chin to encourage her to talk, but the day-old shadow along his jaw looked deadly and made her squirm.

"Well…I guess some people would say that." Merri shifted to stare straight out through the windshield and quietly fisted her hands in her lap. And damned near bit clear through her lip with nervous energy.

"But they don't give you any money now?"

"Uh…no. We're estranged at the moment." Another truth—if you didn't count her trust fund as money.

"I'm sorry. That sounds awful. No wonder you don't want to talk about it." Ty pulled up in front of her cottage and parked the truck.

He turned off the ignition and swivelled in his seat to face her. "No brothers or sisters?"

She shook her head. "No. It's just me."

Ty squeezed her shoulder and lowered his voice. "I can take a guess about the fiancé. I'll bet he was someone your parents picked out for you, right? It must've been hard to break that engagement."

Think, she urged herself in near panic. How was she going to keep talking about this and not come right out and lie to him any more than she already had?

"Um…well… The engagement was arranged, that's true. And it was difficult getting out of it. Sort of."

Ty ran a finger down her jawline and lifted her chin. "You want to tell me the whole story?"

"No. Thanks. I don't." Merri jerked her chin out of his grasp, flipped open her seat belt and hopped down out of the truck.

She beat him to her door, but he wasn't far behind.

"Whoa, darlin'," he said as he caught up to her and took her arm. "What are you running from?"

She spun around and held her purse between them like a shield. "Nothing. I'm just tired and I want to go to bed."

Oops. The minute it was out of her mouth she saw the passion flare in his eyes. But she could also see his struggle to bank the desire.

"I think you *are* running," he said in a steel-edged tone. "But I'm not sure why. You've built a wall around yourself and it's driving me crazy trying to break it down."

"What do you want from me, Ty?"

"A little trust," he began, as a sensual smile spread across his lips. "And another kiss."

"Oh, for heaven's sake," she said with a hysterical little laugh. "If that's what it will take to get you to go away, here…"

Without thinking, she moved close and gave him a quick peck on the mouth. Then…she thought about what she'd done.

Too late.

Ty only took a second to react. He grabbed her shoulders, pulled her close and covered her trembling mouth with his own. It was fast, hot and blood-stirring.

His tongue coaxed her lips open, but she didn't need much urging to fall into his drugging kiss. Their lips and tongues met as if they were desperate for each other. Desperate to touch, taste and nibble.

Merri became dizzy from the sheer pleasure of it and leaned into Ty's body to steady herself. He groaned and shoved his groin against her hips as they swayed together.

Ty clasped his muscled arms tightly around her waist, and she felt his hard arousal pressing into her. It sent shivers down her spine. Digging her fingers into his shoulders to keep from turning to pure liquid and melting totally away, she pressed her excruciatingly tender breasts against his rocky, muscular chest and rubbed. Rubbed hard.

Merri felt, more than heard, the moan escaping from somewhere so deep inside her that it must've begun at her very center.

The sound of her own desire surprised her—and Ty. He broke the kiss and steadied them both.

"Whoa. That was… That wasn't…" Ty cleared his raspy voice and took a step back. "Go inside, Merri."

He looked as stunned by what had happened between them as she was. "It's late and we'll be flying up to Austin tomorrow afternoon. I'll send the dress over whenever it arrives."

"But...what about...?" she stuttered.

"Not tonight," he said with a scowl. "I can't talk about it tonight." With that he turned, silently stalked back to his truck and took off.

Ah, hell, she thought as she watched him go. That had been all her fault. What an idiot she was.

Ty drove toward his ranch in a daze. Needy, frustrated and more than a little bewildered by his own reactions, he tried to dissect their kiss by looking at it dispassionately. But of course, that was impossible.

Back there in two heartbeats, everything he had promised himself, every reasonable thing he had ever told her, all of it had gone south, along with most of the blood in his body. His every good intention—hell, even most of his mind—had heated, gushed through his veins and finally pooled at the base of his spine, where it throbbed relentlessly, making him reach for her when he knew dang well that he shouldn't.

There was not one thing about his relationship with Merri that could be classified as dispassionate. Oh, he'd been telling himself they could have a cordial, boss-employee friendship. But, hell, he knew that was a total fabrication.

Ty had to stop lying to himself about his need for her. After all, he hated liars. From the first moment he'd seen Merri, he'd wanted her in his bed. A person might've thought that a smart man would just acknowledge the fact and begin moving toward that goal.

But, no. He'd been trying to fool himself—and Merri—into thinking they could just be friends.

Okay. He gave up. He had to have her. And after that kiss tonight, he was positive that despite everything she said, she wanted the same thing.

He roared the truck into his ranch's yard, slammed it into Park and turned it off. But he didn't move. Might as well not try to go to bed. There was no possibility for any sleep tonight. Not the way the tension was still humming up and down his spine.

Stepping out of the truck, he quietly closed the door behind him and walked toward the barn. Whenever he wanted peace, he'd always ended up in the foaling barn. There was just something about young creatures that soothed him.

Maybe it was the innocence of youth. Maybe it was the fact that they hadn't had time yet to learn the dangers and suspicions of the world.

When it came to human babies, he recognized that his fondness for them was because they had not yet learned to lie and still trusted everyone implicitly. It was compelling, all that trust.

He'd told Merri that he wanted her to trust him enough to tell him her secrets. But what he'd meant was that he wanted some reason to trust her with his.

Jewel was the only person in the entire world he trusted even a little bit. And she didn't know the whole truth of his pain.

Twice in his life he had completely trusted a woman with his heart and his deepest secrets. Twice in his life he had been, not only disappointed, but totally ripped to shreds and betrayed.

Now his brain kept telling him that Merri was keeping something from him and couldn't be entirely trusted. But his heart and his body were urging him to give her a chance.

Well, he would just have to see about the trust. That was still a maybe. But he'd already made his mind up about giving in to his body. All he had to do was persuade Merri that she was ready, too.

Hmm. His brain started wandering off to images of the ways that he could convince her.

Taking a deep breath of the jasmine-scented night air, Ty realized that those kinds of images were not going to do a damn thing toward allowing him any peace tonight.

But…hey. They would be worth every sleepless minute.

"When you said we'd be flying to Austin this afternoon, I had no idea you meant *you* would be the pilot," Merri told him as she fiddled with her safety belt.

"Does it bother you to fly with me?" Mercy, but he would dearly love to find other ways of *bothering* her.

"No, not at all. You've convinced me that you have all the proper licenses and ratings. It's just surprising."

"When you get to know me a little better, you'll find out that I prefer doing most things for myself. I can't always manage it, of course. For instance, I don't do the maintenance of the planes or the day-to-day running of my businesses and now the Foundation office. In those cases and a few more I have to turn over the work to others."

Though he could think of a couple of things that he would never turn over to anyone else. Like pulling all the pins out of her hair, driving his fingers through the finely textured strands and burying his face in all that sensuous silk.

Every time he was this close, Ty got a faint whiff of lavender and vanilla from her hair. It was enough to wipe his mind clean and leave him with nothing but basic animal urges. Something similar to a lobotomy he was sure.

"I didn't know we would have to stay over in Austin tonight, either," she said, interrupting his thoughts. "Your note to pack an overnight bag was another big surprise."

"It's just about two hours door-to-door and I wouldn't want to feel rushed to leave," he said as he shook off the urges long enough to begin the regular checklist for takeoff. "I also thought it might be fun to drink a toast to the Lost Children Foundation's new Director. I couldn't do that and then get back in the cockpit and fly."

"What?" She jerked her head around to stare at the side of his head. "You mean me?"

He chuckled at the crack in her voice. "I can't think of anyone who would be better for the job."

"But…" Merri couldn't get her mind to settle.

Seeing Ty in the captain's seat of this fabulous new single-pilot personal jet had done a number on her nerves. He was so masculine and so in control that she'd been having crazy butterfly flutters in her stomach, that had nothing to do with flying, ever since the moment they had first boarded.

But now… What would being the Director of his foundation mean? Suddenly it hit her. Publicity. Oh no.

Take a breath. Swallow hard. Think of something. Fast.

"That's quite an honor, but I really haven't had a chance to earn a promotion yet," she gushed, trying to think while she was talking. "I like working behind the scenes for now. Give me a few more months on the job before I start speaking for the entire foundation."

"But you're perfect for the Director's job," Ty argued. "You have that wonderful boarding-school charm and grace. And every donor that has met you loves you. Think about it. You're so much better at the face-to-face stuff than I am."

Merri took another breath and prayed she would say the right thing. "Ty, this foundation is your baby. You were the one who gave the idea wings. It was your money and your time that put it together in the first place. And it's your reputation and contacts that are needed to build a long-term base of donors now.

"No one in Texas knows me at all…" She hesitated over the half truth. Lots of people all over the world knew the face of Merrill Davis-Ross. "Let me stay in the background while we build the Foundation together."

"Well…" He stopped studying the lighted flight displays for a second and turned to look at her. "I suppose you're right. It seems like you usually are. But you have to promise not to let me say or do the wrong thing. I'm not great at this PR stuff."

Merri breathed a quiet sigh of relief. "Don't worry. You'll do fine. I'll be right behind you."

Ty kept silent as he finished his preflight check, radioed to some faraway control tower and prepared to take off. Merri closed her eyes and leaned back while they taxied down his private runway and lifted to the sky. She seemed to have dodged the bullet for now, but could she manage to stay out of the way of the photographers tonight?

Speaking of tonight...

"Where will we be spending the night?" she asked warily once they were airborne and Ty had slid aside his headset and microphone.

"I have a suite of rooms on permanent reserve at the Hilton, same place as the ball," he told her. "Normally I keep them for the use of my lawyers and the lobbyists they hire to work on my interests with the state's legislators. But tonight the suite will be all ours."

"You don't do your own lobbying like you do everything else?" she said with a laugh.

"Not good at the face-to-face, remember?"

Merri thought he was fantastic at some face-to-face activities. But she wasn't about to mention it. He hadn't.

Hmm. He hadn't mentioned that incredible kiss—two kisses—either.

"I'm not going to sleep with you tonight, Ty," she said before she thought it over. "If you had that in the back of your mind, get it out. I presume 'suite' means separate bedrooms and you and I will be occupying *two* of them."

"Didn't say any different, did I?" he told her through a grin.

Ty didn't want to *rush* her into his bed. Or...at least not in his *head* he didn't.

But he had every intention of *easing* her into it. Tonight would just be another step toward the goal.

Cinderella in reverse, Merri thought as she stood looking at herself in the full-length mirror. The dress that Janie sent was just about the worst thing Merri had ever seen. And she'd seen quite a few catastrophes.

Bits of drab rust and military olive clung as if they were tufts of dandelion seeds along the nondescript beige column of the high-necked, long sleeved gown—and spread out like birthday frosting along the ruffles that flared about her ankles. It was a really good thing she would be the one to wear this dress so that some innocent girl would never accidently try on this monstrosity.

Her reflection in the mirror was almost comical. In fact, when Merri lifted her gaze to study her disguised hair and lack of makeup, she actually chuckled. What a pitiful sight she made. Good old Janie had done her job.

This getup ought to discourage pictures. And hopefully it was bad enough to put a damper on Ty's passion for her as well.

Lately, every time he looked in her direction she saw the temperature rise in his eyes. His hotter and hotter need was easy to recognize because she felt it, too.

But Merri had to find a way to cool things down. Ty didn't seem to be the kind of guy to go for one-night stands or short, carefree flings. Everything she had ever heard about him told her that he would be interested in more permanent relationships—if not in marriage.

Which was good and bad news. Good because that

made him a decent guy who tried not to hurt anyone. Bad because she was becoming desperate for him and the two of them were not destined for anything permanent. The minute he had any inkling she'd been lying to him it would be all over between them. And that day was coming—sooner or later.

Sighing, Merri turned to put her compact in her purse, hesitated over the lipstick and decided against it. The more washed-out her face looked next to the hideous dress the better. No one here should be able to recognize her face from her pictures, she hoped. And if she got caught by some wayward camera lens tonight, no one would ever recognize her picture.

A knock sounded on the door to her bedroom. "Merri, are you decent?" Ty called out.

Well, maybe her thoughts about him weren't decent. But if he'd meant to inquire if she was dressed, the answer was *ugh*…if you wanted to call this costume a dress.

"Yes," she answered. "Just let me get my…"

He popped his head into the room, caught her eye and let himself in. "I brought you…" He stopped mid-sentence and stared at her.

Ohmigod. If she was the reverse Cinderella, Ty had definitely done a U-turn into Prince Charming. Dressed in a black tuxedo and crisp white shirt, the man just oozed sex appeal and potent masculine attraction.

It embarrassed her to imagine what he must be thinking about the way she looked. She tried telling herself that this was what she'd wanted. He needed to tone down his desire and there was nothing like an ugly dress and drab hair to cool a man's ardor.

"You look beautiful," he said without moving.

"What?"

Ty saw her confusion and realized he wasn't saying this right. Typical of his bad manners and tongue-tied efforts at being glib, charming words just never came out the way he meant. But it was important for him to make her understand what he felt tonight.

Forcing his feet to move him closer to where she stood, he tried a half smile. "You don't have on your glasses and your eyes are the most spectacular green I have ever seen. They just light up your whole face."

"Oh." She scowled and turned to find the black-rimmed glasses on the table.

"Please don't put them on," he said quietly. "There's no need for you to see anything special tonight. I can tell you what's going on."

The little laugh she gave sounded more like a hiccup. But she put the glasses in her purse and clasped the itty bitty scrap of cloth to her side.

He took another step in her direction. "I brought you this corsage." Looking down at the fiery red bouquet in his hand, he couldn't help but frown. "I thought Janie said your dress would be navy or black. The red roses were meant to liven it up a bit but…"

This time she laughed out loud. "It's okay," she said, through a grin. "For tonight, I can be the one who's wearing clothing that clashes. You look spectacular, by the way. You clean up real good, Tyson Steele. I'm impressed."

He smiled at her in return. Though he knew she was joking, it warmed him to hear her using a less formal way of talking. Maybe she was becoming comfortable with his small-town Texas ways. Good. Maybe that meant she would stay around for a while longer. Like maybe forever.

Letting his gaze move lazily over her, his mouth began to water at the very sight. The dress wasn't much to look at, he had to admit. But it clung to her body in all the right places, leaving not much to the imagination.

His imagination was working double duty anyway. He visualized her standing there before him naked. Breasts tipped up and beaded, waiting for his caress. Hips curved and soft, waiting for the palms of his hands to glide over them. He blinked back a shudder of desire and shook himself free of the strangling erotic dreams.

Nothing was going to happen in that vein tonight. He had promised, and he intended to keep that promise. No matter what. She wasn't quite ready for everything he had in mind. But he sure hoped she would be—soon.

Merri pinned the corsage to her shoulder and then slid her arm through Ty's. "Okay, let's go. Tonight is your night."

No, unfortunately, it wasn't. But he intended to make the most of it anyway. Ten more yards to first down on the way to goal.

He escorted her down in the elevator to the ballroom. Merri glued herself to his side, praying to blend into his shadow so that no one would notice her.

There was the reception line to get through, but that turned out to be a snap. Very few people paid any attention to her at all. Most of the women were so busy drooling over Ty that she became an insignificant blip on their radar. Just as she'd hoped.

The only hitch was the governor himself. He said something kind to Ty, but then turned to her and took her hand in both of his. "And who is this beautiful creature? You can't possibly be a native Texan, young woman. I would never forget meeting anyone so lovely, and I pride myself in knowing all my gorgeous constituents."

Ty scowled but grudgingly introduced them. The governor caught the possessive tone Ty used and chuckled.

"You can't blame a man for looking, Steele," he said with a wink and a nod.

Merri couldn't stop the blush, but she'd never heard anything so ridiculously political in her whole life. She was under no illusions about how she looked tonight.

After three hours of the ball, she'd had enough. She'd sat through a Texas-sized banquet dinner, with platters of two-inch-thick prime rib and baked potatoes. Fourteen awards for charitable service and the acceptance speeches that went along with them. And two hours worth of listening to the heavyset woman sitting on her left who droned on about the good works of her charity to help preserve historic Texas oil derricks from the ravages of time.

Now the photographers had asked everyone to line up for pictures, and she hung back. "You go on," she told Ty. "I'll wait for you over there."

He took her hand. "Come with me. The Foundation needs your pretty face to make the public take notice."

She shook her head and forced a smile. "No. I told you it was your charity...and your night. Just stand there and look important. You'll be fine."

Reluctantly Ty agreed, but before he left her side he leaned in to whisper, "Don't go anywhere. I have a favor to ask. I'll be back in a minute."

Merri's curiosity was piqued. But before she could question him, he disappeared into the sea of people surrounding a spot where flashbulbs were popping away. She looked around for somewhere to sit, knowing full well that he would be gone for ages. If there was one thing she had learned, it was exactly how long photograph sessions usually lasted.

But just as she found an empty spot and sat down, Ty appeared beside her again. "Dang, those guys take forever. Sorry."

"You're done? Are you sure?"

"Oh yeah. They have a regular assembly line going. I stood still and pretended to shake hands with the governor. Then I gave some idiot my name and charity. And that was that. Done, and grateful to be free."

He reached out his hand to help her up. "Dance with me, Merri."

She looked up into the deep blue sea of his eyes. "Is that the favor?"

Ty nodded and pulled her to her feet. "A dance with you will help redeem this disastrous evening."

As he led her to the dance floor, Merri looked around and thought the ball wasn't so bad. The decorations were glorious with all the twinkling lights, ferns and fountains. The hall was set up to look like a spring garden on a warm star-filled evening. And the music had gone from Texas two-stepping to soft slow-dancing ballads.

Walking Merri through the crowded tables, Ty was

startled by the appreciative glances they were getting from all over the hall. She was moving beside him with all the elegance and style of a royalty.

On the dance floor he pulled her into his arms and molded her body to his. She fit perfectly there, with the top of her head next to his cheek, his arm around her waist. As tall as she was, she seemed to be made just for him.

They moved around the dance floor in time to the music. When the tempo slowed, she inched closer and he could feel her warm breath on his neck.

The heat was making him lose track of where they were. His own breath was becoming ragged.

Suddenly, a photographer stepped out of nowhere and began snapping candid shots of all the dancers. Merri groaned and buried her face in his chest, flattening herself along the length of his body. He whirled her away to a darker corner, needing to keep her all to himself.

But the minute they were cast in shadows, his brain went south again. He slowed their pace and let his hand slide down her hip, following the feminine curve of her body. So smooth. So right a fit in his palm.

Too smooth. He *had* lost his mind, because he lifted his head slightly to ask a really thoughtless question. "You're not wearing any panties under that dress?"

"They would've shown through," she told him without embarrassment. "It would've ruined the line of the dress."

All of a sudden the unattractive dress was the most fantastic thing he'd ever seen. He stepped back from her and blinked.

"That's it. Ball's over. Let's go upstairs." He took a deep breath. "Now."

Eight

Ty took her hand and beat a path through the crowds, heading for the elevators. Merri didn't seem to mind leaving the ball and easily kept up with him.

But when he saw the crowds waiting to pack into each upward carload, he shifted direction and moved toward the freight elevators he knew were located down a darkened corridor near the kitchens. A couple of times in the past he had carted his own luggage up or down those elevators. They weren't much to look at due to the thick padding that lined their walls, but they should be completely empty at this time of night.

Sure enough, when they arrived, the freight elevators stood propped open and looking gloriously vacant. Good thing he knew how to operate all the unmarked buttons. One propped the doors open, another kept them shut, one more was an express button to various floors.

His heart was pounding in his chest. The thoughts of Merri, her dress, her nakedness under the dress—it was all too much. He pulled her into the empty elevator and hit the express button to his floor.

He had excellent intentions…that is if his brain had actually been working. He knew they were not going to go all the way tonight. She hadn't given him the signal that she was ready, and he would never push.

He wanted her trust first.

But from the minute she'd told him about not wearing panties, his body had demanded that they leave the ball. He just couldn't have every other man in the world looking at her like that.

"You didn't want to stay any longer, did you?" he belatedly asked as the elevator doors shut.

"No, not at all. I'd had enough…except for dancing with you. That part was great." She gazed up at him through thick lashes that looked like a sexy veil covering those startling green eyes. "You're a wonderful dancer, Tyson Steele. Another nice surprise."

His mouth came down on hers before either of them had their next heartbeat. A pounding staccato beat from his heart skittered down his spine and then moved much lower, driving him to instant hunger.

He backed up to the padded wall and dragged her between his thighs while he kept on kissing her. It was a dizzying sensation. She nibbled at his lips, he nipped at hers. Wet tongues lathed and sucked in a tangled dance.

When he ran his hands up and down her sides, lingering under her breasts, Merri moaned and writhed closer. His pulsed jumped as he licked his way down the column of her throat and palmed her hardened tips through the satiny feel of the dress's material.

Senses on full alert, when the elevator came to a stop and the doors began to open, he reached around behind his back and punched the "doors closed" button and then flicked the "elevator hold" switch. He couldn't have moved away from her right now even if his life depended on it. And he had no intention of having an audience.

"Ty," she gasped and inched back. "What if someone opens the doors?"

"Don't care," he managed. "Trust me."

His mouth came back to hers, and Merri felt the power between them growing. The heat was unbearable. All she could think of was getting both of their clothes off so she could touch him freely. And of having him touch her—easing this terrible need that was making her wet and turning her to butter.

She burned for him. Craved him. Wanted to crawl right inside him. It was madness, but she couldn't help herself.

Ty's hands were everywhere, ranging over her breasts, sliding down her spine and cupping her bottom. She couldn't keep up with him, wanted to touch him in return. But her limbs were weak. Merri desperately threw her arms around his neck and hung on before she turned to liquid right where she stood.

"I need you so badly," he groaned against her hair.

She leaned her head back to give him access as he trailed kisses down her neck and across the flimsy material covering her breasts. When he bent to take a nipple into the warmth of his mouth, she gasped. Heat seemed to sear a hole right through the dress's ugly beige satin.

Electricity zinged along her nerve endings, driving shots of slick lightning to the center of her universe.

Stunned by the sensations, she reached out blindly. Grabbing his shirt front, her only thought was to touch him. To run her lips down the planes of his body, taste salty skin and satisfy this desire. But she couldn't think well enough to undo the studs, so she just clutched at the stark white shirt and hung on.

Ty's hands slid down her hips and bunched her long dress in his palms. He leaned back against the elevator wall, steadying them both while he hiked the dowdy material slowly up her thighs.

Merri felt the whisper of beige as it tickled against her thigh-high nylons. Felt a soft draft of air hitting her bare skin. Then the heat of Ty's gentle touch on her inner thigh brought a startled gasp to her lips.

He captured her mouth as their moans mingled. Shifting her feet, she opened her legs to allow him better access.

"So hot," Ty whispered huskily against her lips. "I have to touch you. Have to…"

Slowly, his fingers edged upward toward the place that ached for him. The trail of his touch set fire to her skin, frustrating her with its too steady pace. She knew he was a gentleman deep in his soul, but he had to go faster now. She had to make him see how badly she needed…needed…

"Touch me," she murmured. The hoarse voice didn't

sound like her own. Desperation was capturing her spirit and making her become someone else entirely.

"Please, Ty," she begged. "Please."

Her needy pleas drifted through the lavender haze surrounding Ty. She was in his blood. In his soul. He knew exactly what she craved and how to take her there.

But he wanted her complete trust first—without reservation. If he couldn't have that tonight, he would take what trust she offered. It told him something, that she trusted him with her body. It was a small start. A beginning to everything he wanted. And enough for now.

He cupped her in his palm and let their combined body heat move through them both. The trembling shock waves of her desire ran up his arm. She was so hot for him.

Merri moaned and pressed hard against his hand, begging for him to take more as she locked her lips on his. Merri the shy, plain sophisticate had become a tigress.

Her aggression didn't turn him off, instead it served to make Ty want more. However, it did manage to remind him of an earlier promise not to take her to his bed tonight. He'd been trying hard not to scare her away, and moving too fast would be the worst possible thing he could do.

He wanted her around for the long-term. Not sure of his own true feelings, he nevertheless knew he needed her in his life. She had become the very best part of his world.

So as badly as he wanted to be inside her, to feel her

surrounding him, he vowed once more that it would not happen tonight. He blocked his own needs and dedicated tonight to giving her pleasure. Allowing himself the supreme satisfaction of watching her come apart in his arms.

Sifting his hand through tight intimate curls, he parted her and stroked across the sensitive bud at her core. She moaned as he slid a finger inside. Finding only more heat and wetness, he added another finger and pushed deeper.

Merri shuddered and he felt her go weak in the knees. Bracing himself against the wall, he dropped an arm around her waist and held tight. Her head fell back and she closed her eyes, mumbling incoherently.

Ignoring his own throbbing desire, Ty's fingers stroked in and out of her heat. Watching the joy drift across her face, he saw the tension building inside her. It was growing in his groin as well, but he bit it back and concentrated on her.

Merri's small cries turned low and feral as she climbed the wall to her summit. Deep, pleading moans seemed to come from some spot buried so far inside her that she was totally unaware of their existence.

She was beyond beautiful in her erotic fog. He bent and licked a path across her jaw that ended in a taste of her lips. He wanted to taste all of her. Every inch. But it would have to wait.

When he pulled back to gaze down at her face again, he realized she was fighting it. Trying hard not to fall off the cliff without him.

He tightened his hold and once again teased her nub with his forefinger. "Come for me, Merri," he murmured. The need in his own voice surprised him but he didn't stop.

"You need to let go, darlin'," he rasped. "Open your eyes. Look at me. Let me watch you going over." His voice was a strangled whisper.

Her eyes opened to meet his gaze and with a last twist of her body, he felt her internal muscles begin to flex.

"Ty," she cried.

With her body sucking at his fingers, Merri whimpered and clung to his shoulders. Over and over she climaxed, making him all too aware that he was not going with her this time. But if he had his way, he would be. Soon.

Breathing heavily, Merri finally sagged against him. "I can't believe we just did that in an elevator."

"I can," he murmured as he slowly released her dress and let it slide back into place. "At last I caught a glimpse of the real you. The you that you keep hidden from the world." He made sure she was steady on her feet.

Her chin came up and she narrowed unfocused eyes at him. "What do you mean?" Ty spotted an emotion that looked like fear, before she hid it again.

He found himself almost chuckling at the sight of her kiss-swollen lips all turned up in a frown. She simply had to be the most exquisite creature he had ever beheld.

Before he answered her, he punched the "door open" button and swept her up off of her feet and into his arms.

"There is a sensual temptress inside you, darlin'. I don't know what's with the prim outfits. But underneath it all, you sizzle hotter than any fire. I dreamed that about you. Now I know for sure."

The adorable scowl that crossed her face struck him as sexy as he reached into his pocket for his key card to unlock the door to the suite.

Once across the threshold, he gently set her back down and locked the door behind them. "Thanks for the nice evening, sugar. Better get some rest. We'll be leaving early." He refused to leave her side just yet, though.

Merri didn't move, but tilted her head and gazed at him with questions in her eyes. "Ty? You didn't…" Stumbling over the words, she tried a different tactic. "Back there. I…uh…and you didn't…uh. Don't you want to?"

He took her hands into his own. "Yes, I want to," he muttered. "More than you can imagine. Desperate might be a more fitting word, as a matter of fact. But not tonight."

"Why not?" She licked her lips and drove him to an edge.

"Don't look at me that way or I might not be able to keep my head. We both need to think about this before we just fall into bed." He released her hands so he could run a thumb over her cheek.

"I don't want to keep my head," she groaned. "I just want you in my bed. Tonight."

"Merri, darlin'." He kissed her and ran his hands over her body to let her know how much he wanted that, too.

When he covered her upturned breasts with his palms, she made an urgent little sound against his lips and reached out to lay a hand over his groin. He groaned, and with a supreme effort, gently moved her hand away.

He shook his head. "Nope." Hearing the wheeze in his voice and feeling the shaky end to his reserve coming close to the surface, Ty stumbled away from her. "I want more than a single night."

"I can't say that will definitely happen," she groaned. "What's so wrong with just tonight?" She looked forlorn, and he thought he must have finally gone over the edge of sanity. What kind of fool would walk away from her?

"You don't trust me yet." He couldn't believe that he was saying these things.

"Trust you?" she laughed wryly. "After what we just did in a public elevator?"

He fisted his hands by his sides and blew out a deep breath. "There will be other nights. I want a whole future full of nights." God. Did he just say that? Was that the way he really felt?

She looked confused and hurt. He didn't want that, but he didn't know how to make it any better at the moment. Two-way trust was the most important thing in his life.

"I don't know what to say, Ty. I don't think…"

"Shush, sugar," he said with a forced grin. "Don't say anything. Let's grab some sleep and we'll talk more about it when we get home."

With those words, he turned his back on her lovely face and stormed off to his bedroom to spend what was sure to be the most depressing night of his entire lifetime.

Merri had been impatiently waiting for their talk—and another chance to touch him—for several days now.

Before they'd even arrived back at home the morning after the ball, Ty had received a phone call from the office of the President of the United States. It seemed the president wanted Ty to join a couple of other oil men at a private conference being held with a cartel in South America. Ty knew all the men and the difficult trade concepts involved and he spoke fluent Spanish. His country needed him there.

But Merri needed him with her, too. Leaning back in the computer chair, she sipped her tea and debated with herself what she'd wanted to happen between them.

Thoughts of the night of the ball danced through her mind, stirring images and emotions to the surface the same way she'd just stirred sugar into her tea. Swirling memories of Ty as he'd been touching her body, breathing warm tingling air against her skin and whispering intimate words about a future between them that could never be.

The sensual thoughts made her breasts tender and achy while warm sensations ranged low in her belly. She was lost. Maybe she had been lost from the very first day she'd met him.

Sighing, she let her shoulders drop and slumped down in the chair. She was falling in love with him.

Merri knew that if he wanted her, she would give him her body. Happily. Gladly. Eagerly.

But she needed to tell him the truth or they could never have any future. Though, the truth would likely destroy anything just beginning between them.

Hell. She couldn't do it. Not yet. Not until she was more sure of his feelings. Not before she had the chance to feel his mouth and hands on her once again.

Now wasn't *that* a really spoiled and selfish desire, she thought with chagrin. And totally opposite the reality she'd once thought she craved. Love the man, but lie to him?

It made her feel only slightly less selfish, knowing that she had turned out to be good at running his foundation while he was gone. But that was merely a small bit of sincerity that she could give to him in her new reality.

He'd called every morning to check on her progress with both the modeling show and the barbeque that they had planned as a thank-you for the Foundation's biggest donors. Their conversations weren't the intimate, private ones she had wished for, but hearing his voice made her days go faster.

The two events would be held only a few days apart. But it wouldn't be a problem because several of the garden club ladies had offered their help with both.

Now, if she could just keep her mind on her work...

The office door swung wide, letting in bright sunlight and a whirlwind who was dressed in resplendent fuchsia. "My goodness but it's hot out there. This has been some spring." Jewel marched into the room with her arms full of notebooks, brimming over with reminders and lists.

"I thought I was the only one bothered by the heat."

"Hardly, sugar," Jewel said with a laugh. She set her bundles down and fanned herself, using both hands. "I brought samples of tablecloths suitable for use at the barbeque. Do you have an accurate count of RSVP's yet?"

"Oh, yes. All these donors are busy executives and they stick to tight schedules. But they also all like Ty and want to see him and meet the kids." Merri reached for a book of tablecloth samples. "There'll be forty guests. Most of them will be flying in that morning and flying right back out that evening after the barbeque."

"Very well," Jewel said absently. "After they're gone we'll get more of your attention on the modeling show."

The guests for the barbeque and the garden club's luncheon would be completely different.

"Everything is coming along just fine for the modeling show," Merri told her. "Janie is ready to provide the outfits as soon as we send her the rest of the measurements, and I've already written much of the narration for the show. The garden club members are doing the publicity and working on the luncheon. We're on schedule."

Jewel sniffed. "Yes, well, a few ladies are upset that you haven't made last-minute decisions on the models. We've given you the lists of those willing to participate and everyone is waiting, none too patiently, for your final roster."

"Uh… I've been thinking it might be nice to have some of the girls from the Nuevo Dias Ranch participate. They have so little to look forward to. What do you think?"

Jewel's face softened into the most blissful expression Merri had ever seen. "Wonderful idea. That really is the kindest thing I've ever heard." Her eyes welled up, but she scrunched up her face and fought back any wayward tears. "Those girls don't have mothers to travel down the runway with them. Won't they be too nervous to model alone?"

"I thought maybe you would find a few local women who don't have daughters that would be available to help," Merri told her softly. "And I'd be willing to be a substitute mom for a couple of the girls myself." She couldn't bear the idea of those sweet kids being disappointed.

"Oh, yes, that should work." Jewel touched her hand lightly. "You are such a dear. No wonder Ty thinks you're so different."

Before she explained that strange remark, Jewel straightened and opened a notebook. "We need to complete the food orders for the barbeque and arrange to have the tables taken out of storage. This party should be a snap since it's just forty people and we'll have Ty's ranch hands helping out."

Merri wanted to go back to the subject of why Ty thought she was different, but she just smiled at the older woman's words about the barbeque instead. It had been positively amazing to find out what a huge operation Ty's ranch really was. As much as he said he wanted to do everything for himself, there were apparently a lot of duties that needed to be done by others.

She only wished he would take care of one very special duty himself. And soon.

"Hey, darlin'. You weren't asleep, were you?" Merri heard Ty ask through the earpiece of her home phone. He'd been gone for ten days and this was the first time he had called her at home.

"No, not yet." The truth was she hadn't been sleeping much at all lately. She would lie here in bed and think of having his lips against hers and his mouth on other tender parts of her body. And it would drive her to sleepless distraction.

"Where are you this time?" she asked wearily. So far he had traveled the globe, conducting further quiet talks with oil drillers, ministers and barons.

"In the far east," he answered with a bone-deep exhaustion that worried her.

"Are you coming home soon?" She didn't like the whiny, nagging tone she heard coming out of her mouth. But she was feeling an acute sense of loneliness without him.

"I just found out I won't be able to get back to the States tomorrow like I thought I would. In fact, I'm going to be lucky to get back by the day of the barbeque. Will you be able to handle things without me?"

Her body's hopes faded and the heat that had been growing deep in her belly began to cool. "Yes, of course," she said despondently. "I dropped by your ranch yesterday to check on the preparations. Everything is progressing nicely. You have an amazing place, by the way."

She sensed him hesitate for a minute before he said, "Thanks, but I wanted to show you the ranch myself. I…"

"It's okay," she interrupted. "I was only inside your office for a few minutes and then out onto the terrace where the party will be held. You can show me everything else when you get back." She hoped he'd meant he wanted to show her the master bedroom. That was all she'd been able to think about lately. Being in his bed.

"Do you miss me, Merri?" His voice was so deep and quiet that she barely heard the question. He sounded lonely, too, and it made her heart stutter wildly in her chest.

"I do," she said in a hoarse voice. She cleared her throat and tried to find something else to talk about… something to take their minds off the distance and time between them. "Uh…when I was in your office, I saw a strange old hand mirror on the edge of your desk. It didn't look like it belonged there. Do you collect antiques?"

"No," he said with a chuckle. "Not hardly. I got that mirror from a weird gypsy while I was in New Orleans. She said it was magic." With those words, he barked out a laugh but didn't sound terribly happy.

Magic? She thought she'd felt something strange about that mirror. When she'd picked it up, it had shimmered in her hand. She had felt a tension and an electric jolt run through her body when she turned it over and studied it. But magic?

"I don't get the magic idea," Ty told her. "It isn't even a real mirror. Just plain glass."

"Of course it's a mirror," she said in a rush. "The reflection was wavy, like the glass was very old. But I saw my image just fine."

Ty was quiet a long time. It made her wonder what he was thinking, but before she could ask, he changed the subject again himself. "Jewel tells me she had a plumber and an electrician out to your cottage, but that you wouldn't let her send a roofer. You like water in your kitchen, do you?"

"The roof hasn't leaked since you fixed it that night." The mention of that night caused goose bumps to run up her arms and the energy to settle back in her gut.

"Good." She heard the slow sensual smile spreading out in his voice. "I'll do it proper when I get back."

There were a few other things she'd rather he do proper first. Mostly having to do with her body. But she didn't want to upset him by begging—not just yet. And she also didn't want him to hang up. So she thought of another topic.

"Speaking of Jewel," Merri began. "The other day she said something strange. She said you thought I was different. What did she mean by that?"

"Merri." He'd said her name like a whispered prayer, then breathed a heavy sigh. "It might not be smart for us to talk about how we feel toward each other while we're still thousands of miles apart." His voice held a sensual quality that she barely recognized—except in her dreams.

Her body responded instantly to the erotic sensation. She leaned back against the pillows and closed her eyes, but found she couldn't make a sound.

"Dang," he said softly. "All right. You're different because you aren't like any of the other women I've ever known—and especially not like the woman I was once engaged to marry. You're very special, darlin'."

She'd heard the pain behind what he'd said. But she also heard the desire. It hummed through her veins and set her skin on fire. Her whole body began to ache.

He wanted her. And, oh Lord, how she wanted him.

Nine

"**T**ell me what happened to your engagement," Merri murmured hesitantly through the phone lines. "Make me understand how she hurt you so badly."

Ty heard Merri's hesitant tone, heard her need to be closer hiding beneath that. His own body had been ripe with desire for her since the first moment he'd heard her sexy voice tonight. Now it sounded as if she felt the same.

He'd known it had been a mistake to call while she was at home. Even thousands of miles and continents away, his body was in a constant hazy state of readiness over just the memory of her. He should've never tried this while it was quiet and still where he was, and even darker and more sensual surrounding her.

The pictures in his head of her in bed, all sleep-tousled and wearing some little scrap of silk for a nightgown, suddenly became too strong. They threatened to shred through every bit of his control.

He sat down on his hotel room bed and toed off his boots. Maybe it was time to trust someone else with his hateful memories. He couldn't think of anyone he wanted to trust more than he did Merri. And maybe the talking would take his mind off of what she was wearing at the moment.

"It's not much of a story," he began. "You sure?"

"Yes, Ty. I'm sure. I want to know you better."

He reached over and flipped off the bedside lamp, leaving himself in rich darkness. "Right." He wanted to know her a whole lot better, too. But he guessed he was honor bound to be the first one to spill his guts.

"When I was in college…and a lot younger and more foolish, I thought I was in love with one of the university's beauty queens," he said through the anonymity of long distance. "The two of us didn't have a whole lot in common, she'd come from a big city in the northeast. But it was a real turn-on to think such a gorgeous creature would want me. I was just a doofus from Hicksville. But I had already managed to rehab my way to my first million in real estate and thought I was so smart…

"It never occurred to me that it was the money she wanted." He decided to rush through the rest of this embarrassing story before he lost his nerve entirely. "Long story short, I asked her to marry me and a month later caught her in bed with one of her old 'friends.' Unfortunately, before they knew I was there, I heard her telling him about what a redneck I was and how if it wasn't for the money, she wouldn't be able to stand being married to such an ignorant cowboy."

The sound of Merri's soft gasp rode along his nerve endings and stirred his blood. He had to gulp down the sudden lust as he leaned back against the headboard.

"I'm so sorry you had to find out that way," Merri told him with honest sympathy. "But she was obviously not worth your spit. Don't give the memories any more of your time or attention. She doesn't deserve it."

"Not worth my spit?" he mimicked with a snort. "Lady, you are starting to sound just like one of us. I'm not sure that's such a good thing."

The high tingling notes of her soft laughter caught him off guard. Mercy, but he was hungry for her. Now. Right now, he needed her more than anyone before.

"Merri, what are you wearing?" The wayward thought popped out of his mouth.

"Me? I was in bed reading when you called so I have on the oversized T-shirt that I usually wear to sleep. It's really old and droopy, you wouldn't…"

"I'd love to see you in it," he interrupted a little too sharply. He lowered his voice to a whisper and tried again. "Is it so old that it's been washed soft?"

"Ty," she sighed. "I wish you were here."

"Me, too, sugar." He took a deep breath and unbuttoned his shirt. "Just keep talking. I need to hear your voice. You're still in bed, aren't you?"

"Are we going to have phone sex?" she asked in a small unsure tone. "I…I've never done that before. I don't think I can manage it." She sounded right on the edge and he figured he was pretty close himself.

"Relax, darlin'. You don't have to do anything. You trust me, don't you?"

"Definitely." The word just jumped out of his earpiece and made him smile. He wouldn't tell her, but he had never done anything remotely like this before, either.

"Merri, do you remember the last night we were together? How I held you close in my arms?"

"Uh-huh."

"Good. Close your eyes then and try to imagine my arms around you now. Can you feel me next to you?"

"Mmm." The little mewing sound hit him dead in the chest with a lust too strong to ignore. He vowed to somehow make this good for both of them.

"Darlin', you are going to have to breathe out loud for me so I can judge how you're doing. Okay?"

"Yes," she said with a wispy sigh. "Uh, Ty, how will I…?"

"Hush, sweetheart. Just listen to the sound of my voice and breathe." He shrugged out of his shirt and unbuttoned the top button on his jeans, positive now it was going to get a hell of a lot hotter in this room at any moment. And wondering if this was a smart idea—or perhaps the dumbest thing he had ever attempted.

"Eyes still closed?"

Merri nodded, realizing too late that he couldn't really see her through the phone. "Uh-huh."

"Picture how it was between us. Feel the heat growing stronger, starting to burn your skin from the inside out."

"Ty, how do you know how I felt? How do you…?"

"Shh, honey. I was there with you, remember? I felt

everything you did. I pulsed when you did and shattered right along beside you."

And he hadn't forgotten one minute of it, either, Merri thought happily. She snuggled down under the covers and listened to him breathing on the other end of the phone.

"All right, darlin'," he began again.

He spoke in a terrifically hushed voice, low and slightly dangerous. And she was taken right back to that night with a flash of fire and wanting.

"Put your fingertips against your lips and think of my kisses," Ty whispered. "Can you feel the need that's pouring from my body into yours through our tangled tongues?"

Merri rubbed the pad of her forefinger across her bottom lip and felt a stirring in her breasts, and lower in her belly. She slipped her finger into her mouth, licked and sucked like she'd done while his tongue was inside her, imagining Ty's kisses.

Her breasts suddenly became tender and achy, crying out for Ty's touch. "Oh," she whimpered. "Oh."

"Yeah, I feel it, too, sweetheart. Keep remembering the way it was. Use your fingers, but imagine they are mine. I want to touch you so badly." She heard him blow out a deep breath and the blood gushed to several parts of her body.

"I want to lick my way down your neck and cover your breasts with the palms of my hand."

"Ty, I feel the heat of your hands on me. It isn't possible." She squirmed and realized her own palm had covered her aching nipple.

"Don't think," he urged. "Just listen and feel. I'm

going to take the hardened tip of your breast into my mouth. I need to. I want you to feel the warmth of my tongue as I flick it over your bud. Is the hot, wet sensation giving you pleasure, darlin'?"

She gasped as a sudden erotic jolt pulsed right through her, traveling from her nipple to the spot between her thighs that was beginning to throb.

Ty chuckled, the noise rumbling deep in his chest. She could almost feel the vibrations running over her skin.

"I have to taste more of you this time," Ty rasped. "I want more than I took before. I want everything."

Merri sighed, too loudly. But it didn't seem to bother Ty on the other end of the phone.

"Mmm," he groaned. "I love the way your skin tastes as I nibble my way across your body. Vanilla and lavender, like cookies in the spring.

"Farther down," he drawled. "Rubbing lazy circles around your belly button with my tongue. Teasing the tender skin between there and my goal."

The images of what they'd done in the elevator disappeared from her mind. And all Merri was left with was the pounding beat of her heart as she truthfully felt his tongue slipping down her body.

Moans filled the phone lines, but she couldn't distinguish hers from his. It didn't matter. Nothing mattered but the sound of his voice and the sensation of her pulse skittering across the edges of her skin. Moving lower.

"I have to touch you," Ty begged. "You're so wet, so hot for me. Mmm. I need to taste all that heat. I want to put the tip of my tongue on the sensitive place that's beating just for me.

"I know how you taste, love," he continued softly. "I've dreamed it a hundred times."

"Oh," Merri panted. Somehow the sound of her voice sounded frantic, too high-pitched and needy to be her own.

"I...I..." She'd stopped thinking and wanted to beg. "Come inside me, Ty. Please. Please. Please. I need to feel you there."

"Yes," he gasped. "It's time. You're wet and ready for me."

She was—more than ready.

But she was also holding her breath...waiting.

"Breathe, sugar. Let me hear how you sound as I slip inside."

"Oh...Oh..." She was about to black out but refused to miss any part of this. Her whole body was throbbing, pulsating with need, soaring to places she had never been.

"Ah. So tight," he groaned. "The fit is perfect...the way I knew it would be. Oh, God. You're so good. So right. Stay with me, love."

The next few minutes turned into a blur of moans and gasps from two sides of the world as his voice took her to the brink over and over again. At long last, the sharp edge of her desire began to crack as if it were a shattered mirror that had started the break with one fine line and spread out from there into a cobweb of a thousand glittering shards.

Afterward, Merri lay back on her bed and tried to catch her breath. Suddenly, something seemed very wrong. This was the time when she needed Ty's arms to hold her close, to cuddle her up and softly stroke her hair.

But he wasn't here. She was all alone and beginning to feel cold and ridiculous. How could she have let her hard-won reality slip away like that and do something so much like fiction?

"Ty?" she breathed into the phone.

"Right here, darlin'. You okay?" His voice sounded rough and she took a small solace in knowing that he was not unaffected by what they'd done.

"Not really," she admitted. "Ty?"

"Yes, love. I'm still here."

"Come home."

The low chuckle she heard coming through her phone from faraway places was stark and bordered on bleak. "Oh, yeah," he growled. "My sentiments exactly."

Ty was edgy and grouchy when he finally made it back to Texas a few days later. Frustrated by not being able to resolve any of the oil trade issues he'd been sent to negotiate, he was beyond frustration whenever his thoughts turned to Merri. Which was more or less constantly.

Ever since the night they'd spent hours on the phone, he hadn't been able to bring himself to talk to her at all. He knew the sound of her voice would just seep inside him, turning the continual hum of his desire into an immediate drumbeat of desperate arousal. He wouldn't have been able to handle *that* across the distances separating them.

Throwing his dirty laundry into a heap on the utility room floor, Ty gulped down his growing hunger to see Merri and headed for the shower. He'd actually managed to tie things up a day early so he could come home for her, and he wasn't about to ruin their reunion by being a smelly pig.

But standing in the shower, with the water beating down on him like a million tiny fingertips stroking and caressing his body, was too difficult. He found himself growing hard and panting, so he immediately toweled off and got dressed.

Not another minute. Ty couldn't stand it until he held the real woman and not the dream in his arms.

A few minutes later he barged into the Foundation office and let the door slam shut behind him. "Merri?"

She didn't answer and he felt a stab of raw nerves from not enough sleep. Within three seconds, he determined that she wasn't at the office, and a low irritation began to settle over him. Where the hell was she?

Ty picked up the phone and cursed under his breath. Why hadn't he insisted that she let him get her a cell phone? He hated not knowing where she was—or if she needed him.

He dialed her house but gave up after twenty-four fruitless rings. Next he called Jewel, who answered on the second ring.

"Where the hell is she?" he growled at his dumbfounded aunt.

"Hello to you, too, Tyson," Jewel said with a sniff. "Welcome home. Now, when are you leaving again so the real Tyson can come back?"

He huffed out a breath and scowled, but Jewel had managed to stick a pin in his anger. "Sorry. I'm just tired…and I really need to talk to Merri. Do you know where she is?" He had to see her and the splitting shaft of panic when he couldn't find her had left him shaken.

"I take it you've been to your ranch. If she's not out there getting ready for tomorrow's barbeque, she'll be at Nuevo Dias Ranch working with the kids. Try there." Jewel stopped talking for a second and he wondered if she was going to hang up on him.

"And try to calm down before you see her, son," Jewel said in a softer tone. "She has seemed a little vulnerable to me over the last few days. I'm worried about her."

Vulnerable? His Merri? Not a chance in the world.

The woman he knew and was beginning to love was strong and true and...

Love?

The word tumbled over his heart and niggled its way to his brain.

He told his aunt goodbye and then began going over his own thoughts from the last few days. Ty realized that he'd actually begun to think of the future. A future that included kids and pets and houses that were never empty when you came home.

A future that centered around Merri.

He waited for the spurt of panic to drive up his spine, but it didn't happen. Why wasn't he afraid this time?

The answer came in a dawning sense of golden glory. He wasn't afraid because he trusted Merri not to hurt him. Drawing a deep, cleansing breath, he actually smiled.

For the first time in his memory, he'd found a woman who could be perfectly truthful and trustworthy. That frustratingly wonderful time on the telephone the other night had proven it to him. How many others would open themselves up like that and let every raw emotion hang out for another person to see—or hear.

He'd turned over his soul to her on the telephone that night and she'd given him back her own. She was brilliant and kind, beautiful and so very real. And he wanted her for his own…for forever.

And right this minute, if he couldn't put his hands on her, he was going to spontaneously combust.

With his thoughts a jumble of hopes and promises, Ty jumped back in his truck and headed for the children's ranch. He wanted to tell Merri how he felt. But first…first he had to actually touch her and feel the beating of her heart under his palm. He was tired of dreaming…and needed…and needed…the real thing.

When he arrived at the Nuevo Dias Ranch, he whisked past a couple of members of the staff and brashly insisted they direct him to Merri. One of the administrators sent him outside to the playground and told him she was working with some of the younger girls.

He didn't care what she was doing now. Only what she would be doing later, when he finally had her alone in his arms. He couldn't concentrate, couldn't think of anything but her.

Slamming the back door and rounding the corner of the building, Ty was nearly running by the time he got to the playground. But when he caught his first sight of her, he froze in his own footsteps.

The sun was high in the sky and painted the background an astonishing shade of cobalt blue. His breath caught in his throat.

Merri was standing there, letting the warm yellow sunshine wash over her, and she looked like an angel. Her hair was pulled back in a smooth ponytail and positively glowed. It seemed a lot blonder this afternoon than he remembered. Maybe it was bleaching out from the sun.

Her face was slightly flushed as if she'd just been kissed senseless. And her green eyes gleamed and twinkled and simply dared her bright blouse to compete for attention.

Dressed in soft jeans and a Kelly green sleeveless top, Merri laughed at two of the little girls who danced around her. Ty's insides turned to mush. He wanted her so badly he could barely breathe.

She was the most gorgeous creature that had ever been put on this earth. Why hadn't that fact managed to sink into his thick skull before now? It didn't matter how she was dressed, the woman was a positive stunner.

Speechless, he stumbled toward her. Merri, Merri, his brain kept repeating. Be mine, Merri. Want me the way I want you.

Somehow, she must have heard his silent prayer, because she suddenly turned to him. "Ty," she mouthed from a distance. "You're finally home."

Holding his breath, he reached out a hand in invitation. "Come with me," he mouthed back.

After a second's hesitation, her eyes lit with a sexy gleam and then she smiled at him. She held up one finger to let him know she would only be a moment, then she turned to talk to the girls around her.

Ty felt as though his chest would burst. He stood quietly watching and waiting as the anticipation rumbled through him.

After what seemed like an eternity, Merri said her goodbyes and headed in his direction. Every step brought his dreams closer to reality.

"Hi, Ty," she said almost shyly when she got close enough to hear.

He couldn't stand it. Reaching out for her, he dragged her to his chest and encircled her in his embrace. Ah. The warmth of her body felt so welcoming. So right.

Not able to wait another minute for a more private reunion, he brought his mouth down on hers and feasted on the honey that was all Merri. He poured everything he'd been feeling into the kiss, telling her without words how much he needed her.

She melted into him and gave back every passion he had been dreaming about. Then she lifted her head.

"It's a little public out here," she laughed. "Can't this wait until tonight? I'll make you dinner…"

He took her hand and headed off toward the truck, dragging her behind him. "Now," he growled over his shoulder. "We're going home…right now."

Ten

"**D**o you really know how to cook?" Ty asked as they sped down the back roads, heading for her cottage.

"I've been practicing making eggs and boiling water," Merri told him with a wry smile. "Maybe you could call that cooking."

Grinning, Ty kept one hand on the steering wheel and took her hand with his other. "You can cook me, darlin'. That's all we need for the time being."

He kept one eye on the road ahead and lifted her hand to his mouth. A whisper of his breath across her palm had her wet and ready long before he placed the gentle kiss against her skin. The hungry sound he made seemed to suggest that her hand was the best thing he'd ever tasted.

The flat of his tongue snaked out as he licked a wide

path across her palm—slowly, erotically. The sensation shoved through her—beginning right there, racing up to her breasts and finally bouncing down between her thighs.

She could no more hold in the gasp that escaped her lips than she could've moved away from him. Paralyzed with need, she blinked her eyes and tried to remember how to breathe.

"Shoot," Ty muttered as they jostled over a bump in the road that he hadn't seen coming. He dropped her hand and left it lying across his thigh so he could hold the steering wheel with both hands.

The bump intensified the sizzle between her legs and had her squirming in her seat. "I'd like to get home in one piece, please," she gritted out. "And I'd like to do it—soon."

He managed a rather self-deprecating grin, pressed his lips together in a determined scowl and drove on like a race-car driver. An electric hum of arousal filled the truck's cab with the silent music of profound desire.

This didn't seem real, this desperate hunger she was feeling. But she'd been blindsided by the obvious need in his eyes when he'd first spotted her out on the playground. The man was driven wild by lust for her and the very thought had turned her on with such a frantic lust she was stunned by it.

No one...not once...had ever needed her that way before. It was thrilling...intoxicating...tempting beyond all reason.

Reason...

Merri pulled her hand away from the stretched

denim that covered his thigh and crossed her arms under her breasts. She needed to think…to plan…to be reasonable.

Yes, she wanted him—was desperate for his body to salve her aching needs. But it wasn't right, not when he didn't know who she was. Their realities were out of sync and if she gave in to her lust again it would no doubt ruin any chance of their being together for the long haul.

Tell him the truth. Janie's warning, sounding loudly in her brain, agreed with her own common sense. Both internal voices vied for her attention. But it was hard to think while Ty's breathing had become so shallow and ragged in the seat beside her.

The truck flew down her gravel drive and Ty jerked it to a stop by her front door. Without a word, he slammed his driver's door and stalked around to her side. Pulling open her door before she had a chance to do it herself, Ty didn't waste a minute reaching for her.

"Merri." He dragged her from the truck and hauled her up to his chest. "I've dreamed of this…of you. I'm sorry, I…"

He caught her mouth in a crushing kiss. Feeling his hunger, Merri wrapped her arms around his neck and melted into him.

One kiss, she thought. What would one kiss hurt?

She knew what it could hurt. Knew it was wrong to lead him on, but she simply couldn't stop him just yet. Not while his tongue plunged so invitingly inside her mouth. In and out, the rhythm of his kiss left her breathless, achy and light-headed.

His hands swept up her back, glided over her tender

breasts and made the nipples harden, while the rest of her flesh went all soft. The exquisite sensitivity moved lower along her spine, heading to the tenderest of spots.

The faraway moan she heard must've been her own because Ty jolted like he'd been shot. She felt him long, hard and throbbing right through the material of both their jeans.

Cupping her bottom with both hands, he pressed her belly tighter against his erection as the heat blazed through their bodies. Wildfire erupted in her veins; sparking, singeing, searing.

All reason and resolve burnt to a crisp and the ashes blew away in the flaming conflagration. As if they had a mind of their own, her hips repositioned themselves so that she could touch him to her center, to the pulsing desperation at her core.

"Key," he gasped.

It took her a second before she understood. But he scooped her in his arms and was flying toward the front door before she could dig in her purse. She held on to him, not wanting this to end but vaguely remembering that it should.

In a whirlwind of hands, groans and kisses, Ty dumped out her purse, found the key and had her inside the cottage and half undressed before she could take another breath. He seduced her mouth with his tongue, backing her down the short hall to the bedroom.

"Taste you," he moaned between kisses. "I want to taste…"

Merri tumbled backwards onto the bed as she continued her inner struggle. She should… She shouldn't…

With two quick tugs, Ty dragged her top over her head then pulled her jeans down and off her legs. She lay back on the bed in her skimpy white teddy and stared up at him.

"Dang." He shook his head in amazement. "I wondered what that contraption would look like on you. I like it."

He stripped off his own shirt and kicked off his boots. "But I'll look later. Take it off. I want…" He reached out and slid the straps down her arms to speed up the process. "I have to see you."

The look in his eyes drugged her with an urgent warning. His passion had become irresistible.

Reality suddenly broke apart, leaving her in a fraudulent fog of dreams. Dreams of what he could do to her with just a slight touch—or the simple sound of his voice. The sensual images took over her everyday world.

Merri shimmied out of the one-piece garment and let it glide to the floor. She was naked in her need, lying before him now and it almost slapped her out of the erotic trance.

Almost. Ty's eyes darkened, his jaw set and his nostrils flared. His obvious pounding lust was the biggest turn-on in her life.

Her nipples tightened unbearably and stretched up, begging for his touch. "One of us has too much on," she squeaked as she held out her arms to him.

"Oh, sweet mercy," Ty groaned. He dug in his pants' pocket for the foil packets he'd put there earlier and tried breathing through his mouth to stem the need.

It took two tries, but in sixty seconds the packets

were on her night table and his jeans were flung into a corner. He loomed above her, silently praying for enough strength to make this good for her.

"A taste," he mumbled. "Just let me…"

He bent, meaning to lightly brush her lips with his own so he could build the tension inside her to a slow burn. But the tension between them was too hot. She dug her fingernails into his shoulders and pulled him down.

Rolling to the side, he let his hands range over her smooth skin, while his lips teased, lathed and nipped everything within reach. He tasted lavender on her shoulders and neck, vanilla as he drew a puckered nipple into his mouth. And finally, he tasted the salty musk that was all Merri as he allowed his tongue to roam down the crevices of her body.

Turning her flat on her back, he nudged her thighs open and fit himself in between. He felt hot and heavy and damn near gone as he maneuvered a hand between them. She was pooled and slick, a sexy invitation he couldn't resist.

Leaning over her, he used the fingers of one hand to roll and tug the bud of her breast until she cried out. His other hand feathered lightly across the wetness at her most sensitive area.

The pad of his finger opened her to his exploration. Until he found her tight little nub and flicked his thumb.

She jerked, her whole body arching up to his hand. He gazed down into her lust-filled face and saw a wanton, wild look in those green eyes that absolutely undid him.

"Damn it," he muttered. He sat up and grabbed for

a packet. "I meant for this to go on all night. I wanted to drive you totally insane first."

"Later," she said with a husky voice that mimicked his. "Look. Taste. Insanity. All later. I promise."

The honeyed sound of her voice traveled across his nerve endings and made his hands shake. He struggled with the foil and cursed as Merri reached out.

"Let me," she soothed. Using one finger, she traced a line up his length and absently licked her lips.

Ty ripped the packet in two with his teeth and sheathed himself in an instant. Near explosion, he flipped her over on her stomach, raised her hips and flattened his palms against her groin.

"Mmm. Just like that," he said as he moved behind her.

Merri grasped the bedspread with both hands and held on as he began to pulse at her entrance. She went up on her knees as he tilted her hips, sliding inside easy and deep.

They both gasped with the pure pleasure of it—of finding the one place that felt like home. Ty began to run his hands over her body, fingertips to knees, as if he were a blind man and wanted to learn every inch.

He was driving her higher with his hands…wilder as his fingers glided along her skin. She ground her hips against his groin and took him deeper still. Ah.

Kissing the back of her neck, Ty began to rock. Slow and steady. He eased out so that only his tip teased against her.

"No…" she sobbed. Merri wanted hard and fast. Needed an ending to all this tension.

Ty only chuckled and eased back inside her. She pushed against him, tears of passion blurring her eyes.

"Tell me, darlin'. Tell me what you want," he whispered in her ear as he withdrew again.

Merri wanted to scream as he reached under her to roll, first one nipple and then the other, between his fingers. Then he tugged at each unmercifully.

She wasn't raised to ask for the things she wanted. Her mother's "kind" never spoke of sensual things... never said what would make them really happy. How could she manage it now when she hadn't even told him the truth?

His hand felt warm and wide as he ranged it low on her belly. He inched his fingers downward until he reached the tiny taut bud that needed his touch. The shock of it moved her at last to speak.

"There," she cried out. "Now, Ty. Please. Harder." For the very first time, she wanted another human being to share all her pleasure. And she was willing to ask for it.

He picked up the pace and their bodies came together over and over. She was so close she could scream. Desperate, Merri reached back and dug her fingers into his hardened thighs, begging without words until she felt him start to come undone inside her.

In the end, she did scream as the ripples of pleasure pulsed from him to her and then washed over them both with a red ocean of sensation. He gave his own low, raspy shout, wrapped her in his arms and rolled them together over on their sides without breaking the connection.

He spooned against her back and kissed her temple, holding her close as their pulses began to subside. She found herself crying, but didn't want him to know.

That was the most beautiful thing that had ever happened to her.

She wanted to keep him just here...right beside her for a lifetime full of beautiful times. But she knew it wasn't going to happen.

Oh, maybe she could keep him from finding out the truth tonight. But sooner or later she would have to tell him. She wanted him to hear it from her though, and not have to read about it in the papers, knowing that would mean the end of their beautiful nights forever.

A cold draft of reality wafted over her sweaty body, leaving her suddenly chilled and shaken. Then what would she do? Where was she to go—and how would she ever forget him?

Merri snuggled herself back up under his chin and stretched her body along the warm length of his. She felt him growing hard again inside her, and tried desperately to block out the future. For tonight...maybe for a few more nights...she would have what she'd always dreamed about.

Twenty hours later Merri once again stood in the bright sunshine, staring down into the gigantic barbeque pit that Ty's ranch hands had dug. She had heard the term "a whole side of beef" before, but had never known what that meant.

Now she did. Below her on a spit above the fire, the main course for this afternoon's barbeque was slowly rotating and turning dark brown.

Everything was ready for the guests, who should be arriving at any moment. Merri backed up a step, staying out of the smoke coming from the pit. She'd just finished taking a shower and dressing in her new western outfit for the barbeque and would rather not trade after-shower splash for the smell of mesquite smoke.

She was actually surprised that she could stand at all after the long night of lovemaking with Ty. Thinking back on it, she remembered how shaky her knees had been when Ty had dragged her into the shower in the middle of the night. A low purr of approval ran along her veins as the images came back to mess with her mind.

It had been the most wonderful night of her life. And she wanted more. A lifetime of more.

"You look happy," Jewel said from behind her. "Is it because everything's ready for the barbeque...or because Tyson got back in town last night?"

Was what she'd been feeling so obvious on her face? What had happened to all that great acting she'd thought she'd been doing?

Merri took a silent breath and turned to smile at Jewel. "Maybe a little of both."

Jewel nodded her head and winked. "I took notice of my nephew's expression when you came outside a minute ago. I'm guessing both of you are plenty glad he's finally home."

Merri automatically looked over Jewel's shoulder to find Ty. It seemed her eyes had the man on radar today, because with one quick glance she found him standing over by the barn talking to his attorney.

Ty just plain oozed masculine sexuality. In his navy long-sleeved designer shirt and fresh new jeans, he looked good enough to gobble whole. Mmm.

"You've certainly made a world of difference in

the way my nephew looks...and acts," Jewel said when she saw where Merri's gaze had gone. "I hope my instincts are right about you—that you're really serious about him and not just playacting to get a better job."

The question nearly doubled Merri over with panic, but she managed to tell Jewel a partial truth. "What I feel for Ty is very serious." *In fact, I love him more with every breath I take.* "And I don't want or need a better job. I like the one I have."

"I'm glad," Jewel said. "I love Tyson and I know he can be too intense sometimes. But since you've been here, those rough edges have smoothed over some. And..."

Jewel hesitated and Merri could see that she was considering how much to say. "Well, for the first time in my memory, the raw look that's always been there in his eyes is gone. That's your doing, honey. And I can't thank you enough for it."

The pain? Yes, Merri remembered that there was a kind of hidden pain in his eyes when they'd first met.

"If you don't mind answering a too-personal question, what caused that raw look?" she questioned Jewel. "He's told me of the awful breakup with his fiancée in college. But there's something more, isn't there?"

The other woman crossed her arms under her breasts and her expression turned sober. "He's never been willing to talk about it. But I've always guessed it comes from when his parents were killed in that accident when he was five.

"Tyson had never spent any time away from his mother before then. When my sister left him with me, he cried and cried. She promised him she would be back before dark…"

"But she never made it?" Merri guessed.

Jewel sniffed. "That night and the months that followed were probably the worst of my lifetime, and I know they must've changed Tyson forever. All he kept screaming was, 'But Mommy promised me. And she *never* tells lies.'"

Jewel's voice hitched but she continued. "From then on, I don't recall ever knowing him to believe someone at face value. Not even that Diane person who hurt him so badly in college. If he'd really thought she was being truthful with him back then, he never would've snuck in and caught her with another man."

Merri swiped at her face, holding back the unshed tears welling in her eyes. She ached for the little boy—physically hurt—knowing the pain that the man she loved must have endured.

She turned her face, trying to locate him again over Jewel's shoulder. The connection between them had obviously grown magnetic because at that very moment he looked up to find her, too. Their gazes met across the expanse of barnyard, locked together and held steady.

I will never be able to live with myself if I hurt you like that, my love. Merri decided then that she had to tell him—and soon. She'd been entirely too selfish, letting him believe in her lies.

She vowed to tell him—tell him everything—before they made love again. As hard as it might be for her, it was time to back away before her lies destroyed him. And left *her* with no reason to live.

* * *

Ty felt Merri's gaze and knew even from this distance what she needed. He wanted her, too. But the *way* he wanted her would have to wait until they could be alone.

Still, the blunt power between them drew him in and made his body throb with arousal. He was sure that in an entire lifetime he would never be able to get enough of her.

"Steele? Where'd you go, bud?" Frank shook his shoulder but donned an easy smile as he said, "As if I couldn't guess." They were standing near the barn, waiting for other guests to join them.

Ty turned away from the distant sight of the woman he loved long enough to finish the conversation he'd begun with his attorney. "Isn't she something?" But he couldn't quite get his mind off Merri yet. "Just look at how fantastic she looks in that new denim skirt and top. Man…"

"Right," Frank said with a grin. "Uh. We were discussing the progress, or lack thereof, to our investigation into your magic gypsy in New Orleans."

Ty tried to focus. "Yeah. I don't understand why you can't get a line on her. Both my cousin Nick and I saw her on the same corner and I described her in great detail. She has to be working at tarot reading or something similar, and I'd bet her place of business would be near that corner."

Frank sighed. "The P.I. firm I hired has questioned every tarot reader and gypsy they could find in the entire Quarter. Giving them the name 'Chagari' helped. One of the tarot readers once knew of a woman known as Passionata Chagari. But nobody had seen her around town in years."

"Where did she last work? Someone must know where she's working now."

That brought a smile to Frank's lips. "Gypsies are… well…gypsies. They don't exactly leave forwarding addresses, you know."

Frustrated, Ty's mind and gaze went back to something much more pleasant. "Can you do me another favor?"

"Sure. Name it."

"I wanna promote Merri to be Chairman of the Foundation. I think she'd make a terrific public spokesman for the kids, don't you?"

"No question. She's really blossomed since she's been here. And she sure loves those kids. What can I do?"

"Call our publicist in Dallas," Ty directed. "Get her to send down those reporters she's always bugging me to be nice to. I want to surprise Merri with an announcement right after the mother-daughter modeling show tomorrow.

"She'll be all rigged out then, substituting as a mother for some of the Nuevo Dias Ranch girls," Ty continued with a grin. "Those news guys should be able to get great shots of her with the kids. It'll make a terrific PR story for the Foundation. Merri will be so pleased."

"Yeah…once she gets over the shock. I don't believe women like surprises."

"Just do it. Let *me* worry about Merri's reaction."

Eleven

Promises should never be broken. Especially promises that you've made to yourself, Merri decided.

But here she was two days after she had vowed to tell Ty the truth immediately, and she still couldn't find the way to say what she needed to say.

Every time she came close to telling him the truth, he would kiss her or take her in his arms and make her pulse jump. It was no good. When he was that close she couldn't think, let alone say the words that would send him away.

Sighing, Merri quickly finished dressing for the modeling show, which was to take place in a couple of hours. She slipped on the stiletto heels that were required for the first of her mother-daughter assignments.

She and little Rachel Garza would be dressed in

bright red party frocks as they walked down the runway this afternoon. The rest of her eight outfits would
be waiting for her in the ladies dressing room at the garden club's luncheon.

The Nuevo Dias girls were so excited. It would be
Merri's pleasure to let them show off in pretty dresses
for the first time in their lives. Still, she was beginning
to worry about dressing up and walking down the runway in a public place.

Merri checked her image in the full-length mirror
and didn't like what she saw. She looked way too much
like the Merrill Davis-Ross from her previous life. The
life she wished she could banish entirely from her reality.

"You decent in there, darlin'?" Ty's voice coming
from her front room surprised her.

"Yes, come in."

"Too bad. I was hoping you wouldn't be decent just
yet." He opened the bedroom door and slipped inside. "I
was wishing for a chance to make you late. You…" As he
first spotted her, he paused with his mouth hanging open.

She turned in a tight circle so he could approve the
dress. "Is it okay? Don't you like the color on me?"

"I…" He swallowed hard. "Give me a minute to get
my heart started again. That may just be the sexiest
dress I've ever seen. You sure you wanna wear that out
in public?"

A girlish giggle popped out of her mouth and caused
her to frown at her own stupidity. This was too complicated. She wanted him to like the way she looked,
wanted him to want her. But she didn't want him to like
the "old" look of Merrill Davis-Ross at all.

Damned confusing lies.

He cleared his throat and the sound made her lift her chin to check if he was all right. When she really focused on the man for the first time today, her own heart skipped a few beats.

The light gray Armani suit with the white silk shirt and maroon tie simply took her breath away. He was absolutely the most gorgeous man she had ever seen. This business-shark look was even sexier than the fancy tux from the governor's ball had been. *Whoa,* as Ty would say.

"Merri…sweetheart," Ty murmured as he took a few steps in her direction. "I have a couple of surprises planned for you today. All good—I hope. But now…"

"I'm not much for surprises. What…?"

He gently took her hand and the sensitive expression in his eyes surprised her into speechless wonder. "I was going to save this one for later when we could be alone, but seeing you in that dress made it seem a lot more urgent all of sudden. I feel like I've known you forever, somehow, and I want to nail this down before the show."

He sounded so ominous she panicked. "Uh…"

"You and I have a special bond, Merri Davis," he began, oblivious to her tension. "I've never felt this close or trusted anyone as much in my life. We think alike, you and I. You want to do everything for yourself just like I do. You value trust as much as I do. We'll be perfect together.

"Marry me," he urged. "Be my partner and my wife…the mother of my children."

She gasped and tried to drag her hand from his, but

couldn't manage to say a word. This was the dream that she was not allowed to have.

He held on to her hand and narrowed his eyes. "I don't like that look in your eyes, darlin'. And I really need to hear what you have to say. Tell me what you're thinking."

Oh, no. She couldn't stand seeing the hurt expression in his eyes when he discovered she had been lying all this time. And on top of that, she desperately wanted her one last opportunity to help the Nuevo Dias kids at the show this afternoon. Why did he have to ask now?

"Uh, Ty. We've only known each other for a few weeks. This is too soon."

He dragged her into his arms and kissed her furiously. It was beyond flash and heat. Beyond frantic and passionate. Ty was telling her through their bodies what was in his heart.

At last, he broke the kiss, took her by the shoulders, leaned back and let his needs shine through his eyes. "Tell me *that* is too soon," he demanded in a hoarse voice. "Tell me you don't feel the connection."

Her throat was closing. Tears threatened. And she could only manage to shake her head.

"You love me, I know you do," Ty gasped.

Through watery eyes she saw the tears welling in those deep blues of his too. "I…"

"Say it," he pleaded. "Say that you love me."

Past all the lies. Past every vow she had ever made and broken. Merri found that this one time, she could not bear to lie to him again.

"I love you," she mumbled miserably. "But…"

He crushed his mouth down on hers and moaned

deep within his chest. "That's all we need, sweetheart," he told her when he finally lifted his head. "You and I are a team. Love will take care of the rest."

"No." She pushed out of his arms and took a step back on shaky legs. "You need to know something about me. I have to tell…"

"Hush, darlin'. Whatever it is, it's from your past, and I don't care. All I care about is what's between us now. Nothing else matters."

He reached out and ran his thumb lightly under her eye to catch a wayward tear. "We can have a serious talk later, if it's so important to you. After the modeling show tonight. Okay?

"Right now, let's just get used to the fact that we love each other." He took her hand again. "And I do love you, Merri. You've crept into my soul. I want to share my bed and my life with you. I want to wake up every morning and see your familiar face."

Thank heaven. Damn it. Her relief at the idea of being able to put off the truth made her furious with herself.

Merri had become her mother, after all. No matter that she had fought to escape her fate. Or that she'd tried boldly to change her whole life. She had turned into Arlene Davis-Ross, a spoiled and selfish rich-witch who was greedily grabbing at a few more hours of being someone else. How could she have let this happen?

But it had, and she sighed, nodding her head. "All right. We'll put off our talk until after the show. But then…"

"Ah," Ty began with a smile. "Then—we'll spend the night in each other's arms, telling every secret in our hearts. It will be the first night of the rest of our lives."

The idea was so tempting…so compelling and wonderful that Merri almost lost her cool again. Almost let herself fall under the spell of his love.

What wouldn't she give to have a magic wand right now? If she had a magic wand, she would wave it over herself and become the person he thought she was. Erase the reality of her life and turn into the person that was worthy of his love. The person he saw through the eyes of love.

She sniffed and let him wrap her up in his embrace one last time. Too bad there was no real magic in the world.

Passionata Chagari swiped at her cheeks and cursed softly over her crystal ball. Was her father's gift to be wasted after all?

Was this brash young man going to rush headlong into a version of the truth and never discover the real magic? Would he throw away his once-in-a-lifetime chance for happiness?

Her crystal fogged over and the gypsy looked toward the heavens, trying to explain to her ancestor's spirit. "I cannot make him see the light, father. The time and distance is too far for me to interfere this time. I have tried to honor your legacy. I, too, owe a debt to Lucille Steele, and this young Steele *is* worthy of the gift.

"He is so close to his heart's desire. So close…and yet he continues to shun the magic. I can do no more than watch and hope. If he never looks in the mirror to see the truth of his own selfishness, all will be lost.

"If the problem is due to my bungling of the gift-giving, then I am truly sorry Forgive me…"

Standing outside the 4-H arena where the luncheon was to be held, Merri felt a stirring of cold wind against her skin and it gave her the chills. But when she looked up, the winds were calm and the heat of the afternoon sun bore down on all the females who were awaiting their turn to walk down the runway. Sweat was beginning to show across several feminine foreheads.

A sudden panic jolted across Merri's skin, raising the hairs on the back of her neck. Something was not right.

But when she gazed down into the smiling, happy faces of the girls from the ranch, she struggled to ignore the deepening sense of foreboding. Merri had made sure no photographers were on the guest lists, so it couldn't be the fear of being discovered that worried her.

Perhaps what she was experiencing was guilt about not telling Ty the truth. Her desperation to make time stand still so that tonight would never arrive must be making her paranoid.

"Ms. Davis, you sure look beautiful without your glasses," little Rachel told her as they waited in line for their turn. "You should be a real model. I bet you could be a big star in Paris or New York."

Her glasses? Oh, my gosh. It had been days since she'd even thought about putting on those fake rims.

She'd gotten too comfortable here. The place felt too much like the home she'd never known and always wished for. She had become careless.

Taking a deep breath, she thanked Rachel for the compliment and felt her heart sink. The truth was, she'd simply fallen head-over-heels stupid in love with the place…with the people…with the man who ruled her soul.

Biting back the tears, Merri plastered a smile across her lips as they entered the darkened backstage area. Just a few more hours. She would make the kids happy, raise as much as possible for them this afternoon, and then it would be all over. She would tell Ty the truth and take the consequences.

She would once again be on her own. Alone with her guilt and her unfulfilled love—and more miserable than ever.

"You did what?" Frank asked him incredulously.

They were standing out in front of the 4-H arena, getting ready to go back inside and take their seats for the end of the show. They'd been hanging around outside for a few minutes, making sure the reporters had arrived and that everything was ready for the big announcement.

"I asked her to marry me," Ty answered and felt the goofy grin break across his face.

"But why?"

Ty's lips narrowed into a scowl. "Because we love each other. Why else?"

"You two hardly know each other. What do you really know about Merri's background? You should've let me check her out more thoroughly first. She's worked out fine at the Foundation, but as a wife?"

"Don't push it, pal. I don't care about her background."

"What if she's really another gold-digger—just better at it than all the rest?"

"Keep that kind of talk to yourself, Frank. I know who she is inside. She can't be like that."

"All right, fine. But at least let me draw up a prenup agreement for her to sign. Be a little practical here."

The fury blinded Ty and he nearly grabbed Frank by the throat. "Never say anything like that again," he growled. "I don't want you to slip and mention such a thing when she's around. She loves me and I trust her. Don't ruin it by making it seem that we need a written contract to be able to trust each other with our future."

Frank shrugged but knew enough to keep his mouth shut. He had said too much already. Taking his leave from Ty, he hurried over to talk to one of the reporters who had gathered up in front of the main door.

Ty leaned back against the wall and let the sunshine wash over him, soothing his anger and calming him back down. He closed his eyes and took a breath. It wasn't Frank's fault. Not really.

No one knew Merri like Ty did. He had seen into her soul and found the other half of himself.

The acid smell of cigarette smoke disturbed his reverie. He opened his eyes and saw a couple of the professional photographers standing apart from the others and within a few feet of him. They weren't paying a bit of attention to who was nearby and suffering from their smoke.

Too bad he needed them for the publicity photos or else he might just be tempted to tell them what they thought about rude strangers in this part of Texas. Ty clamped his mouth shut.

"You have got to be kidding," one of the reporters said to the other. "What the crap would someone like her be doing in such a hellhole as this? It's barely civilized here. There isn't even a damned Starbucks in this whole section of Texas."

"Dude, I've spent hundreds of hours studying her pictures and a thousand more trying to get a lead on where in the world she'd disappeared to," the other guy argued. "It's her. I'd stake my next big shot on it."

"Well…well." The first man took a last drag and pitched the cigarette a few feet away. "I'll be damned. Looks like this gig isn't going to be as boring as I first thought."

"Yeah. Hell. The sleaze rags will pay in the six figures for a decent shot of her. Maybe we can even get her to give us an interview. Shit. That'd be worth millions."

"Shut up about it," the other man said in a stage whisper. "Don't let the other guys figure it out. We have to get to her first."

Ty was suddenly beyond curious. Who were they discussing? He'd grown up with every single person in this part of Texas. There couldn't be anyone famous here that he didn't know about.

There couldn't be…

"Just think of it," one of the men said with a wistful grin. "We ambush the infamous Merrill Davis-Ross and we'll be famous, too. And rich. What a kick. We must be living right for a change."

Merrill Davis-Ross. Merri Davis?

Ty's breath whooshed out of his chest, leaving him stunned and sick to his stomach. He felt as if the ground had opened up and was about to swallow him whole.

He fisted his hands at his side and fought for clarity. No wonder she looked so much like a danged fashion model in that dress. No wonder she had seemed so familiar to him the last few days and especially this morning.

It wasn't because she was the missing piece in his life and his heart had recognized her spirit. It was because she *was* a fashion model—a tabloid queen he'd remembered from the front pages at the grocery store—and a damned liar.

Wanting to hit something, Ty fought the pain in his chest and shoved away from the wall. How could he have let himself be taken in—again?

He stalked around the idiot reporters in silence. Gritting his teeth, he made his way toward the back entrance that had been turned into the model staging area for today.

This time he wasn't going to back away and let the pain take over his life for years to come like the last two times he had been fooled by women. No way.

Ms. Merrill Davis-Ross was going to have to explain herself. If she could find some excuse for lying, that was.

Ty's whole body shook with rage. There was no excuse for lying. And, by God, she was going to hear him tell her so before he ran her out of town and sent her packing back to her plastic life forever.

Twelve

Trying to ignore the deepening premonition that something terrible was about to happen, Merri stepped out the back door of the arena and into the heat. The place was packed and they were bound to raise a lot of money for the kids at the ranch. Still the uneasy feeling persisted, making her check over her shoulder every ten minutes.

She'd heard that reporters were out front waiting to take publicity pictures after the luncheon. But she knew how to duck them. That couldn't be where this strange feeling was coming from.

Dressed in her last outfit of the day, Merri looked around for the little girl who would be wearing a matching lilac linen tea dress. As she recalled, this girl was the tiniest one of the bunch, a mere four years old with big wide eyes and as cute a smile as could be. Merri spotted one of the matrons from the ranch but the little girl was nowhere in sight.

The Mexican-American matron waved her over. "If you're looking for Lupe, we had to take her back to the ranch," she said with a chuckle. "I'm sorry, but it was a mistake to let you schedule her for last. *Pobrecita.* She's too little to understand and too young to wait around for an hour without getting her dress all dirty."

"Oh, no." Merri felt like a moron for not thinking of that. "I'm the one who should be sorry. I'll have Janie send her another dress, and I'll come out to the ranch to try and make it up to her."

The other woman shook her head and smiled. "She'll be fine. Don't worry. They were planning on getting her an ice-cream cone on the way back. She'll never be disappointed with her day after ice cream."

Merri nodded but she still felt like a jerk. How could she be so stupid?

Sighing, she chalked it up to yet another example of her selfish ways. "The show is nearly over. Our models are about to be served lunch. Then we can get them all back to the ranch."

The other woman opened her mouth to reply, but stopped as her attention was drawn to something over Merri's shoulder. A shadow fell across Merri from behind and the cold wind once again raised goose bumps on her arms.

"You can't leave until they take the publicity photos, Ms. Davis-Ross."

She didn't need to turn around to know that was the

voice of her beloved. Only his tone carried an edgy, bitter sound that she'd never heard before.

And he'd called her—Davis-Ross. Oh. My. God. *No!*

Merri spun on her toes to face him. "Ty…"

"Excuse us a second, will you?" He glared at the matron, who quickly walked away.

"You *know,*" Merri mumbled as her heart sank.

Ty drove his hands through the short strands of his hair and frowned. "Of course, I know. You didn't think I could be fooled forever, did you? Regardless of what you must think of me, I'm not a completely backward redneck."

His voice was flat, the look in his eyes was dead. She had never seen him like this. Always when he gazed at her in the past, there had been a sexy glimmer in the depths of those steel blue eyes. This afternoon all of that was gone.

"I'm sorry…I tried to tell you this morning. I didn't want you to find out this way."

"Gee, thanks," he said in a voice that dripped of sarcasm. "How kind of you to worry about me."

"Ty…"

"You lied to me, dammit! To Jewel, and to all of us. And for no good reason except to make us look like fools. Was this all some kind of publicity stunt?"

She raised her chin and straightened up. "Never. If anything, it was exactly the opposite." Her voice caught and she had to swallow hard to go on. "At first, I was just trying to escape from my empty, useless life. I wanted to do something worthwhile…I wanted to physically help others instead of throwing money at the world's problems like my parents had always done. I wanted to find out for myself what it was like to lead a normal life—no servants—no fuss. I…"

"You lied to *me*. Why? I would've understood. I would have let you be normal. Why did you have to hide the truth from me?" His voice cracked and he scowled.

His pain was killing her. This was what she had dreaded the most. This was what she'd tried so hard to avoid. And yet, she'd let her selfishness override her good sense and here she was after all, facing devastation.

"I wanted to find out if anyone could like me for just me. So I did something really ironic and stupid and became someone else. Someone kinder, more real.

"But by the time…other people…befriended me, it seemed so hurtful to confess the truth that I…"

"Continued lying?" he said through gritted teeth. "After you lied your way into our lives—and our hearts—you kept on lying?

"Was everything a lie?" Ty turned, paced a few feet away then swung around for one more bitter dart. "You've been acting…fooling everyone. I don't give a rip about your previous useless life, but did you lie again this morning when you said you loved me? Are you that good an actress?"

She shook her head violently, but the words backed up in her throat as she fought not to break down.

He turned and paced again, hands fisted by his sides. "Damn you," he muttered. "I trusted you. I thought I knew who you were. I wanted to make you the public face for the Foundation and promote you to Chairman."

"You do know me," she sobbed into her hands.

"Now," he continued right ahead as if he hadn't heard her words. "Instead of publicity photos with the kids, the reporters will all be trying to catch a shot of the famous runaway tabloid queen. Thanks a lot. For nothing."

The reporters? So that's how he found out. They must've spotted her.

"Oh, Ty, I'm so sorry." The pain was searing through her chest, the tears blinding her eyes. "I never meant for this to happen. I really tried to keep you and Jewel out of the glare of the spotlight I've always hated. Let me try to fix things with the paparazzi, and then I'll just go."

"Fix things?" he exploded as he paced back. He wanted to strangle her, cause her as much hurt as he felt. His own naive stupidity at letting yet another woman get to him was beyond belief. Had he learned nothing about women in his life?

She stiffened and winced at his tone. "Let me try, I can…"

"You can just get out," he growled. "Go back to jet-setting and leave us be. We don't need your kind here. I'll have someone pack your bags and fly you wherever you want to go."

The pain in her eyes nearly made him reach for her, but he held himself back. His own pain was too overwhelming.

"No, thanks," she said tightly. "I've found out I can take care of myself. And for that I'll always be grateful to you and this whole town."

He couldn't stand watching her. She was trembling and holding herself together with her arms crossed over her waist, as if one wrong move would break her in two. Turning his back on her, he squeezed his eyes shut and held onto the last vestiges of self-control.

"Goodbye, Tyson," she whispered. "And…I wasn't lying when I said I loved you."

Ty couldn't move. He wanted to scream "liar" at her one more time, but his wounds were too great to speak.

Hearing her steps as she walked away drove nails into the empty space that used to be his heart. This time it would definitely kill him. She was the last one to punish him this way by taking his soul with her as she left.

Never again, he swore silently—never again.

Several hours later, as purple dusk crept over the range, Ty found himself still pacing. But this time he was pacing up and down the main aisle of the foaling barn, the one place that should've been able to soothe his battered heart.

But nothing was working. All he could think of was never having Merri in his arms again. Never being able to touch or stir or taste her. It was driving him crazy.

He'd made a mad dash back here after he'd walked away from her at the arena, hoping to rid himself of the scent of her, of the sound of her pain in his ears. But he could still smell her. Still hear her in his heart. Still feel her on his fingers and his tongue.

Dammit. To top that off, he'd had to shut off his phone because all of a sudden every tabloid in the world wanted to interview him. He'd even been forced to post ranch hands as guards along the main gate to keep the fool reporters out. Idiots.

He used the toe of his old comfortable boots to kick

violently at the dirt. This pacing wasn't making him feel a bit better, so he started out across the barnyard heading for the house. Maybe he would try to work in his office for a while. Anything to take his mind off of Merri and what might be happening to her right now.

When he'd almost reached the house, Jewel drove up and parked. Odd. She rarely came out to his ranch except for parties or emergencies.

Jewel got out of her car and stormed toward him, her eyes shooting sparks and her whole body tensed for a fight.

"What brings you all the way out here?" he asked warily when she got close enough.

"I have something to say to you, Tyson Adams Steele. And I'll say it inside. Now."

He followed her as she stalked through his kitchen, down the hall and into his office. When he walked into the room, she slammed the door behind him and rounded on him with such a furious expression across her normally sweet face, it made him take a step back.

"What's the matter? What did I do?"

"Give me a minute to get over that mob out at the front gate," she said as she hissed in a breath. "Jackals. The whole lot of them."

"I'm sorry, Jewel. If you'd let me know you were coming, I would've sent someone to help you through."

With one hand, she reached out and gingerly patted his arm while putting the other hand against her breast. "Not your fault. At least not *that* particular part of this mess isn't."

Underneath the glaring look she was giving him, Ty could still see the love and concern shining in her eyes.

It hit him out of the blue that here was a woman who had never lied to him. A woman he could trust completely never to betray him. He'd always known he loved her, but now he could see why he'd clung to the idea that somewhere out there was another woman he would be able to count on.

Another woman just like Jewel. Too bad it wasn't the woman that he'd stupidly fallen in love with.

"I love you, Jewel," he told his aunt before she could say anything else.

"Don't go saying sweet things to me, son," she said with a scowl. "Not until you explain why you felt it necessary to destroy that gentle young woman."

"Merri? But I was the one…"

"I'm so disappointed in you I could just spit," Jewel told him. "Merri never did anything but work hard to please you and the whole community. And you turned all that on its head and made her out to be some kind of pure evil. She made a mistake. Get over it."

"She lied to me," was all he could manage to say.

"Tell me I didn't raise such an idiot," Jewel frowned and gave him a backhanded shot across the upper arm. "She loved you, and you sent her out alone to face the dreadful hordes by herself."

"Merri should be used to the paparazzi by now," he said coldly. "After all, her whole life before she came here was one stunt after another. Let her get herself out of whatever mess she's in."

Jewel narrowed her eyes at him and frowned. "If you'd taken a moment to let her explain instead of running home with your feelings hurt, you might have learned that the reason she was hiding from the lime-

light in the first place was because she'd tried to help
a friend. But when the going got rough, that so-called
friend betrayed her. Used her to take the heat off himself and then turned her over to the jackals so they
could pick her clean."

"Did she tell you that?"

"Some of it," Jewel replied. "The rest I bribed out
of one of them no-good reporters."

"Bribed?"

"With a couple of the garden club's raffle cakes. No
better way to get the truth out of a man."

A tender shift in Ty's heart took him by surprise as
thoughts of Merri wound through his mind. She had
worked hard at learning things she probably had no
idea how to do. She'd charmed the Foundation's
donors, made sense out of the office and gave the kids
at Nuevo Dias Ranch a reason to smile. Everyone who
knew her loved her. Including him.

"But she didn't have to lie to me," he whined in
spite of everything else. "Not to me." The hurt and be-
trayal were still strong in his heart. Too strong for for-
giveness.

"Argh," Jewel muttered. "How can you be so foolish? You hurt her bad, boy. And stubborn pride is going
to hurt you, too. Maybe worse than ever before.

"I can't stand to watch you behave like this and ruin
a once-in-a-lifetime opportunity to be happy," Jewel
said with a snort. "If you're determined to sit here pout-
ing and suffering, you're going to do it by yourself. I'm
going home to bake and garden. And hope to hell I can
get the sour taste of your bitterness out of my mouth."

Ty rubbed at his temples as Jewel stormed out of the

house, slamming doors behind her. Damn it. He wasn't the bad guy here. He hadn't lied.

He took a deep breath of cleansing air, but stopped when he smelled the sugar scents of lavender and vanilla. Those weren't Jewel's scents. Hers were almost always the tangy smells of Ivory soap and cinnamon.

No, the soft scents he'd just noticed were all Merri's. Ty looked around his office. She had told him she'd been in here while he was out of town. Maybe the musky smells of her had lingered until now.

Or maybe he was really going insane and would never get her out of his mind completely. Oh, God.

Starting around his desk toward his heavy high-backed chair, Ty ran his fingers lightly around the edges of his polished wood desk. Thinking that Merri might've touched these same places, he could just imagine feeling her touch still warm through the mahogany.

Suddenly his fingers and his gaze landed on the gypsy's antique mirror, lying facedown on the desk where he'd carelessly left it several weeks before. Strange that now he remembered, Merri had mentioned seeing her reflection in the mirror.

It had been the one time before today that he'd thought she'd told him a lie. This look-alike mirror was nothing but plain glass. But then, just as now, Ty couldn't imagine why Merri would choose to lie about something so meaningless.

He reached to pick up the golden mirror and then plopped down in his chair and leaned back. Closing his eyes, he tried to remember what Merri had looked like when she'd first come to Stanville and he'd fallen for her. So innocent, so sweet.

But there had been a wounded look in her eyes back then. Had she been afraid of him? Afraid that he would give her away by accident?

Fighting that uncomfortable idea, Ty thought he heard a voice speaking to him. He really was going nuts.

"Turn the mirror over, Tyson Steele. It will reveal the truth, no more."

His eyes opened wide and he stared down at the scrollwork with his name embedded in the back of the mirror. That had been what the gypsy had told him. The mirror would take him to his heart's desire.

Slowly, filled with trepidation for no good reason but still determined to take a look, Ty turned the mirror over in his hand and stared down at the glass.

The damned thing seemed to be alive all of a sudden. Swirls of haze and fog obscured the mirror and seemed to rise up to encircle him within its mists. He would've dropped the creepy thing immediately, but his fingers felt as if they were glued to its handle. He noticed the gold had begun to warm under his hand and was heating up to somewhere past normal room temperature.

Ridiculous. There was no such thing as magic.

Just then the fog began to clear and Merri's face came into view. *Merri.* His heart lurched at the mere sight of her beautiful smile.

It was like every other time she had appeared before him. His blood began racing through his veins and his erection hardened with a sudden throbbing beat.

Looking closer, trying to focus on her sparkling green eyes, Ty was taken aback by the vision before him. It wasn't Merri—and yet it was.

Somehow the image in the mirror had become a combination of both the sweet, shy Merri Davis and the sexy, gorgeous model, Merrill Davis-Ross. He would've thought that the latter would repel him, remind him of her treachery.

But nothing about her turned him off.

Instead, rippling changes of scene zipped past in the mirror right before his eyes. Merri crawling under his desk to find her shoes. Merri falling on her butt in the rain and kissing him senseless while the water poured over their heads.

Next he saw Merri telling him she didn't want anything permanent, begging him not to force himself into her life. Then came the vision of pure lust shining in her eyes as he saw himself bending over her, tasting and cherishing—

Rubbing at the spot on his chest that had begun to ache, Ty could scarcely believe the next picture. It was of a stunning Merrill Davis-Ross in a red dress and stiletto heels with soft green eyes and a panicked look on her face.

"I love you, Ty," she had said. "But you need to know something about me. I have to tell…"

Ty groaned and felt the tears stinging at the back of his eyes. It was as plain as the image before him. She *did* love him. And…she had tried to tell him the truth.

He had pushed her, run right over her feelings in his zeal to have her. And in the end, he *had* rejected her.

Jewel was right. He was a selfish bastard and didn't deserve anything as wonderful as being loved by Merri.

He *was* determined to make it up to her, however. Maybe he had hurt the woman he loved beyond repair.

Though he could barely stand to think of that idea at the moment.

But regardless of whether she forgave him, it was time to act like a man and make things better for her.

Merri heard a bigger commotion than ever at the back of the café where she'd stopped running and let the paparazzi catch up. At least she was miles away from Stanville, Texas, and all the wonderful people there.

It was her time to stand and face the music. Which she intended to do, if she could ever hear a reporter's question through all the yelling and screaming that was going on in the back of the room.

Several strobes flashed in front of her eyes and temporarily blinded her.

"What about your relationship with Tyson Steele, Merrill?" someone called out from the crowd.

"There is no relationship," she squeaked. "None at all. He just happened to be in the town I picked. He never knew a thing about me."

"Wrong," came a familiar-sounding shout from the back.

"Aw, come on, babe," a nasty voice snarled from behind another snapping bright light. "Tell the world about him. Did he turn out to be gay, too? Maybe it's just *you* that forces guys out of the closet. Maybe you emasculate the men around you. Maybe…"

The guy's words were suddenly halted and Merri swirled, trying to see what was happening. When her vision cleared, she saw Ty, breaking though the crowd and spinning the vicious reporter by the shoulder. Ty reared back and took a swing, pasting his fist right into the photographer's jaw.

"Say what you want about me, creep," he growled. "But don't you ever say anything like that about her again. Got it?" Ty still had the man by his shirt and reared back to take another shot.

"Hold it," the guy cried. "I got it. And you're going to hear from my lawyer, dude. This is assault. You'll be paying for it for a long time."

Ty released him and looked over to Merri. "Are you okay?" he mouthed.

She nodded but wanted to tell him to go away. He was just going to make things worse.

At that moment, about a dozen sheriff's deputies came out of nowhere and began dispersing throughout the room, rounding up and herding the reporters out the door.

A tall man with a tan hat and a silver badge pinned on the pocket of his western style shirt walked up to where Ty and the obnoxious photographer were standing. "I saw everything," he grinned at the reporter. "Too bad it was so crowded in here that you accidently ran your jaw into Mr. Steele's elbow. You coulda knocked your eye out."

The reporter spun to address the rest of the paparazzi. "Did anybody get a decent shot of this cowboy hitting me?"

A rumble went around the room, but everyone else was being escorted outside. The man who had been "accidently" hit lifted his camera and pointed it at Ty and the sheriff.

"I don't believe I'd do that, son," the sheriff told him.

"Not if you want to keep that camera…and your fingers…for future use. Come on, let's take this outside. You're trespassing on private property here."

When they were alone in the café, Merri turned to Ty. "Why did you hit him? I was holding my own with them. Now he's going to sue you and make a big fuss."

"Forget him. He's not a problem." He reached for her but she slithered away from his reach. "Merri, darlin'."

"Why did you follow me?" she asked. "I thought you said everything that needed to be said. What more is there? You were clear enough. I'm on my way out of your life."

She'd been crying, he could tell. And it ran stabs of pain through his soul.

"I don't want you out of my life," he whispered. "I want you to forgive me for being a bigger jerk than that idiot photographer."

"Why? Nothing has changed. I'm still never going back to being the shy Merri Davis you thought you fell in love with." She hesitated, swallowed and then kept on talking. "I'm never going to be Merrill Davis-Ross again, either. I couldn't go back to that. Not after…you."

He moved in on her then. He was compelled to wrap his arms around her body, keeping her safe and warm.

"How about if you don't go back to either one?" he asked softly and tightened his arms around her. "Why can't you just be Mrs. Merri Steele from now on?"

"Ty?" she said breathlessly. "I don't think we can…"

A momentary panic gripped his stomach and he knew if he had to get down on his knees and beg, he would do it gladly.

She would listen to him. She would hear his words in her heart. She just had to.

He leaned his forehead against hers and closed his eyes. "I have been an arrogant fool for most of my life, Merri. Letting anger at my mother's death color all my relationships with women.

"I wanted to be loved so badly that I shoved myself down people's throats and then sat back, waiting for them to betray me."

After chuckling over the idea that his own method of hiding his true feelings had been so much worse than Merri's disguises, Ty drew a deep breath and continued. "Most of them didn't disappoint me. But you were different. You held back and made me see the real you first. And I did, darlin'. I really saw your soul first."

She gasped, threw her arms around his waist and clung to him.

"I don't care what name you use…or how you look on the outside," he said gently in her ear. "None of that matters.

"It's what's between us now. Who we are when we're together as a team. That's all that truly counts."

She pulled back, putting inches of air between them and lifting her chin to look in his eyes. "Really, Ty? It hurt so bad when I thought I would never see you again. I…"

"I'm so sorry, sugar," he mumbled past a lump in his throat. "I was hurting too…and stubborn as hell. Give me a few hundred years to make it up to you."

"I'm not exactly blameless in all of this," Merri said with a slow sexy grin. "But I *do* love you, Tyson Adams Steele. And I'll be more than happy to spend the next hundred years or so letting you try to convince me that this was all your fault."

He couldn't help himself. She was so tempting standing there, gazing up at him with love shining in her eyes. He bent and lightly kissed her lips, knowing full well some horrible tabloid would carry a picture of them like this on their front page tomorrow.

But what the hell. None of that mattered anymore. Not when he had the other half of his soul beside him at last. Not when he could taste her and hold her and keep the rest of the world at bay forever.

They could do anything…go anywhere. As long as they stayed together.

He still wasn't sure why he had been so honored, but their love was his legacy, given by the gypsy and Lucille Steele. And no one could take that away from them.

Not as long as he held on to the magic.

Looking down at the bewitching face he hoped to see everyday for the rest of eternity, he realized that he really did hold the magic right here in his arms. Merri was the real magic.

And he would never again let her go.

Epilogue

"**W**ell…" The old gypsy sat back in her chair as the crystal ball grew dim.

"Very nice," she murmured to herself. "Tyson Steele has finally captured his heart's desire. But it was too close to a complete disaster to suit me."

Passionata gazed at the heavens above and addressed her ancestor once again. "The *next* recipient will be much more difficult to help, my father and king. I cannot sit idly by with him and watch the 'lost' Steele descendent squander or misuse his legacy.

"This next time I *must* intervene on your behalf."

Steely gray clouds opened up and bolts of lightning crisscrossed the midnight sky. "Not to worry. I shall keep a close rein on young Chase Severin. Your gift of magic shall be used for its proper purpose.

"I swear it."

* * * * *

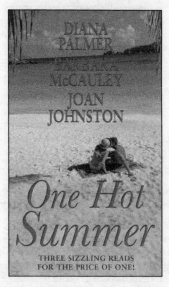

Queens of Romance

The Australian Outback breeds men who are tough to resist and dangerous to marry!

Master of Maramba

Catrina Russell jumped at the chance of a job as governess on a North Queensland cattle station. But while his young daughter and Carrie really got on, Royce McQuillan wondered if beautiful Carrie could be content living an isolated life with the master of Maramba.

Strategy for Marriage

Tough, eligible and determined cattle baron Ashe McKinnon took one look at Christy Parker and swept her off her feet. Ashe was impossible to resist, but he made it clear that any marriage to him would be on a business basis only. Why then was Christy fast falling for him?

Available 15th June 2007

Collect all 4 superb books in the collection!

www.millsandboon.co.uk

M&B

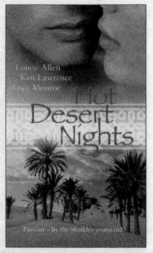

FREE!

2 Books
and a surprise gift!

We would like to take this opportunity to thank you for reading this Mills & Boon® book by offering you the chance to take TWO more specially selected titles from the Desire™ series absolutely FREE! We're also making this offer to introduce you to the benefits of the Mills & Boon® Reader Service™—

- ★ **FREE home delivery**
- ★ **FREE gifts and competitions**
- ★ **FREE monthly Newsletter**
- ★ **Exclusive Reader Service offers**
- ★ **Books available before they're in the shops**

Accepting these FREE books and gift places you under no obligation to buy, you may cancel at any time, even after receiving your free shipment. Simply complete your details below and return the entire page to the address below. You don't even need a stamp!

YES! Please send me 2 free Desire books and a surprise gift. I understand that unless you hear from me, I will receive 3 superb new titles every month for just £4.99 each, postage and packing free. I am under no obligation to purchase any books and may cancel my subscription at any time. The free books and gift will be mine to keep in any case.

D7ZEF

Ms/Mrs/Miss/Mr ....Initials ....

Surname .... **BLOCK CAPITALS PLEASE**

Address...

....

....Postcode ....

Send this whole page to:
UK: FREEPOST CN81, Croydon, CR9 3WZ